MW00986798

# WHITE SPHERE

*a novel by*

# D. F. BAILEY

White Sphere
Copyright © D. F. Bailey 2021
ISBN: 978-1-9995405-9-3 • Registration #1188501
Published by CatchwordPublishing.com

**All rights reserved.** No part of this publication may be reproduced, stored in or introduced into a retrieval system, or transmitted in any form, or by any means, graphic, electronic or mechanical, including photocopying, recording, or otherwise, or by any information storage or retrieval system, without the prior written permission of the copyright owner, except where permitted by law, or in the case of brief quotations embodied in critical articles and reviews.

*White Sphere* is a work of fiction. The resemblance of any characters to real persons, living or dead, is coincidental. All names, characters, places, brands, media, situations, and incidents are either the product of the author's imagination or are used fictitiously.

**Acknowledgments.** I am extremely grateful to Lawrence Russell and Stephen Bett for reading an early draft of White Sphere. Their insights and advice helped to shape the final version of the novel. I'm also indebted to my "review crew"—Barb Stoner, Bonnie Burskey, Marc Brown, Dave Henry, Dennis J Horner, Jeffrey R. McMillan, Joanne Lawson, and Teresa Collins—the team of whip-sharp editors and proofreaders who polished the final draft of the novel. Last but not least, I have to thank Marc Brown for sharing his expertise in firearms.—DFB

A Downed Airliner
A Plot For Revenge
America in Disarray


*We are facing a future in which*
*all information is untrustworthy*
*because the environment in which it exists*
*has become so corrupted.*
*— Nina Schick, Deep Fakes*


Subscribe to D. F. Bailey's newsletter
www.dfbailey.com/VIPclub.html

For Lawrence Russell,

The first reader of every Will Finch novel.

Thanks for the wink and a nod.

# WHITE
# SPHERE

# CHAPTER ONE

SAN FRANCISCO — 16 FEBRUARY, 2021

A sharp, hard blast.

The sound swung his head around, but when Will Finch looked back at the woman, he knew it was too late to save her. The bullet had pierced her forehead. She slumped sideways then collapsed in an awkward spiral at his feet. A few minutes after she'd blurted out her confession to Finch, Myfanwy lay dead on Vallejo Street.

He let out a gasp and stumbled backward on the sidewalk. "My God," he whispered. Her face mask slipped under her chin to reveal her nose and mouth. Her eyelids fluttered—then froze in an open, vacant stare.

Finch held a hand to his lips and spun around to search for help. He saw the motorcycle race over the crest of the hill and down Vallejo Street towards North Beach. He glanced at the pair of lovers walking arm-in-arm toward him, but when they saw the corpse sprawled across the sidewalk they both

1

screamed in horror.

"Call 911!" he yelled.

Before he could say another word, they turned and ran down Kearny Street toward Chinatown. He muttered a curse, but he understood their sense of fear. They were just like everyone else in San Francisco these days. Terrified.

He dropped his courier bag onto the sidewalk and stared at Myfanwy's face. An inch to the left of the bullet hole he saw the tiny, strawberry birthmark on her forehead. No mistake about it. The same woman he'd met last year in Rapid City, South Dakota. Myfanwy something. He didn't know her surname. Never bothered to ask.

He drew his phone from his pocket, slipped his mask under his chin, and called 911. The emergency responder took his name and the street address of the apartment building to his right. Then he checked the time. 9:17 p.m. The cops would want to know this—and everything else that transpired over the previous ten minutes.

While he waited for the police to arrive, he walked to the vehicle barrier that closed the cul-de-sac on Vallejo and stared down the walkway below. He decided to call his wife. As expected, he was shunted into her voice mail. Just as well, he thought. He decided to leave a generic message. No need to alarm her. "Hey, Eve. Looks like I'm running late tonight. Not sure when I'll be back, but I'll call again if this goes long. Kiss the baby for me, okay. Love you."

In the distance he heard the sirens wailing. Then the flashing red and blue lights reflected on the adjacent buildings as an SFPD squad car approached the top of the hill. Finch waved a hand in the air and the driver parked at an angle to block on-coming traffic. The two cops inside the car conferred for a moment then stepped onto the street.

"You the one called this in?" the driver asked. "Will Finch?"

"Yeah, that's me," Finch said. He noticed both officers wore face coverings and drew his mask over his mouth and nose.

The second cop kneeled beside the corpse, tugged on some latex gloves, and pressed his index and middle fingers to her throat to probe for a pulse. After two or three tries, he glanced at his partner and shook his head. "Nope. She's gone."

"All right." The driver turned to Finch and drew a notebook from a pouch on his vest. "I'm Officer Benton, this is Officer Taskasaplidis. I'll take down the details while my partner calls this in."

Finch studied Benton's eyes. Because of the mask covering his face, it was impossible to get an accurate read of the man. Finch felt the gravity of the moment and nodded to confirm that he'd comply with whatever Benton needed.

"You got some ID? Driver's license'll do." His head tipped to one side. "And a business card if you've got one. In case I have to follow up."

Finch slipped his wallet from his pants pocket and handed his license and card to Benton. The officer photographed the documents with his cell, made some notes, and returned the license.

"So depending on what went down here, you may have to come over to the precinct station to give your statement." He shook his head to suggest this would not be in Finch's interest. "However, with the Covid virus this bad, you really want to settle things right here if we can. You understand?"

"Sure," Finch said with a light cough. He struggled to find his breath. He looked at the corpse on the sidewalk. A dark pool of blood trickled from the back of her skull across the smooth concrete toward the gutter. He'd seen this kind of butchery before. And much worse in Iraq. He shook his head and drew a long stream of air through his lips. *Myfanwy*. He still couldn't believe it.

"I'm going to record what you say on my cell, okay?"

Finch nodded as he tried to absorb his situation. The shock of the murder stuck in his throat.

Benton clicked an app on his phone and attached it to a clip on his jacket. "So let's take this from the top, Mr. Finch. Did you witness the shooting?"

"I did. But, uh…" His voice faltered again. He rubbed a hand over his face in disbelief. Had it really happened? The gunshot. The motorcycle roaring past him and down the slope. "This bike came from behind us, up over the hill. Then circled back to her." Finch pointed at the hilltop where the squad car stood—lights still flashing—and swung around one hundred and eighty degrees to the concrete wall that formed the barrier of the Vallejo cul-de-sac.

"A motorcycle?"

"Yeah. Mid-size I'd say." He shook his head. "I'm not sure what make."

"The shooter rode a motorcycle?"

"He went around that parked car"—he pointed his hand to a

green BMW—"coasted up to us and stopped. Then he asked her something."

Benton paused and lifted his pen from his notepad. "Asked her what?"

Finch gazed at the litter next to the curb as he tried to recall the exact words. "Her name. He said, 'That you, Myfanwy?' "

"What?"

"Myfanwy." Finch's shoulders rolled up and shrugged back into place. "A Welsh name."

"Say it again."

He pronounced it phonetically. "Mif-awn-we."

"Can you spell it?"

Finch spelled her name letter by letter as Benton struggled to write in his pad. He repeated the spelling to Finch to ensure he'd recorded it properly.

"All right. Myfanwy. You get a last name?"

"No."

"So the perp said her name. Then what?"

"She turned to him, and said, 'Yes.' Then the shooter said, 'I've got something for you,' and pulled a gun from a shoulder bag. Then shot her. That was it. Boom. One shot to her head." Finch held up a hand as if he'd witnessed a magic act. Some lethal sleight of hand. "Then pulled a wheelie and disappeared." His chin tipped toward the squad car and the hill below.

Finch and Benton turned towards the crest of the hill but the squad car blocked their view. Perhaps the killer would miraculously reappear. A shiver ran up his spine and rippled through his body.

Just past Myfanwy's body, Officer Taskasaplidis began to string bands of crime scene tape to block off the body.

"Can you describe the shooter?"

"No. He wore a mask."

"How 'bout the bike? Brand name? Color?"

Finch reflected on the questions. "Definitely not a Harley or BMW. But it was cherry red. And in good shape. New looking."

"What about the weapon?" He leaned forward slightly. "Pistol or semiautomatic?"

Again Finch tried to recall the details, then lifted his empty hands. "No idea."

"After the shooting"—one hand swept across the road —"did the shooter pick up a brass shell?"

"Maybe. I'm not—" He paused. How could he miss this detail? "Honestly, I just don't know."

Benton drew a deep breath and studied Finch's face. "Okay. What else did you see?"

Finch raised his eyes to the gray clouds massing above the street. Yes, there was something else. Something didn't fit. "You know I'm not sure."

"Not sure about?"

"That the shooter was a man."

"You think a woman shot her?" Benton's eyebrows flexed to reveal a row of creases in his forehead.

Finch shut his eyes as he considered the shooter's voice. "Yeah. Maybe." An uncertain look crossed his face. "It's a possibility."

Benton turned to Taskasaplidis and said, "Hey Mr. T, looks

like the shooter came and went on a mid-size, red motorcycle. Could be a woman. Call out a BOLO on it. Then check the road for some brass. One shot only."

Under the cover of his mask, Finch smiled. With a name like Taskasaplidis, he understood why the cops abbreviated it to a single letter. It was all Greek to them. To anyone.

Mr. T's phone rang. He took the call and turned to Benton. "Forensics is on the way. And looks like she's got a wallet."

"Yeah. But don't touch nothing, T," Benton replied. "Just call it in."

Taskasaplidis waved a hand to Benton, a thumbs-up gesture, and walked across the pavement scanning the asphalt for the bullet casing, the phone pressed to his ear as he relayed the crime scene situation to the dispatcher.

"All right." Benton paused to gather his thoughts. "So you talked to her before she was killed. That right?"

"Briefly." Finch drew a long breath. He knew he had to be careful now. What he revealed might put him in jeopardy. Especially if he was caught in a lie.

"Yeah?" Benton's eyebrows rose with a look of surprise. "What'd she say?"

"It was one of those awkward times when you mistake somebody for someone else." He tipped his head to one side. He'd made the same error himself. Who hasn't? He waved his hand at his face. "I guess because of the masks."

"So, like she passed you on the street here and said hello?"

"Something like that. Except she came up behind me. Back on Kearny Street."

"What'd she say?"

Finch broke off eye contact with a shrug. He had to find a way to fudge the details without lying. "Like I said. It was mistaken identity. I told her my name was Will Finch. I even slipped down my mask so she could see my face."

"And that's when the shooter killed her."

"Not long after that." He held up a hand as if he needed to ward off any more questions. "Look, I've gotta say, I'm still shaking from this thing."

Benton nodded with a hint of sympathy in his eyes. Then a white van crested the hilltop and parked behind the police squad car.

Taskasaplidis called over to his partner. "You want me to walk Forensics through this?"

Benton clicked off the recording app on his phone and tucked it into a pouch on his belt. "No, I'll handle it."

The police hierarchy. Again Finch's smile went undetected under the cover of his mask. Benton was top dog. Mr. T, a mere pup.

"Okay, you need anything more from me?" Finch asked. The interruption had stopped Benton from probing any further. With luck, Finch could now walk home knowing the cops wouldn't link him to the murder victim.

Benton shook his head. "Not now. Someone will be in touch if we need more info." He took a few steps toward the two women on the forensics unit who slipped under the crime scene tape and stood above Myfanwy's body. Then Benton shifted and glanced back at Finch.

"One last question." His chin lifted at a slight angle toward Finch.

Finch waited, but Benton stood there, ten feet away, eyes wide open as if an insight had just struck him.

"What's that?"

"Who did she think you were?"

Finch ran a hand over the top of his scalp. He couldn't speak.

"The mistaken identity," Benton said. "So what was his name?"

Finch struggled to find his voice and adjusted his face mask. "Joel Griffin," he mumbled.

In the distance a car horn honked. Benton cupped a hand to his ear. "Who?"

"Joel Griffin," he said.

"Joel Griffin." Benton repeated it to him. "That right?"

"Yeah." He stared at Benton and blinked. "You got it."

As he turned away, Finch felt as though he'd slipped over an edge into the void. And over the next day, he realized that he'd entered a dark, hollow—almost infinitely empty—space without walls or floors or any discernible ceiling. A place where he could wander lost forever.


FINCH walked down the pedestrian passage through the cul-de-sac on Vallejo, turned left on Montgomery, and walked the two blocks over to Alta Street. When he reached the cottage, he opened the door and dropped his courier bag next to the potted Bird of Paradise plant that Eve had purchased last spring. He tugged off his jacket and hung it on the coat tree. He paused and listened for sounds from the baby. Nothing. Then he dragged a hand across the scruff of his beard and wondered how to approach Eve without alarming her. As soon as he considered the options he knew any deception would be impossible.

"You home?" he whispered. This time of night, they both dreaded waking Casey, their eleven-month-old daughter.

"Living room," Eve responded in a heavy whisper.

Finch stepped along the hallway in his sock feet and peered into the living room. Eve sat on the sofa next to the gas fireplace. The iron logs radiated a dry heat through the room. Looks like she's been sitting here for an hour, he thought.

"She down?"

"Just five minutes ago."

Her left foot pumped the base of the rocker in a steady pulse. Snuggled under the flannel blanket, Casey turned her head to Finch. Her lips burbled and a spittle of saliva slipped onto her chin. Eve leaned over and wiped it away with her thumb.

"Let me get something to drink." He pointed to the kitchen. "Want anything?"

"There's fresh tea on the counter. Enough for both of us." Eve smiled and patted the cushion beside her.

Finch returned with two mugs of Eve's favorite brew, Afternoon in Paris. He put one mug on the side table at Eve's elbow, then sat beside her and sipped the tea to assess its temperature. Hot. He set the mug on the coffee table to wait for it to cool.

"I got your message," she said. "Good walk?"

"Not really."

In those two words she detected the edge in his voice. Since the lockdown—which began not long after their wedding—Eve and Finch traded an hour's solitary break every evening after dinner. And every night each returned to the cottage somewhat refreshed. Despite the nearly empty streets and the haunting vacancy of the city, their walks around Coit Tower or down the hill to North Beach provided a sense of renewal—of what everyone called the "new normal."

"Soooo…" She gave him a long look. "What happened?"

"A woman was shot." He paused and held a hand over his lips. What to tell her? Everything, he decided. "She was killed standing beside me. Like *right* beside me." The palm of his hand rolled open and hovered above the floor. As if Myfanwy lay at their feet.

"What?" She glanced away, then turned back to face her husband. "My God. You were there when it happened?"

He shrugged. "Close as I am to you."

"Jesus, Will. That's horrible." She took his hand in her own and leaned toward him. "Tell me. What happened?"

He knew he could put her off for an hour, maybe two. Ask her to wait until tomorrow. But eventually it would all have to come out. No, now was the time. When the death was still fresh in his mind.

"Just let me think." He took a sip of tea and settled his back on the sofa cushions. "All right. You remember when I drove to South Dakota last year."

"Of course. With Brock and Klare."

He nodded. Brock, Eve's nephew, had disappeared with his girlfriend. A week later Finch returned to San Francisco with both of them in tow. They were emotionally bruised but alive and well.

"So there's a coffee shop in Rapid City where I had breakfast every day. The Alt Fuel café."

"Okay."

"And there was a server there. Maybe twenty-three, or twenty-four. Her name tag said Myfanwy." He paused to see if the name was familiar to her.

"Welsh, right?"

"It is." He stared at the far wall, summoning the memory of his encounter with the server. "So when I got to the cash register, I talked with her. Just a few words like everyone does. I mentioned her name. She seemed impressed that I could pronounce it correctly. Then I used Joel Griffin's MasterCard to pay for my meal."

"Okay." Her lips curled with a so-what expression. "Same as always, right."

"Not this time." Finch's look suggested his story was about to turn a dark corner. Joel Griffin was the alias that he'd created years ago to permit him to travel under the radar when one of the stories he'd covered for the *San Francisco Post* had become too dangerous for him to appear in public. To keep his alias alive, every month he charged a meal or minor purchase —socks, underwear—to Joel's VISA or MasterCard accounts. Eve had done the same with her alias, Alice Shaw.

"So when Myfanwy noticed the name on the card, she said she knew a Joel Griffin in Florida. But that he'd died. She was obviously troubled about it. Then embarrassed that by saying he was dead, it might cast some shadow on me. Which is ridiculous, right?"

"I guess." Eve frowned and nodded for him to continue.

"And that was it. A coincidence. You shrug it off with a laugh and move on." He shook his head as if he needed to shrug off the memory, too. "Until tonight."

"So what about tonight?"

"As I was walking up Vallejo, she called out to me. From behind." He paused to consider this. "Now that I think about it, I'm sure she'd been following me."

"She called your name."

"No. She called me *Joel Griffin*. So I turned and said something like, 'Sorry,' and kept walking. But she ran ahead of me and blocked my way. Then she said, 'No. You're the man I met in Rapid City. I was a server at the Alt Fuel.' I knew it was her right away. I could tell by this little mark on her forehead."

"A birthmark."

He nodded. "Strawberry colored. A perfect oval, the size of a fingerprint. Same color as her hair." He took another sip of tea and considered the worried look on Myfanwy's face when she'd confronted him. "I could tell she was in some kind of trouble, so I asked if she needed anything. She said, no, but she was glad she'd tracked me down."

"Tracked you down?"

He shrugged as if he couldn't believe it, either. "Turns out, she kept a copy of my MasterCard slip. At first I thought she had some kind of fixation with Joel Griffin. One of her friends, Emily Somebody"—he waved a hand to suggest Myfanwy didn't know her last name—"works for MasterCard. Myfanwy got her to trace my card to our address here on Alta Street."

Eve's eyebrows rolled up in a bewildered frown.

"I know. Believe me, it gets stranger. It turns out that the real Joel Griffin—the dead version—was Myfanwy's roommate's father."

"The MasterCard friend?"

"No. The roommate. And she lives here, over in The Haight." He hooked a thumb in the direction of Haight-Ashbury. "Which is where Myfanwy moved last summer. The two of them share an apartment." He stopped to take a long sip of tea as he puzzled over Myfanwy's story.

"So what does all this have to do with you?"

"I don't know." He shook his head and stared at the flames licking the glass window of the fireplace. "But I'm pretty sure she's been following me for a few days."

"Really? You've seen her?"

His shoulders rose up to his ears, then slumped back into place. "Just a hunch. But she definitely wanted to tell me something. Like a *confession*. She felt guilty." He paused. "In fact, that was the last thing she said to me. 'I feel really guilty about this, so I have to tell you what happened.' Then she said, 'I think the game is getting dangerous now.' "

"The game? What game?"

A mute weariness rolled through him as he continued to stare at the orange flames curling together, breathing their heat into the room.

"She said it was *dangerous?* "

"Yeah. Her exact words." He drew his eyes away from the fire to study Eve's face. "It was the last thing she said to me. Then she was shot in the head."

WHEN Will Finch heard the banging at the front door he rolled onto his side and wrapped his hand across Eve's hip. She held the baby cuddled against her right breast. Both of them sleeping. Thank God, he thought. Casey had woken at least twice, and Finch had walked her back and forth along the short hallway between the master bedroom and the baby's room—an addition they'd built onto the second floor of the cottage last fall.

Another knock. Two more, then a third. Finch managed to focus his eyes on the clock. 8:30. Later than he imagined.

"Wha-issit?" Eve murmured.

Finch swung his feet to the floor. "I'll get it. Go back to sleep."

The knocking continued as he wrapped a bathrobe around his shoulders and made his way to the front door. He peered through the spyglass and felt a surge of energy pulse through his chest. A man and woman in suits. Both wearing virus masks, both six-footers. Finch slid the security chain across the door and cracked it open.

"What's going on?"

The male took a step forward. "Will Finch?"

He nodded. "Who's asking?"

"I'm Special Agent Jeremy Saxx. This is Special Agent Sandra Keely." He opened a flip wallet to reveal his badge. The top half showed Saxx's picture. The bottom held a gold FBI shield.

Finch examined the badge for a moment. What the hell are these two doing at the door? Then the more disturbing question came to him. Are they really FBI agents?

"Give me a sec." He closed the door, stepped over to his courier bag, and found his phone. He clicked on the camera app, eased open the door until the steel chain stood taut between the door and the doorframe.

"Show me your badge again." He held the face of his phone to the three-inch gap above the chain. "Pull down your mask."

Saxx let out a cynical chuckle. "Finch, we're not kidding around here."

"Me neither. But I've been burned too often to know better. Badge up, or come back with a warrant."

"All right," Saxx muttered, tugged his mask beneath his chin, and held his badge to the door.

Finch took a picture that included Saxx's face and badge in one frame. "Okay, next up."

Keely removed her mask, held the badge to the gap and Finch captured a second image. Then he closed the door and inspected both pictures. Their faces and ID images matched. They looked legitimate. Maybe. But he couldn't count the number of stories about police impersonation *The Post* had covered over the past five years.

He opened the door again, chain on, and decided to take a more conciliatory approach. "Okay, so how can I help you?"

"Mr. Finch," Saxx offered, his voice stern, "we need to talk to you. But not through a locked door."

"What's this about?"

"The murder last night on Vallejo. You called it in, right? Now we're following up." He slipped his badge back into his jacket pocket. "You're not under suspicion. We don't have a warrant."

"And we know we don't need one," Keely added. Her voice rolled in a brassy, contra-alto tone. "Look. We need to get to the bottom of this. Can we come in, please? It's either here or down at the regional office."

Finch pressed his lips together as he considered her request. If the FBI had pulled this case from the hands of the SFPD, then they'd discovered something much bigger than a drive-by shooting. The amber alert in his mind now flashed red.

"Sorry. Not with the Covid pandemic. I've got my wife and eleven-month-old baby inside. Let me get dressed. I know where you are. I'll drive down to your office and meet you there in an hour. That work for you?"

Saxx shook his head with an impatient look. He was about to reply when Keely took a step forward.

"Okay, one hour." Her frown revealed that this wasn't her first choice, but that she could compromise. "I'll meet you there at the reception desk."

"One hour," he repeated. He shut the door again and sent a text to Eve. Then he crept up the stairs. Eve rolled over to watch him gather his clothes from the closet.

"What's going on?"

"The FBI. Don't worry, it's not an arrest. It's about Myfan-wy."

She sat up, now on full alert. *"The FBI?"*

"Look, I sent you a text with their ID and badge numbers. See if you can find out anything on them." He paused to ensure he had her attention. *"Anything,* okay?"

She pulled the sheet and blanket over her breasts. "If the feds are involved that means the murder last night wasn't some local killing."

"I know. It's worse." Much worse, he thought, but couldn't say the words out loud.

He tugged on his jeans, shirt, and socks then plodded downstairs to the main floor and slipped on his shoes and jacket. He thought about brewing a coffee and dismissed the idea. Better to get this over with now.

FINCH joined Saxx and Keely on the thirteenth floor of the FBI regional office on Golden Gate Avenue. Almost fifteen years ago he'd been in the same room for a private debriefing when he'd broken a story about the Five Knives Killer—a story that launched his career at *The Post*. Back then he never imagined that he'd return to be interrogated for another federal investigation.

To accommodate the pandemic social distancing rules, the interview room had been renovated to support a sheet of plexiglass that separated Finch from Saxx and Keely. Finch set his courier bag next to a wastepaper basket and draped his jacket over the back of a steel-framed chair. Two tables abutted one another—separated by the long, quarter-inch-thick sheet of plastic. The makeshift solution created the illusion that they shared a single table as they peered at one another through the plexiglass. He slid the top of his mask below his chin and took a sip of the coffee Keely had offered him after they entered the main office. The brew was thin, lukewarm, bitter.

Both agents took off their face masks and settled into the two chairs opposite him. A long, hooked nose bisected Saxx's square face. A ridge of six or seven worry lines furrowed his forehead up to his hairline. His dark, swollen lips reminded Finch of a high school friend nicknamed Liver Lips. He adjusted his weight in the chair with a lumbering motion as if he were a baseball catcher squatting behind home plate.

Compared to Saxx, Keely bore a fine set of delicate features. Everything about her appearance suggested that she'd been a contender for any number of school and college pageants. Her high cheekbones and smooth, tanned skin made Finch wonder if she was cut out for the rough and tumble demands of the FBI. As she turned her head to open a file folder on her desk, her blue eyes caught the light from the overhead fluorescent lamps. Finch glimpsed a spark of intelligence. He realized he needed to be wary around her. Saxx might cover home base but she called the pitches.

"Mr. Finch," she began. "As I said before, you're not under suspicion for anything related to the murder of Myfanwy Thomas last night."

Finch nodded. So far, so good. She'd pronounced Myfanwy's name correctly and provided her surname, too. New information for Finch to process.

"Okay. What I don't get is why her case was bumped from the SFPD to the FBI in-box."

"We can only reveal so much," Saxx put in, "but the circumstances of her death involve an ongoing federal investigation. Whether we wanted the case or not, we own it. Lock, stock, and barrel."

Finch had heard it all before. It sounded like Saxx was quoting from an FBI orientation manual. He chuckled to himself. "Look. I'd like to help in any way I can, but I gave a complete statement to Officer Benton last night. I assume you read it?"

"We did." Keely held a transcript up to the plexiglass. A glance told Finch that everything was signed, sealed, and delivered according to official SFPD protocol. "But we need more information."

"Fine." Finch shrugged. "Fire away."

"All right." She put on a smile. "Joel Griffin." She paused as her eyes settled on his face. "Does that name ring a bell?"

Finch leaned back in his chair and shifted his gaze to his coffee cup. They had him. On her first pitch, she'd nailed him with a down-the-line fastball. He knew it would be a huge mistake to deny any knowledge of Joel Griffin. Lying to the FBI was a federal offense. That alone could land him in jail. But first, he needed to see what they actually had on him.

"Yeah, it does."

Saxx's head ticked to one side. "And what, *exactly*, do you know about him?" A false smile creased his puckered lips.

Finch shrugged. "You tell me."

Keely let out a brassy, spontaneous laugh. She pushed the file to one side. "Mr. Finch, *please*. Believe me, you are *not* a suspect here." She glanced at Saxx. He nodded. "I'm going to be completely transparent with you. Would you really like to know what we know about you?"

A surprise move. He leaned forward and set his elbows on the table. "As a matter of fact, yes, I would."

She opened the front flap of a second file folder to a summary page clipped to the inside cover. "Okay. So, first the fun stuff. You're a leap year baby. Born February 29, 1980. Last year you celebrated your actual birthday—your fortieth? Your tenth?—by marrying Eve Noon, the mother of your baby, Kelly-Céline." She said Céline with a French accent, *Say-lean.* His French-Canadian mother's name.

He nodded. "We call her Casey."

"Well, either way, congratulations."

"Thanks."

She turned her eyes back to the file. "Let's continue. Parents deceased while you were still a young man. Your mother, then your dad. Just nineteen when your father died." Her eyebrows knit together in an expression of sympathy. "Earned a bachelor of journalism from NYU, 2001. After 9-11 served four years in military intelligence while posted in Iraq as a first lieutenant. In Abu Ghraib Prison, of all places. Awarded the Distinguished Service Cross. Honorably discharged 2005."

She looked from the file to Finch. "The award notation says you killed two Iraqis in a skirmish that saved your commanding officer's life."

Finch drew a breath. "That's correct."

She gazed at him with a deliberate look. "Well, thank you for your service."

He shifted his hands as if to wave off her comment. He never knew how to respond to this easy cliché. "There's more?"

"Much more." She scanned the summary sheet. "After your tour in Iraq, you completed an MA in journalism. From Berkeley." She hesitated while she pondered another line in his profile sheet. "You had a previous marriage and a son. Cecily and Buddy Finch. Both deceased." She shook her head as if she regretted bringing this up, then skipped ahead. "And since oh-eight you've worked as a crime reporter for the *San Francisco Post*—and more recently you became a best-selling crime writer with what? Three books under your belt?"

He felt his throat tighten as he tried to swallow the memory of his first wife and son. He hated to reveal his remorse. Not to these two. Not here. Not now. "Look, I think you've covered all the bases."

She held up a finger with a school teacher's wag. "Just a little more. You've also killed civilians in the course of your investigations." She closed the file and nudged it aside. "More than once. Am I right?"

"Only in self-defense."

"Yes. Which takes us to last year." She notched her head back to examine him again. Then she tapped a fingernail on the top of her desk. A signal that brought Saxx into the conversation.

"Outside Rapid City. Under Mount Rushmore." His voice carried a meaty self-assurance. "Three people killed in a shoot-out. You were part of it. And the only survivor."

Finch turned to face Saxx. He appraised the hooked nose, the liver lips, the ridged forehead. An ugly face by any standard. "Have you got the transcript of my statement? From Sam Avery, the Assistant DA in Rapid City."

"I do." Saxx held up the stapled document which bore a South Dakota state seal on the top corner.

"Then you know I was exonerated of any criminal culpability." Finch drew his forearms across his chest. "In fact, the DA commended me on my service to the state."

"Yes. Duly noted. And we might come back to that." He set the file aside. "But we're more interested in the fact that you impersonated Joel Griffin while you were in Rapid City."

Finch blinked. Now he could feel the long arm of the FBI as it reached into his inner world. He knew they had the power to toy with any American anywhere in the world. But Joel Griffin was an invention. A mirage. Finch also knew that impersonation was not an offense—unless it was employed in the course of a crime. He decided to play the innocent. "All right. So you've got a record of my credit card expenses."

Saxx's heavy lips parted in a smile of fond regret. What did the German's call it? Schadenfreude. Reveling in someone's misfortune. "Just your MasterCard. We could have searched your VISA and bank transactions. Your book royalties. But—"

"But we *didn't,*" Keely cut in. "Look, Mr. Finch, let's jump to the chase. As I said from the beginning, we didn't bring you in here to interrogate you. Frankly, we're after something completely different."

She blinked and paused to consider how to continue. "We need your help."

"My help?" Finch slumped back in his chair as if a weak punchline had just been delivered in a long-running joke. Too long. "What are you talking about?"

Keely glanced at Saxx again. When he nodded, she continued. "Have you checked the Twitter feed for Joel Griffin?"

"The Twitter feed?"

"How about his Facebook account. Or Instagram?"

"Never. It must be some other Joel Griffin."

"No. All his social media accounts are linked to you."

23

He felt his stomach churn. Someone is catfishing me. Who? How? He didn't know how to respond. "All right. So you tell me. What's going on?"

"Take a breath."

He did. And at that moment he understood that she had him. *They* had him. They knew more about his secret world than he did. He felt as if he was standing knee-deep in the ocean as a riptide flushed the sand from under his toes.

"Joel Griffin—*your* Joel Griffin—is one of the leading voices in the anti-vaxxer movement. Across his social media platforms, he has over a million and a half followers."

"Over twenty thousand new followers a week," Saxx put in.

The two agents paused to let the burden of facts weigh on him. Then Keely broke the silence.

"As you know, the new president has identified the battle against Covid-19 as *the* number-one government priority. We have to establish herd immunity this year. That means vaccinating seventy to eighty-five percent of the population. He's targeting two hundred and eighty million vaccinations by October. And everyone requires a double dose." She pursed her lips in a tight frown. "You do the math."

"Even Einstein couldn't do it," Saxx said with a laugh.

A ridiculous joke, but they all sputtered out a weak chuckle. Yet Finch was glad to hear it because somehow it confirmed their claim that they needed him. That he was on their side. More important, they were on his side.

"Now the darknet is buzzing with something new." Keely lay both hands palms down on the desk.

"Which is?"

"Some of the anti-vaxxers are planning to sabotage the vaccine supply."

"Sabotage. What kind of sabotage?"

She shrugged. "That's what we have to find out."

"That's where you come in," Saxx offered, his voice soft now, contrite after his earlier sneer.

"Where *I* come in?"

"It was Myfanwy Thomas who created your online persona," Keely said. "She posted all your tweets. All your Facebook and Instagram posts. Through her, we can track your followers. But now that she's dead, the game changes."

"Whoa." Finch held up a hand as if he needed to stop the flow of traffic. "How does this involve me?"

"First thing we did after we picked up her murder investigation was to confiscate her laptop," Saxx replied. "It took our tech team less than an hour to break her password. She was strictly amateur hour. Now we're in control of all Joel Griffin's accounts. All of them."

"It took less than ten minutes to break her VPN," Keely added.

A Virtual Private Network, the digital shield that should have screened her activities on the internet. "Okay." He waved a hand in the air searching for direction. "So what?"

"So now that we've taken over Joel Griffin's posts," Saxx said. "We want to use Griffin to penetrate the conspiracy to sabotage the vaccine program."

"In other words," Finch added, "The FBI is now the ghost behind the mirage."

"Exactly." Keely smiled, pleased by his phrasing. "And there's a meeting coming up. A meeting we need Joel Griffin to attend."

"A meeting." Finch smirked. "And you want me to be Joel Griffin?"

"Just for a day." Keely stared at him with a neutral expression. "So we can identify the other players in the conspiracy."

"What? You can't be serious. I'm a civilian." He waved a hand to dismiss the idea as if he were brushing away a housefly. "Get one of your masters of disguise to handle your undercover work."

"We'd like to," she continued, "but Myfanwy pirated your picture. It's on the net."

"And apparently she swabbed your DNA," Saxx added.

*"My DNA?"* Finch felt his stomach churn. "How the hell did she get my DNA?"

"We're not sure," Keely's hand rose in a gentle patting motion as if she might be comforting an angry child.

Finch felt a hazy dizziness swirl through him. "Wait a second. Just hold on." Again he held a hand in front of his chest. "How can you be sure it's my DNA?"

"Look, Finch," Saxx said and leaned toward him. In a whisper, he added, "We just know."

Finch felt his fingers trembling. He bunched them into fists and hid them in his lap below the table. Was it possible? The FBI possessed his DNA profile? As a reporter, he'd covered crime and corruption for fifteen years and he'd never experienced anything close to this level of personal violation. He felt himself digging deep for a way to respond.

"No." Finch's voice bore a hard, determined edge.

"No what?" Keely asked.

"No, I'm not going to do it." He felt the muscles in his face harden in a gesture of defiance. He decided to simply walk away from their game. "Yesterday, last night, I stood at her side when Myfanwy Thomas was murdered. Do you think for one minute I'm going to expose myself—*my wife and daughter*—to this crazy scheme you've put together? The answer is no. Forget it."

"So what *are* you going to do, Finch?" Saxx looked genuinely curious.

He leaned forward, not quite certain that he had the answer to untangle himself from their subterfuge. "To begin with, I've got the facts on my side."

"And just *whose* facts are they?" Keely asked. "You think we'll corroborate anything we've told you today?"

"And don't imagine that the FBI will permit this story to see the light of day. In *The Post* or anywhere in the USA," Saxx added.

Finch felt the air seeping from his lungs. "All right. So maybe you can block the press," he conceded. "But only for so long. Eventually, this bullshit will all come out. But no matter what, I'm not playing your crazy game."

He stood up and lifted his jacket from the chair.

"One more thing, Finch." Saxx gave him a penetrating look. His face revealed that he was about to pitch a low, underhand lob that he'd lined up over the past ninety minutes. "The shootout at Mount Rushmore. Three people dead. I said we might come back to that. Well, here we go. You emptied two full clips from a Ruger LC9s Pro that was not registered in your name. Furthermore, you transported said weapon across state lines. Both of those are felonies. Worst of all, you used an alias—Joel Griffin's credit card—to purchase lodging, food, and gasoline in the course of committing those crimes. That's false impersonation. We could—and I emphasize *could*—arrest you on three federal charges. So take a moment to consider what ten years in prison will do to your family life."

A rush of blood pumped through Finch's arms into his fists. He took a few seconds to reel himself in. He grabbed his courier bag and slopped the coffee cup into the wastebasket where it landed with a heavy splash.

"Go screw yourselves," he growled as he turned toward the door.

Saxx didn't respond. But Keely nodded as if she understood his anger.

"Finch, wait," she said. "I have to sign you out of the building."

He turned back to her, the red scowl still flush on his face.

They walked down the hall without exchanging a word. When they reached the security station, she turned to him.

"Look, it doesn't have to go this way. We need you as much as you need us," she said. "Take a day. Think it through. Call me when you change your mind."

"You threaten me with ten years in prison?" He shook his head with a look of contempt. "How about this. You call me when you change *your* mind."

TWO days later Eve took a call from Gabe Finkleman, the

revered researcher at *The Post*. As *The Post's* CEO and largest shareholder, she'd instructed him to uncover anything he could about Agents Saxx and Keely. Ten years ago she'd been a fresh recruit on the SFPD and she gained first-hand knowledge of the layers of secrecy that shrouded FBI investigations—and the agents responsible for them. Consequently, when Finkleman called, she wasn't expecting much.

"Hello Ms. Noon," he began.

"Gabe, thanks for getting back to me." Eve held her phone in one hand and braced Casey under her left elbow. A diaper dangled from her fingers. She walked into the kitchen, passed the baby to Finch, and tossed the diaper in the bin next to the door.

"She needs a change," she whispered to him and sauntered into the living room.

"So. You find anything beyond what's on the Bureau's website?" She dropped into the loveseat with a sigh. Finally, a chance to get off her feet.

"Yeah, not much there," he said. "I also ran a search on both their names and facial images using Go-Pic. Go-Pic found a few hits. Six on Saxx. A little more on Keely. Seventeen, actually."

Go-Pic. This was Finkleman's proprietary search application that he'd designed to find and report images that might be hiding anywhere on the internet. It was brilliant. Perhaps, too brilliant. Eve feared that one day he would leave *The Post* to launch a tech startup company based on the app. Every week millions of dollars were funneled into ingenious new ventures and fantasy schemes in the Bay Area. Finkleman could be next week's poster boy.

"I'm looking at them right now."

Eve could visualize Finkleman facing three computer screens in his one-bedroom apartment. When the first wave of the pandemic hit California, she'd given the order for all *Post* employees to work from home. Lou Levine, the company lawyer, drafted a policy regarding "home-based worksites" during the shutdown. The policy required every employee to send him images of where the company computers and other corporate assets were located in each household. Finkleman's photo, a selfie, showed his lean, almost seven-foot frame towering above the triple computer array in his kitchen. He even managed to put on a smile. Like many *Post* employees, he seemed to prefer working on his own.

"So what's the scoop?"

"Okay, so Jeremy Winston Saxx was born in Dallas in 1978. He's married, has one son, sixteen. Graduated from Baylor—major in biology—in ninety-nine. He spent the next five years in the army, stationed in Germany. I think that's when he was recruited to the FBI because after his military discharge he disappears."

"Disappears?"

"In the virtual sense. You have to remember the internet was in its infancy back then. Especially social media. Which didn't actually exist." He paused as if he might be scrolling through one or two screens. "Next, he reappears in 2011 as part of a team that busted a fraud case that was run out of Berlin."

"You mean from Berlin into the US?"

"Yup. Money laundering. A pre-Bitcoin operation the FBI

dubbed Water Born."

Eve smiled to herself. She knew a lot about Bitcoin. When she met Finch, they broke open a massive Bitcoin fraud together. After several twists of fate, she inherited a Bitcoin fortune that allowed her to purchase *The Post.*

"Then in 2017, he was part of a cybercrime bust right here in San Francisco. Maybe you remember it. Operation Cats Eye."

"I do. It was a huge score for the Bureau. So Saxx was in on that?"

"Uh-huh. Since then it looks like he was drafted into the regional Bureau's cyber crimes unit, officially called the Internet Crime Complaint Center—or IC3. There are five of them on the regional cyber team. One of them is Agent Keely."

"Okay. So, now her."

"A completely different story." He laughed as if he'd discovered a pleasant surprise. "She's thirty-five. Born in Baltimore. Her parents adopted her shortly after her birth and moved her to their home in Boston. She was an early bloomer and they enrolled her in The Winsor School."

"I've heard of it. A top drawer academy for gifted girls."

"She is certainly that. And more. Graduated from Winsor at fifteen. Four years later she finished a masters degree in mathematics at Harvard."

"A masters at nineteen. Really?"

"She jumped from undergrad to grad studies after her second year. Then get this. After Harvard, she moves to Kyoto, Japan and spends a year training in Aikido at the Budo Center. Which happens to be the oldest military martial arts training center in Japan. Then she returned to the US, straight to San Francisco. Likely that's when she was brought into the Bureau. My guess is they put her on a desk in intelligence. Then just like Saxx, her digital trail is wiped clean. At least until she appears with him in 2017 on Operation Cats Eye. For the last four years, she's been his partner in the cyber crimes unit."

Eve tried to visualize how the pieces fit together. "So she's smart, she's tough and she's independent."

"Just wait until I send you her picture. She's like ... well, outstandingly beautiful."

Eve smiled. Finkleman had a shy, private part of his personality that he rarely revealed. Admitting that a woman might be attractive would be a huge risk for him.

"Really? *That* good-looking?" she couldn't help baiting him.

"Yeah. I found one image from Harvard where she's sort of posing. Like Kiera Knightly. Only with short hair."

"Ha-ha!" Eve couldn't stifle the laugh. "Okay, Gabe. Great job. Can you send the file to me?"

"You bet."

"And cc it to Will, okay."

"Yes, Ms. Noon."

So formal, she thought. "By the way, how's everything going? You dealing with the pandemic all on your own?"

"Yeah. Umm ... good."

She sensed he had more to tell her. Likely his girlfriend was in his bubble, but he'd never reveal that either. Perhaps his hesitancy was another manifestation of his obsessive privacy. She waited a moment and when he didn't continue she said,

"All right, Gabe. Thanks. Call if you need anything."

AFTER Finch settled the baby in her crib, he stepped downstairs to the front door and checked the mail. He pulled two packages from the box. The first was sealed in a fat, nine-by-twelve-inch paper envelope. He checked the return address. Gerard & Associates. He knew this would be the new contract for his latest book—apparently delayed in the mail due to cutbacks in the postal service.

The second package was addressed to him in square, hand-printed letters. Wrapped in a four-by-five bubble pack, it showed no return address and was bound in layers of transparent tape. He squeezed it between his fingers and felt a lump inside. Something the size of an eraser. No, smaller. Maybe a computer thumb drive? Every year or two, an anonymous source sent him a digital drive loaded with "evidence" of crimes. Only once had the allegations led to a story that he could report in *The Post*. Nonetheless, he always treated these tips with respect. Someone had taken the time and effort to contact him. Hit or miss, he always honored their intentions.

He carried both envelopes into the living room and sat in the chair opposite Eve. She finished her call with Gabe Finkleman and offered him a smile.

"You got Casey down for a nap?"

Over the past six months, Kelly-Céline's name had morphed to her initials, KC, then to the more fluid Casey. At first, Finch resisted the change, but when Eve's sister Megan Rivers caught on, she wouldn't let it go. "Come on, Will," she'd said. "You love baseball. Think of Casey Stengel. And the Giants'

Casey Schmitt. And hey"—she waved a hand at him—"every-body knows 'Casey At The Bat.' It's the perfect girl nickname. I guarantee she'll be famous before she's in kindergarten." They all laughed at that and when Megan's son and his girl-friend, Brock and Klare, adopted the name, Finch conceded the battle.

"Yup. She's down for the count." He washed a hand over his face. He'd barely slept the past two nights as his encounter with the FBI rolled over and over in his mind. He felt cornered. Trapped in a dangerous game.

"That was Finkleman on the phone. He's got some intel on Saxx and Keely. They run the local cyber-crimes squad. IC3."

"That fits."

"He's sending us the file. Knowing Finkleman, it's already in our inboxes."

"He sent it in email?" Finch was skeptical. A few years ago some of his email correspondence had been hacked. His friend Jerome Rickets and Jerome's wife had been murdered as a result.

"No. Encrypted in Signal. You know Finkleman. He thinks email's for dinosaurs. Anyway, let's read what's in the file and think about what to do next." She noticed the envelopes in his hand. "Got some mail?"

"Looks like the contract for the new book." He plunked the larger package on the cushion. "And something else. You never know what." He lifted the bubble-wrap envelope in his fingers. It felt feather-light.

"Open it."

"I'll need scissors. It's sealed in about ten layers of tape."

She opened the narrow drawer in the coffee table and found the safety shears with rounded nubs on each point. "Throw it over."

Finch tossed the envelope over the coffee table and Eve snagged it in her right hand. Unable to find a gap in the sealing tape, she scissored off a narrow strip of the wrapper from one end. Inside she found a small, unsealed white envelope. She pulled it from the bubble wrapper, opened the flap, and looked inside.

"My God." She let out a hiss of air.

"What?"

She took a few seconds to read a message on the back of the white envelope. "Don't touch it," she said. She drew a tissue from the Kleenex box on the table, wrapped the tissue around the small package, and passed it to Finch. "Just look. Don't touch anything with your fingers."

Inside lay the brass casing of a discharged nine-millimeter round. He closed the flap and read the message printed across the face of the envelope in square, upper case letters.

PLAY THE GAME
OR YOU'LL END THE SAME.

ANOTHER day passed as Eve and Finch explored the universe of Covid-19 vaccine information on the internet. They sat facing one another at the kitchen table, clicking hundreds of links on their laptops as they tried to sort the science from utter fantasy. Eve had devised a way to nurse the baby while she tapped her keyboard with her right hand. When she felt Casey easing up on her nipple, she prepared to pass her over to Will.

"It's hopeless," she concluded. "Maybe twenty credible institutions are broadcasting the facts—all confirmed by the Centers for Disease Control, the Mayo Clinic, the National Institutes for Health—compared to thousands of anti-vaxxer sites."

"Which are mostly tribal cults," Finch added as he closed another chatroom claiming that the virus was transmitted by 5G networks. In the UK, cellphone towers were set on fire. Days later, the mania had spread to other countries. "They all drank the Kool-Aid."

"Except they think *we've* drunk the Kool-Aid." She shrugged off the irony.

"Yeah. The world is flat. The sun circles the earth." Finch rubbed a hand over his beard. "Look, let's get back to basics. This isn't about who's right or wrong. It's about how we get out of this mess."

"Agreed." Eve sighed with pleasure as the baby unlatched from her breast. She gazed into Casey's eyes as she buttoned her blouse. "Mmmm. That was good, huh baby?"

Finch hoisted Casey's chest up to his shoulder and stroked her back. It was part of their routine. After Eve nursed the baby, she passed her on and he would burp her. With luck, Casey would drift off and Finch could slip her into the crib without a fuss. As they approached Casey's first birthday, Eve planned to wean her as soon as possible. International Freedom Day, she called it.

"Look," he murmured, "tomorrow morning you two are moving in with your sister."

He walked back and forth along the kitchen floor hushing the baby's soft cries as he patted her back in a slow, hypnotic rhythm. When she settled he turned back to his wife.

"We can't waste another day like this, Eve." His voice conveyed a sense of urgency. "We know three things for sure. They murdered Myfanwy. They know where we live. And they've threatened me if I don't play along."

Eve nodded and glanced away. She felt the fear gnawing in her belly. "I know. You're right," she conceded. "But I think you should come with us."

"Let me put her down," he whispered when he heard Casey expel a long, wet burp. "Then we'll decide."

Eve watched him carry the baby upstairs to the nursery and wiped a hand over her mouth and nodded to herself. She knew Will was thinking clearly. Above all, they had to protect Casey. Funny, she'd never had to confront that burden before. She'd felt the protective, maternal instinct the moment her baby was born. The life-shifting impulse coursed through her like a shot of adrenaline. But with a real threat at hand, her determination hardened. An hour after the mysterious bullet casing appeared, she'd gone up to the lockbox in their bedroom and found her Ruger LC9s Pro. She took a moment to examine the weapon and the matching bullet clip. Just like the old days when she was a beat cop with the SFPD. But now she slept with the gun in the night table drawer next to her pillow.

When Finch crept down the stairs to the living room, she smiled at him. "She go down all right?"

He nodded and sat on the sofa next to the gas fireplace.

"Okay, I agree," She began. "Tomorrow we'll go to

Megan's. But I still think you should come with us."

He shook his head. "No. I stay here." His voice was firm. "Whoever this is"—he pointed to the bubblewrap envelope —"they can find me. They're smart. And fearless. But if I stay here, they have no reason to go after you and Megan. That's better for them."

Eve's face softened. "All right," she conceded. "I know. It's just so ... *fucked.*" She struggled to catch her breath. "It's like they've already won."

"No, not yet. We haven't even made our first move. Getting you and Casey over to your sister's in Berkeley is the first step. It's like castling a king in chess. Once the defense is set up, then we start the middle game."

"And that begins with the brass bullet shell."

"It's all we've got." A sense of weakness seeped through him. But he knew it was temporary. "So far," he added.

IT might not be a great plan, but at least they had something to work with. Yesterday Finch wondered if he should deliver the envelope holding the brass shell and the cryptic note to the FBI. Let Saxx and Keely's unit run a forensic analysis and report their findings to him. Did the brass match the slug that killed Myfanwy? Had it been fired from a revolver or a semi-automatic pistol? Could they track the brass and slug to the owner? Were there trace elements of DNA on the package? Fingerprints? Within hours the FBI could bring their resources to bear on all these questions—and more.

But he'd hesitated. Collaborating with Keely and Saxx would drop him blind and defenseless into their bullpen. Exactly what they wanted. From her years of experience, Eve knew the FBI would never share their findings in an active operation. Instead, she suggested that they take the envelope, the brass, and the two-line note to Leanne Spratz. Leanne used to work in the SFPD forensic lab when Eve launched a sexual harassment suit—which she'd won—against the department. A few years later Leanne joined a biotech startup called 123-DNA. Since then she'd provided Eve with fast-track forensic analysis on request. In addition to her lab work, Leanne served as an expert witness in dozens of state and federal criminal prosecutions. More important, she had the signing authority to notarize forensic discovery documents that satisfied the state court's evidentiary criteria.

"So. You want me to take the package over to Leanne?"

Finch considered the two options one last time. Deliver the mystery package to the feds or Leanne?

"I do," he said. "It's our best move. If nothing comes out of Leanne's analysis, then I can give it to the feds later. We can't do it the other way around."

She nodded. It was the better sequence.

"If you want to take it over to Leanne while the baby sleeps, I'll stay home and get my head around what comes next."

Which would lead to his third move. Myfanwy's roommate. Gabe Finkleman had tracked down Sheila Griffin's home address.

"Sheila lives pretty close to where she works. At the California Academy of Sciences in Golden Gate Park," Finkleman said.

"What street?"

"Lyon." Finkleman spelled the street name and added the house number.

Finch entered the information into Google maps.

"You get bonus points if you can name her next-door neighbor." Finkleman's voice brightened with an expectation of surprise.

"Her neighbor?"

"Yeah. Back in the sixties."

"No idea." Finch wasn't in the mood for surprises and his voice showed it. "Just tell me."

"Janis Joplin. She lived at 122 Lyon."

"Thanks, Gabe." Finch offered a smile and closed his phone. He narrowed his eyes as he considered his plans.

All right then. Tomorrow he'd visit Joel Griffin's daughter, Sheila. Who knows, he wondered. Maybe she doesn't like surprises either.

# CHAPTER TWO

DOBB'S FERRY, NY — JULY 3, 1988

Up until that Sunday morning, Joseph Tull's world was almost perfect. He had tons of friends, a small but loving family, a new Casio watch, and a twenty-five-inch tall, remote-controlled Omnibot 2000. He'd scored one hundred percent in every math test throughout the school year and in June he'd won the school spelling bee. The day after the spelling bee, he'd hit a stand-up triple that drove in the winning run against the Hastings Giants. And although it made his stomach churn with excitement, on the last day of classes, the extremely cute Sally Kitterson said she had "a thing" for him. *A thing.* He knew that meant something special and began to conjure up her beautiful face as he lay in bed at night.

When he reflected on the course of events, Joseph decided that his almost perfect life came to an abrupt end when Janice Graham, his babysitter, tore down the staircase to stand at his side. When she put her hand on his shoulder. When the strangers asked if they could come into his house.

The day before his world ended, Janice had invited her boyfriend to spend Saturday in Joseph's house while his parents were out of town. The boyfriend, Paul Snipes, had brought a bottle of Southern Comfort into the tidy home on Chestnut Street in Dobb's Ferry, New York. After Janice and Paul drank off two-thirds of the whiskey and fumbled their way into the guest bedroom, Joseph stationed himself in front of the TV and watched a five-hour marathon of *Tales From The Darkside*. To provide a little comfort of his own, Joseph began to sip what remained of the honey-flavored whiskey straight from the bottle. By three a.m. he dropped into a heavy sleep on the sofa. It wasn't until he heard the knocking on the front door that his eyes blinked open. He dragged a hand over his face and checked his new digital wristwatch. 11:23.

His father had given him the watch for his twelfth birthday —on the day before he and his mother left for an international science conference in Tehran. Joseph had set the display to the 24-hour mode because it was cool. Besides, the 24-hour mode was the military standard.

"Jeez," he muttered and sat up in a sudden panic. For a moment the knocking felt like it was hammering inside his head. He tried to shake off the pain and rubbed both hands over his face. Could it be his parents? No, they were scheduled to land at Kennedy International Airport at 13:15. In less than two hours.

Then another thought struck him. Where was Janice?

"Janice?" he called out.

"Yeah, I'm just getting dressed. Joey, answer the door,

okay."

As he made his way to the front door he could hear fits of laughter upstairs. Janice and Paul fumbling to get dressed in a panic.

The moment he opened the front door, he understood that something fundamental in his life was about to change. A tall, thin man wearing a crumpled gray suit stood beside a woman who clasped a black leather briefcase in her left hand. She had curly blond hair and put on a fake smile.

"Hello. Are you Joseph Tull?" She paused as if she didn't quite know how to continue. "The son of Richard and Anya Tull?"

Joseph knew something terrible had happened. Except for his mother, nobody called him Joseph. To everyone else, he was Joey.

Janice appeared behind him at the door. The man looked at Janice and leaned forward. He had a hopeful look on his face. "Are you Joseph's babysitter?"

"He's not a baby," she said with a shrug. "But, yes."

"Right. Sorry," the woman apologized. "I'm Heather Sisman. And this is Mr. Frank Besweatheric. May we come in?"

Janice put her hand on Joseph's shoulder. He could feel his skin sizzle as her fingers pressed against his collar bone. She took a step forward and asked, "Who are you?" Her voice was taut. "Like, why are you here?"

"We're from Children and Family Services."

The lady smiled again. She wore heavy makeup, Joseph thought, but not enough to cover the sadness in her face.

"We should sit down together. I'm afraid we have some bad

43

news."

JOSEPH sat in the Kennedy International departures lounge waiting for Aeroflot Flight 62 to board. He gazed through the window watching the jets land in three-minute intervals which he timed on his Casio watch. Something was soothing about their routine. As if he'd discovered that the world had a reliable structure after all. Considering the upheaval he'd endured over the past two weeks, the orderly world inside the airport felt almost normal.

"You still have ticket, Josef?"

"Uh-huh." He pulled the boarding pass from the outside pocket of his backpack and passed it to Alena. She examined it briefly and returned it to him.

"And passport?"

"Yes." His lips rolled into a frown.

Alena Budanov had been kind enough to him during the past ten days, but over the last hour, she had him double- and triple-check everything in his bag. His boarding pass, US birth certificate and passport, school records, Soviet citizenship papers. And most important, the address and phone number of Uncle Valery in Tver.

"You want anything before you get on plane? Any food? Something for drink?" She studied his face, marveled at his good looks. His thick red hair.

"No. I'm fine." But he wasn't certain. What does anyone need when they fly alone over 4,500 miles? Tomorrow he'd be welcomed by his mother's brother, Uncle Valery—his only living relative. He'd spent the past three summers at Uncle

Valery's lakeside home. Joseph's mother Anya insisted that he master the Russian language and his father Richard agreed that two months in the countryside outside Tver would benefit Joseph. Now the prospect of living permanently with Uncle Valery stirred Joseph's broken heart with a dash of hope. His parents were dead. *Dead.* He still couldn't say the word aloud.

When his uncle offered to bring the boy into his family—and due to the new spirit of detente—the Americans and Russians agreed to Uncle Valery's proposal. Joseph would live with his uncle and aunt. He would attend public school. However, the Americans and Russians agreed that when he graduated, depending on his academic performance, Joseph would be granted admission to a university in the USA. Furthermore, any compensation from the Americans along with his parents' meager estate would be held in trust and a portion distributed to him annually. The arrangement was reported in the press as an example of the new US-Soviet collaboration.

"It's good that your mother booked this flight last month," Alena said. "This is your third summer with Uncle Valery?"

He shook his head. "My fourth."

She smiled and a glowing look of sympathy filled her face. Three days after his parents died in the air disaster, she'd taken the Hudson Train from Grand Central Station to Dobb's Ferry and walked the few blocks to his house. She wanted to give him comfort, to let him know that while another life was possible, he would have to adapt. Every morning she worked from the consulate office to make the necessary arrangements for his journey from New York to Moscow. And every second afternoon she took the train to his home to prepare him for the chaotic world she knew awaited him in the USSR.

"Yes, your fourth visit. I forget." She gazed at his hair. The light streaming through the windows brought an orange tinge to the curls. "And each time you visit in the middle of July?"

He nodded. Because she already knew about his annual visits, he suspected that she was making conversation for its own sake. Maybe it made her feel more comfortable. Last week, she revealed that she was an orphan, too. "But it didn't stop me from making a life of my own. You can too, Josef. You'll see that one day."

She looked into his eyes and spoke in Russian. "Never forget that you are Russian *and* American. You are both. Yes?"

Her voice sounded very much like his mother's. He liked to listen to Alena talk. The Russian words flowed in a soft stream from her little mouth. As the week passed Alena spoke more Russian and encouraged him to reply in her native language.

"Ty ponimayesh', chto ya govoryu?" Do you understand what I'm saying?

He nodded.

Her head ticked to one side. "Please, answer in Russian then."

"Konechno. Kazhdoye slovo," he said. Of course. Every word.

"This is a new time for Soviet-American relations," she continued in Russian. "Together Gorbachev and Reagan are making a new world. It's because of detente that authorities on both sides have agreed to let you live in Tver. Five years ago? Impossible." Her hand flicked through the air to dismiss the thought. "But soon there will be a place for a smart young man who is fluent in both languages. However, it won't be given to you, Josef. You must *seize* it." She wrung both hands together as if she were squeezing water from a towel.

"Do you think so?"

It felt good to hear the Russian words roll off his tongue. His mother had loved to hear him speak. "All that is good about Russia lives in the language," she'd told him.

"I'm sure of it," Alena said.

The departure gate doorway opened and the check-in attendant announced his flight departure.

Alena walked Joseph to the gate. She leaned over and caressed his cheek. "Now we part like Russians."

He slipped his backpack over his shoulders and shrugged as if he didn't understand.

"We kiss. On both cheeks." She kissed him once, then again. Waiting each time to feel his lips graze her skin. "Good. Now you're Russian. Go. And do your duty."

JOSEPH found his seat in the second row next to the window on the starboard side and nudged his backpack between his foot and the chair frame. He stared out the window and watched the ground crew attend to the operations on the tarmac. He recalled the procedures from the last few years when he'd traveled to Moscow to visit Uncle Valery. It all seemed so routine. So normal. For a moment the fear of a mid-air disaster filled his chest, but he curled his fists around the armrests and drew in a deep breath. Yes, you could die, too, he told himself. But then you'd be with Mom and Dad. Then he corrected himself. With Mama and Nana. It didn't matter that his father was British.

His mother was Russian. She was the one who'd guided him. The one who sent him to Russia every year to be with Uncle Valery. That was the routine that would save him now.

"So you're Josef Tull." A stewardess with blonde hair pinned up at the back of her head leaned toward him and smiled. A dusty pink lipstick enhanced the warmth of her perfect lips. "My name's Katiya, but you can call me Katie."

She held out a hand. He lifted his right palm from the armrest. As they shook hands he could feel the smooth tenderness in her skin.

"I spoke to Alena from the Russian Consulate. She told me to take special care of you." She smiled again. She had beautiful teeth, too. Then she spoke in Russian. "She told me you speak Russian."

"Da."

"Good, then from now on we speak Russian. Do you know how to buckle your seat belt?"

"Yes."

"Good."

She watched as he buckled in and then she leaned over to tighten the slack from the belt across his waist.

"Once we're underway, Alena gave me a present to give you. A surprise."

"What is it?"

"I just told you, Silly. It's a surprise. I'll be back soon." She winked and then walked along the aisle to check on the other passengers.

When the pilot announced that they'd reached their cruising speed and an altitude of 35,000 feet, Katiya returned to Joseph and passed him an envelope. She rubbed her fingers back and forth across the paper as if she were trying to guess what might be tucked inside.

"Could be money. No, too thick." She winked again. "Unless it's *a lot* of money." Her look suggested she couldn't fathom what might be tucked inside.

Joseph took the envelope and read the words written on the front. *To Josef Tull. You have to know the truth. Best of luck, Alena Tal.*

He broke the seal with his index finger. Sure enough, ten ruble banknotes were held together by a paperclip. Four 50s, four 100s, and two 500s. Folded underneath the money was a newspaper article clipped from the Soviet paper *Pravda* dated July 4, 1988. Joseph knew the word Pravda meant *Truth.*

*US Missile Downs Iranian Airbus*
*290 Passengers and Crew Perish*

*Yesterday all 290 passengers and crew died when the USS Vincennes, an American guided-missile cruiser, fired an SM-2MR surface-to-air missile that destroyed Iran Air Flight 655.*

*On July 3, the Airbus A300 departed Bandar Abbas at 10:17 Iran time. Before the attack, the aircraft was transmitting IFF squawks in Mode III, a signal to identify it as a civilian aircraft.*

*The Vincennes illegally entered Iranian territorial waters and shot down the Airbus as it passed through Iranian airspace over the Persian Gulf. Crew on the Vincennes incorrectly identified the Airbus as an attacking F-14 Tomcat. The F-14 is a US-made fighter jet, once part of the Iranian Air Force.*

*American authorities claim their ship was in international waters off the coast of Iran and entered Iranian territory after one of its helicopters drew warning fire from Iranian speed-boats.*

*Soviet satellite tracking records confirm the Iranian claims. In this illegal act of war, the US contravened five articles of the United Nations Convention on the Law of the Sea.*

*"Once again, the US military has broken its international commitments," said Yuri Apalkov from the Ministry of Foreign Affairs. "Once again, the moral bankruptcy of the imperialist regime is exposed for all the world to see. The fact that a Soviet citizen lost her life on Flight 655 could delay—if not halt—the progress we are making toward detente."*

*Anya Tull, a Soviet academic, was returning on Flight 655 with her husband from an international conference in Tehran. The married couple was part of a goodwill exchange initiated in 1975. They met and lived in New York City where each held a fellowship in paleontology at Columbia University. They leave behind their only child, American-born Josef Tull, age 12.*

*Soviet officials have initiated contact with American authorities to provide the necessary support for the child.*

Joseph read the article twice, then held the newsprint in his hands as if it were one more identity document that Alena insisted he check and double-check on the passage to his new life. After a few moments, he tucked the article into his backpack and stared through the window. The *truth,* he thought. Pravda. As he watched the still clouds hover below the aircraft, he swallowed the pain of his loss. Pushed it down into his belly where—silently, slowly—it gnawed at his gut. Already he could feel it growing. He wondered if one day it might become a monster.

WHEN his flight arrived at Sheremetyevo International Airport, Joseph felt relieved to be on firm ground. After he cleared customs, his uncle welcomed him with the gruff smile that exposed his crooked teeth and immediately broke into tears as he clasped Joseph in his arms.

"My child, my child," he whispered. "We have both lost Anya. She died twice to us. Once as your mother. Once as my sister. She can never be replaced."

The two of them cried arm-in-arm until Joseph had to break away. He'd blocked the pain for over two weeks. But now the burden of his broken heart felt too heavy to bear. His tears spilled onto his uncle's shoulder. Maybe it was a mistake to come to Russia. But where else could he go?

When their sobbing ebbed away, Valery released his nephew and took a step backward. "Let me look at you." Uncle Valery wore a leather sailor's cap with a tattered peak that cast a narrow shadow on his forehead. After a moment he nodded his head. "Despite your tears, you look fine. Bigger than last summer. Maybe three inches taller."

"Maybe."

"Are you still called *verkhnyaya chast' morkovi?"*

Carrot top. His mother's nickname for his red hair.

"Not anymore."

Valery saw how his question hurt the boy. He decided to try another approach. "Here in Russia, we'll call you Josef, not Joseph. Like Josef Stalin. A hero."

Joseph nodded and looked away. What did it matter? "I have to pee."

"Okay."

They walked across the concourse to the toilets. On the way to the queue waiting for the airport ground transportation, they passed the food carts stationed near the exit.

"Uncle, can I buy something?"

Valery hesitated. "They didn't feed you on the plane?"

"Not much."

"Well." He had to think about it. "I don't have the car this year. Our bus to Tver leaves from downtown in forty minutes. Let's get to the bus depot and decide once we're there."

Their drive into the city ran late. As soon as they stepped into the terminal they had to dash to the bus bound for Tver.

"Still hungry?" Valery asked as they took their seats.

"A little." Joseph sensed that his hunger posed a problem. On the drive into Moscow, Uncle Valery explained that "circumstances had changed since last year." He'd sold his Volga GAZ, and Aunt Tanya had lost her job at the pharmacy.

"Our bus stops after an hour in Reshetnikovo," Valery continued. "A half-hour stop. You can eat there. If you still feel the need."

Joseph checked his watch. It would be close to three in the afternoon before he ate. 15:00. He decided to squeeze his belly and wait.

"Oh, you have a watch now." Valery's face brightened. "A Casio."

"For my birthday. It has push buttons," he added and clicked a button to show the display as it shifted the date and time settings.

"Best not to show that off." Valery's voice wavered with a cautious tone. "You never know these days."

When they arrived in Reshetnikovo, Valery led them into the cinder block station. It smelled of diesel gas and urine. Joseph pinched his nose and searched for a food cart. He pointed to one parked next to the toilets. "Can I get us something, Uncle?"

"Hmm. You still like the pigs in blankets?"

"Yes." Joseph felt his hunger rise from his belly through his throat and onto his tongue. "Yes, I almost forgot about them."

Valery nodded. "Josef, did they give you any money?"

"Money?"

Every year Joseph was given two hundred US dollars from his mother. "You give this to Uncle Valery," she'd instructed him.

"Yes, from Alena." He showed the envelope to his uncle.

"How much is it?"

"Sixteen hundred."

Valery almost gasped. "Dollars?"

"No, rubles."

Valery's thin lips rolled together. "Well ... it all helps. Better give it to me. I know how to put it to good use. But first, let's buy some piggies in blankets." He led the way to the food cart and waved a hand at the old potato-faced babushka tending the stall. "Two piggies."

She nodded to Valery with a tired frown. Then offered a brief smile to Joseph.

Uncle Valery gestured to the old woman again and held up two fingers. "And we'll have both servings with sauerkraut."

He wrapped his arm around his nephew and whispered, "Just to celebrate your welcome home."

# CHAPTER THREE

SAN FRANCISCO — 22 FEBRUARY, 2021

Finch sat in his Toyota RAV 4 and studied the immaculate house on Lyon Street. The three-story Victorian charmer stood a block and half north of Haight Street and half a block south of the Golden Gate Park panhandle. The structure was an outstanding example of the Queen Anne architectural revival that followed the 1906 earthquake which destroyed most of the city. While it was unique, Finch knew the building was one of twenty-three homes in the real estate portfolio owned by Tru-Hip Properties. All of them money-spinners.

After Finch's request for assistance, Gabe Finkleman had generated a list of tenants who rented the Lyon Street building over the past decade. Since 2019 Sheila Griffin, registered as the legal tenant, shared the house with one roommate, Myfan-wy Thomas. Finkleman's profile of Sheila showed that she'd moved from Florida to San Francisco the year after her father Joel Griffin died from anaphylaxis. Her mother, diagnosed with early-onset dementia in 2011, still lived in a long-term care facility in Tampa. Sheila graduated from the University of Florida with an honors degree in computer science. She'd spent one year on a student exchange in Moscow. She didn't have a driver's license. Her grad yearbook identified her as a "Computer nerd who learned to code at the age of eight and can squeeze fresh lemonade from a database about moon rocks."

The jibe made Finch chuckle. It was one of the better backhanded compliments he'd heard. To Finch, it meant she had no social life but could unravel deep mysteries hidden in numbers. She was twenty-five, single, and employed by The California Academy of Sciences, located in the heart of Golden Gate Park. Despite its highfalutin name, local residents thought of the Academy as an indoor zoo. A good one, to be sure, but not an academic hive abuzz with Noble Prize winners.

In October, when the severity of the Covid-19 pandemic throttled the national economy, the Academy closed its doors to the public. However, Sheila was considered an essential employee, and the museum's IT systems required her attention every day. While the pandemic altered the routines of most citizens, Sheila's schedule appeared to be governed by a broken clock.

Over the past three days, Finch followed her as she walked through the park to her office. She left her house between nine and nine-thirty. It took her about half an hour to reach the museum on foot. At that point, any semblance of routine ended. The time she spent in the Academy varied from thirty minutes to five hours. Based on the evidence, Finch figured he had no more than the time she took to walk back and forth—at most an hour—to break into her home and learn what he could about Sheila and her deceased roommate, Myfanwy Thomas.

Finch sat in his RAV4, biding his time. It had been years since he'd staked out a property from his car. He'd learned to be patient and to remain alert through unbroken stretches of boredom. While he waited he ate the last wedge of his egg sandwich and washed it down with a long sip of coffee from his thermos. As Finch screwed the top onto his thermos bottle, Sheila descended the eleven steps to the sidewalk and made her way towards the park. Through the rearview mirror, he watched her cross the road. When she turned onto Oak Street he pulled his mask over his face and slung the strap of his courier bag across his shoulder. Then he climbed out of his car and crossed the street to her house.

A gateway next to Sheila's house led to the rear door. During previous surveillance, Finch learned that the back door opened into the kitchen. He also knew the bolt was a heritage warder lock that he could jimmy with his lock pick tools. When he reached the door, he set his bag on the deck and tugged on a pair of latex gloves. Then he drew a leather case from his back pocket. He had a fondness for the little kit, one of the few gadgets he'd kept from his days in the US army's military intelligence unit in Iraq. He selected two picks and applied them to the lock. Ten seconds later he felt the catch release and he stepped inside. He pulled his face mask below his chin and stood for a moment in the kitchen, his senses tuned to the ambiance of the house. He heard the swish and hum of warm air streaming from the gas furnace through the vents. Otherwise, nothing. The house appeared to be empty.

The air smelled of coffee and meat stew. He approached the gas stove and saw a dutch oven sitting on a cast iron element. He leaned forward and the aroma of meat, vegetables, and household spices filled his nostrils. He chuckled to himself. For whatever reason, he'd assumed she was vegetarian. Dead wrong. Not only that, but from the spicy aromas, she appeared to be a decent cook. He strolled into the adjoining dining and living rooms. The tables, the furniture, the chairs, and sofas all maintained the Queen Anne style—ornate, overstuffed, ostentatious. Furthermore, everything was tidy and well ordered. Was she somewhat compulsive? Not uncommon for computer coders. Finch wondered if obsessive cleaning provided a way for Sheila to cope with her roommate's murder. Cover it up, hide it away until the past disappeared.

He walked to the front door, turned, and studied the hallway. A narrow, carpeted passage led to a small bathroom containing a toilet and sink. Beyond the bathroom, the hallway returned to the kitchen. On the right, a staircase rose to the second floor. There he found two bedrooms separated by an updated four-piece bathroom. A second staircase climbed up to an attic loft that served as an office. On the desk sat three computer monitors surrounded by an elaborate array of peripherals bound together by a jumble of wires and cords. He wondered if this was Sheila's secret lair, the place where she and Myfanwy concocted Joel Griffin's schemes—the deep fakes that ensnared Finch in the FBI's subterfuge. He pressed a gloved finger on the keyboard. The screen refreshed with a prompt for him to enter a password. Finch shrugged. He could spend hours here and get nowhere. He took pictures of the computer and monitors. When he returned home, he'd forward them to Gabe Finkleman. Perhaps he could reveal something useful about the equipment

He decided his time would be better spent investigating Myfanwy's bedroom. The stairs creaked as he stepped back down to the second floor. The room facing Lyon Street appeared to be the master bedroom. The queen bed was covered by an embroidered duvet. Two lace puff pillows lay against the headboard. On the dresser, a collection of framed pictures showed Sheila and a middle-aged couple whom Finch assumed was her father and mother. Two professional family portraits showed all three of them together. Everyone in the pink of health. A long, sheer curtain covered the triple-pane bay window. He pulled the curtain aside with one finger and studied the sidewalk and road below. The view stretched from corner to corner. Finch realized that Sheila could easily have seen his car parked halfway up the block. Had she bothered to look?

He drew a breath and moved to the second bedroom. The door was closed. Perhaps Sheila's way of sealing off the loss of her friend. He turned the handle and stepped across the bare floorboards which groaned under his weight. A pair of black-out drapes shuttered the tall window. He found the light switch, clicked it. The overhead fixture cast a weak light into the room. Before him stood a double bed on a brass frame, the mattress bare, without linens or pillows. To the left of the bed a lone side table, another Queen Anne antique, sat as if waiting for a layer of dust to cover the bare wood. He walked over to the only other piece of furniture, a four-tier dresser with bowed drawers. He grasped the twin loop handles mounted at each end of the top drawer and tugged it open. Empty. The second, third, and fourth drawers—all bare. He opened the closet door. The single rail held a dozen wire hangers. There were no boxes, no shoes—not a trace of Myfanwy Thomas to be found.

Maybe the emptiness itself was evidence of something. A deep cleanse. Of someone's need to make Myfanwy disappear. Finch used his phone to take more pictures. The bed, the dresser, the closet. He realized the answers he needed must be hidden somewhere else. He was about to leave the room when a sense of curiosity tugged at him. He stepped over to the window and again with one finger, pulled the heavy drape aside. The neighboring house—Janis Joplin's hippie lair—stood about five feet away. Between them, a narrow passage led from Lyon Street to the backyard.

He saw a shadow move. Fast, dark—then it disappeared around the corner toward the kitchen door. A moment later he heard the lock rattle. Two, three times. Then the sound of the hinges creaking open sent his heart on a run. Who could it be? Not Sheila. She would have entered through the front door as she'd always done every day when Finch followed her home from the Academy. A stranger—perhaps Myfanwy's killer—looking for … what?

Finch knew he had two choices. First, he could hide here, in Myfanwy's closet. In which case the intruder would likely do the same thing Finch had done and open the door. But when Mr. X discovered Finch hugging the back wall, then what? What if he had a gun? Myfanwy's murder proved the assassin wouldn't hesitate to kill him, too. He chose a second option. Exit ASAP.

He clasped his courier bag to his chest, drew a deep breath, and stepped into the hallway. He inched toward the landing and gazed down the stairs. Now he heard steps pacing along the hallway from the kitchen to the front door. Two men. He decided to hold his ground up here. If they had weapons he'd dash through the master bedroom, smash the window with his bag and try to swing onto the front porch below.

Now he saw their masked faces, their shoulders.

"Hey!" His voice bellowed down to the two intruders at the foot of the stairs. *"Who the fuck are you?"*

"FBI!" They turned in unison, pistols aimed at his chest. "On your knees! Hands in the air!"

Finch recognized the FBI tactical vests. They had him. He could follow their commands or absorb five rounds from each of them. Better this, he decided, than diving through a glass window onto the street. His hands floated above his head and he eased onto his knees. From that moment on, everything followed a script. They ordered him to roll onto his belly, swing his hands behind his back. A pair of handcuffs clipped around his wrists—"too tight," he whined—then they braced him in their arms and they stumbled down the stairs, walked through the back door, down Lyon Street to a windowless van parked near the corner of Haight Street.

"DAMN it, Finch, what are you thinking?" Agent Jeremy Saxx wore an N-95 face mask but it didn't hide his expression of scorn. His eyes seemed to bulge from his eye sockets. "You have no idea what you're up against. Who'ya think you are, Clark Kent?"

Sandra Keely leaned toward the two agents who'd shoved Finch into the back of the van. "Uncuff him," she whispered. Her voice sank with weary despair as if she'd already dealt with a dozen SNAFUs this morning. "Wait in the observation car. Keep an eye out for the O.M."

Once his hands were free and he peeled the latex gloves from his hands, Finch rubbed the chaffing on his wrists. "What's the O.M?"

Saxx chuckled at that. "Persistent bastard, aren't you? Ask yourself something, Finch. Should we add breaking and entry to the charge sheet we've already got on you?" He pointed in the direction of Sheila's house. "It's one thing for you to be stalking Sheila Griffin every day. But far worse to screw up an ongoing federal investigation. In my experience, guys like you who jump from Little League to the Majors—chumps like that —all of 'em strike out."

Finch shrugged. So they'd been tracking him while he was tracking Sheila. A shadow on a shadow as he wandered through an invisible labyrinth. Okay, he had to admit, maybe I am playing out of my league.

Saxx let out a fizz of disgust. "By the way, you got a face mask with you? Something tells me it's risky breathing the same air as you."

Finch nodded.

"Put it on."

Finch adjusted the gaiter mask wrapped around his neck. He tugged it up past his chin and over his nose.

Saxx scoffed when he saw the cloth mask. "You know those things are useless, right?"

Finch shrugged off the complaint and adjusted the mask around his ears.

"Look, Mr. Finch," Keely said, her tone lukewarm. "You're going to have to make a decision. Before you step out that door"—she pointed to the hinged doors on the van—"you either accept the offer we made to work with us or face arrest and prosecution if you interfere with our operation again. Do you understand me?"

"And make no mistake, Finch," Saxx added. "You *will* go down. Hard."

Finch closed his eyes. He needed a moment to think. Then he turned his attention to Keely. "First, they murdered Myfanwy Thomas. Then I was threatened. I'm only acting in self-defense. You both know that's a justifiable defense in any court."

"Yeah, well you could try that, I guess," Saxx scoffed. "And I can hardly wait to testify against you, pal."

"You were threatened?" Keely asked. "Do you have any evidence of that?"

Again Finch had to pause. He knew that at some point the brass shell and the note on the envelope would come to light. He had no way out.

"Yeah. I do."

Keely studied him a moment as if she expected him to divulge more. "Okay. What've you got?"

"The day after we met, an envelope landed in my mailbox. It contained a brass shell. Brass from a nine-mil bullet. The envelope had a message printed on the front." He paused. "It said, 'Play the game or you'll end the same.'"

D. F. Bailey

"Play the game or you'll end the same," Saxx repeated as if he'd committed the rhyme to memory. "And where's this note now?"

"Don't worry. It's secure."

"Secure? Where?"

"At home."

"Jeezus!" Saxx scoffed. "You realize you've withheld evidence in an ongoing criminal investigation?"

"Not if I give it to you," Finch said. "Especially if I agree to the offer you made." He turned to Keely. "But first I want to know what you know."

"Mmmm." Her mouth flattened as if she had to carefully consider his request. "I'm not so sure that deal is still open."

Saxx, Keely—and Finch especially—understood any offer was tentative at best. More likely a lost opportunity. And the chance that he'd ever know the full extent of their operation was less than zero.

"Let's talk about maybes. Maybe there *is* a way we can make this work." She leaned toward a utility box bolted to the van floor and passed him an evidence bag. "Slip the message and the brass into this bag. You know the drill. Use your gloves and don't contaminate anything. Got it?"

"Yeah."

She checked her wristwatch. "Then meet us back at regional HQ at four this afternoon. That fit into your busy schedule?"

Finch didn't appreciate her sarcasm. It made him wonder how much he could trust her. "I can make it."

"Then we'll brief you. Just so you're clear, we can only tell you so much."

*"Need to know,* means just that." Saxx's voice offered no concessions. "And not a word more. So don't be digging for dirt underfoot. You got it?"

He nodded.

"Okay. Go." Saxx waved a hand toward the back door as if he were chasing off a mosquito. A pest that he'd decided to let live rather than crush with a brisk slap.

AFTER his interrogation, Finch called Eve to apprise her of what had happened in the FBI van. In case they were being tracked by Myfanwy's killer, they agreed to meet at Caffe Trieste. It was their favorite café in North Beach, a few blocks downhill from their cottage. Meeting here wasn't perfect, but they knew they'd be safer in a public space than if they had to confront Myfanwy's killer at home.

Finch stepped into the Trieste and ordered a cappuccino from the barista. The room was almost empty. He counted eleven patrons sitting at four tables on the sidewalk and spotted Eve sitting at the furthest table, tapping on her phone screen. Once he had his coffee in hand, he made his way back outside.

"Oh hi." She clicked an icon and turned her phone upside down on the table.

"Hey."

"Any more threats?" She notched her head to one side as she tried to gauge his mood.

"Just the letter and shell."

He sat in the chair beside her and put on a hopeful smile. "To be honest, I'm more worried about the FBI right now."

"Since your call I've been thinking. The way they busted

you at Myfanwy's house?" Her voice rose to emphasize the question. When he'd phoned to tell her about being dragged into the FBI van her mind filled with a myriad of possibilities. "Maybe the feds are our best hope. They're holding all the cards, Will. We've got to bring them on our side."

He knew she was right. Working solo had gone off the rails.

"I know. And once I hand over the brass and the envelope to them, we won't have any other options." He shrugged, a gesture of surrender. "Speaking of which, did you get the package?"

"You're lucky. Leanne just dropped it off."

Finch breathed a sigh of relief. Finally, something had gone right. When he'd told Saxx and Keely that the envelope and brass were securely stored at home, he was flying on nothing more than a wish and a prayer. As far as he knew, Leanne Spratz's forensic analysis could fall weeks behind schedule.

"So you met Leanne here?"

"Less than an hour ago." She opened her purse to reveal a sealed bag containing the envelope and brass slug. "You want it?"

Finch glanced around to ensure no one was observing them. He nodded and then Eve transferred the evidence into his courier bag. He pulled the zipper tight and set the bag next to his feet beneath the table. "So what's her verdict?"

"There's good news and bad." Eve glanced across the street into the bleak midwinter air. She hated the cold and the past few months spent in lockdown seemed to drop ten degrees from the thermometer. "There's no prints or DNA residue on the brass. Leanne figures whoever put the package together wore gloves. The handwriting itself reveals nothing. Especially since it's written in caps. Maybe if we ever find a suspect's handwriting to compare it to, an expert *might* be able to make a determination."

"A determination? What's that mean?"

"At best a fifty percent confirmation that the same person wrote the message on the envelope."

"So, no better than a guess."

"Nope." She ran her fingers over her cheek. "But there is something else."

"The good news."

"Right. So whoever wrapped the sellotape around the bubble wrap got a little frustrated. You know how it can bunch up around itself?"

"So?"

"So Mr. X took off his gloves to re-seal the tape."

Finch leaned forward in anticipation. "There's fingerprints on the tape?"

"Better than that." A hint of pleasure seeped into her voice. "The prints are only partials. But they hold enough DNA to convict another Charlie Manson."

"And Leanne preserved that? It's on the record and secured as evidence?"

"Uh-huh," she whispered. "As good as live testimony in court."

For the first time, Finch felt they'd scored a point. Maybe two. "Okay, let's keep this to ourselves for now. Our ace in the hole. The FBI will soon know everything we do about the package."

"And more. Especially if they find a DNA match."

"Right. And then I can't be accused of withholding information."

She considered the possible legal pitfalls. "Yeah. I think you're safe."

He leaned back in the chair and felt the weight lift from his shoulders. Now that he could relax, his mind turned to Casey. "So you met Leanne here and left the baby with your sister?"

"Yeah. It's a good set-up. I don't know why we didn't think of it before," she added. "Brock and Klare are there, too. They pitch in every day. Changing diapers. Whatever."

Given the threat they faced, the pandemic did provide a few advantages. Eve's sister, Megan Rivers, her son Brock, and his girlfriend Klare lived together in Berkeley Hills, just east of UC Berkeley. In early January the campus had locked down after a spike in viral transmissions. Now, most classes were delivered online. Almost everyone prepared to hunker down until the pandemic exhausted itself, or some sort of herd immunity snuffed the viral spread. Two or three promising vaccines, anticipated by billions around the world, were in production. A broad vaccination program was rolling out across the USA. Brock and Klare believed the virus biotechnology was so advanced that everyone in America could be vaccinated within a year. Who knew?

While Finch continued to live in the cottage on Alta Street, Megan's home in Berkeley provided the perfect safe-house for Eve and Casey. As *The San Francisco Post's* owner and CEO, Eve worked remotely and kept the business on life support until the staff could return to the downtown office. To everyone's surprise, although they worked from home, the reporters' productivity increased. However, revenues continued to drop every month as the economy slumped. Consequently, Eve turned her attention to the business ledger. While she worked the phones, Megan thrived as she tended to the baby.

"It's perfect," Eve said. "It's the first time I've seen Megan this happy since Daniel died."

Finch still remembered the morning Daniel Rivers was shot in front of City Hall on New Year's Day. Something he'd never forget. His empathy for Megan deepened with every passing month. After losing his first wife and child Finch understood the full meaning of an expression he'd picked up in Iraq. Fatal wounds never heal.

"So, okay. You're going to meet Saxx and Keely at four." She checked her watch and nodded to the sandwich board on the wall behind the barista. "You want to have some lunch with me before I drive back to Berkeley?"

"I guess I have to settle for that." Finch smiled. It had been three days since they'd slept together. "But I'd like to do a little more than *eat* with you."

"Whoa. Down, boy." Her chin tipped to one side. "Maybe when you come visit me in Berkeley," she purred in her best imitation of Mae West. "You can taste a little something from my special menu."

"Yeah. Maybe." He could play the game, too. "Maybe I'll do just that. Order something special."

FINCH joined Saxx and Keely in the same room where he'd been interrogated the day after Myfanwy's murder. He sat in the same chair and studied his inquisitors through the sheet of plexiglass that separated them. He sat facing the two agents and placed his paper coffee cup on the Formica table. When they removed their masks he slipped his gaiter mask under his chin.

"So. Here we are again," he said with a droll laugh. Anything to lighten the anxiety he felt when he'd been arrested at Sheila's house and tossed into the FBI surveillance van.

"Just get to it, Finch. You brought the brass and the note with the so-called threat?" Saxx's eyes expressed his doubts.

"Right here." Finch unzipped his courier bag. To comply with their protocols, he'd taken a moment at the Caffe Trieste to transfer the brass casing and the envelope to the FBI evidence bag.

He leaned around the plastic barrier and passed the bag to Keely. She rose a few inches from her chair, took the bag in her right hand, and took a moment to examine the brass and the message.

"Play the game or you'll end the same," she recited and passed it to Saxx.

He leaned forward to study the package as it lay face up next to his hand.

"Okay. Just like you said," he acknowledged.

"*Exactly* like I said," Finch waited while they considered the evidence.

"When we're done here, I'll walk this down to Connie's lab," Saxx said to Keely. He turned to Finch. "Till then, we wait and see."

As Finch observed the hesitancy in Saxx's eyes a new

suspicion struck him. What if someone in their forensics team claimed the note and brass weren't evidence of anything at all? A fraud. "Fake news," the common jargon during the last election.

"Wait and see?" Finch waved his hands above the table as if he were treading water. "So what's next?"

"Two things." Keely set her elbows on the table. She pivoted her head to gaze into Finch's eyes. "Our intelligence tells us that within the next week there's a meeting with a group called White Sphere. Five leaders of the Anti-vaxxer community will be there. One of them will be you. That is, Joel Griffin. But in the dark web, he's known as Brass Shoes."

"Brass Shoes." Finch stifled a laugh. "What's that mean?" He shook his head, amused by the pseudonyms that internet gamers invented to shroud their identities. A ruse adopted from their adolescence playing Nintendo.

"From our email intercepts between Myfanwy Thomas and Sheila Griffin we learned that Joel Griffin was a tap dancer as a kid. Back home in Tampa, he was considered a *phenom*." He pronounced it *fee-nom* and grinned as if he belonged to a hip inner circle. "I don't know if you caught wind of this from Myfanwy, but he died of anaphylaxis following a routine shingles vaccination in his doctor's office. Died within minutes apparently. Which inspired Sheila and Myfanwy's crusade. Using your bogus credit card ID."

Saxx shrugged as if the women's reaction was understandable. Even righteous. Then he turned in his chair and set a hand on a thick file. "These are transcripts of the Brass Shoes internet posts over the past year. Twitter, Facebook, Instagram. And more from the dark web. Much more. From places most people never heard of. These can't leave the room, so when we finish here, stay behind and memorize as much as you can."

"Here?" With every passing minute Finch felt more ensnared by their plotting.

"No worries, Finch." Saxx chuckled at what seemed to be an inside joke. "The coffee might not be fresh, but it's free."

Finch rolled his eyes. "All right. So what's White Sphere?"

"White Sphere?" Keely glanced at the ceiling as if the answer might be written there. "So there's what we know for sure. Then there's what we think we know. And there's what we don't know at all." She shifted her eyes back to Finch. "We know where they'll meet and when. And we're almost certain they're planning a conspiracy to sabotage the president's national vaccination rollout."

Saxx continued. "The president is announcing details soon. But if White Sphere sabotages the campaign before it gets off the ground, it'll mean disaster."

Finch considered the dynamics. Over the past year everyone had been wandering blind in a fog of fake news, promises, lies, innuendo. Who could tell fact from fiction? For the first time in his life, Finch began to doubt his own ability to cut through the mass of BS. Keely was dead wrong. Sure, there's what you know and what you think you know. But when you can't tell one from the other, everything becomes unknown.

"All right," Finch pushed on. "So Joel Griffin attends this White Sphere meeting." He swung an open hand in the air as if he needed to clear the mist from the room. "I still don't get it. The first time we met you said you'd confiscated Myfanwy's laptop. And that someone inside the firm here continued her Tweets to keep his ghost alive. So why do you need *me?*"

"I also said they have your DNA. How did they get it?" Keely glanced away and then turned back to him. "Now we know. We found a file on Myfanwy's laptop. After she met you in the Alt Fuel Café in Rapid City—and realized you had the same name as her friend's father—she kept your coffee mug and asked someone to profile your DNA."

"She was smart. Cunning, really. And the way she catfished you into becoming Joel Griffin? *Phu-wee.*" Saxx let out a gust of air. His eyes expressed a grudging admiration for her ingenuity. "End result? Your DNA is now in the hands of White Sphere."

Saxx paused to let Finch absorb the extent of Myfanwy's deception.

How could he have been so naïve? Finch shook his head in disbelief. "I still don't get why you need *me* for the White Sphere meeting. Get your Joel Griffin impersonator to attend." He pointed to the interview room door as if another spook stood on the far side with an ear pressed to the door.

"To sit at the table," Keely continued, "everyone in White Sphere submits a real-time DNA sample. These days it's the only fake-proof form of ID."

Finch leaned back in his chair and dragged both hands through his hair. He felt as if he were sealed in a vault. Brick by brick the walls rose above his head. "Okay. Okay, for the sake of argument, let's say I attend the meeting. What do you hope to get from me?"

"Two things. To confirm what we think we know and don't

know." Keely held up her index finger. "One, to ID the White Sphere leader. We need a physical description, his real name, where he sleeps at night. In other words, all you can get on him. And two"—she raised a second finger—"learn how they intend to sabotage the vaccine roll-out."

*"That's it? That's all?"* He scoffed and looked away. He'd slogged through four years in military intelligence in Iraq. Long enough to know that nobody penetrated the inner circle of any conspiracy in a single meeting. "You're delusional."

"Not at all," Saxx said. "We have two things going for us. First, Brass Shoes is a known sympathizer. His daughter and Myfanwy firmly established his online credentials over the past year. But this is the first time White Sphere will convene an *in-person* meeting. Why? The answer provides our second advantage. They're short of time. They need to hit the vaccine roll-out before it achieves momentum. They've got two weeks at the most."

Finch gazed at the far wall as he assessed his situation. A new thought struck him.

"Am I going to get paid for all this?"

Keely looked as though she'd expected his question. "We pay a standard consulting fee. This job fits into the half-day rate. A thousand dollars. Scales up to two grand a day if things go long."

"Go long?"

"But we're not expecting that," Saxx put in. "This is your classic one-and-done."

Finch closed his eyes as his chin rolled from side to side in contemplation. The money didn't matter to him. So what to do?

He'd asked himself the same question at least twenty times since Saxx and Keely knocked on his front door back on Alta Street. He could refuse to work with them and walk out right now. But without the support of the FBI, he and his family would remain vulnerable to an attack by Myfanwy's killer. Or he could insert himself into the White Sphere conspiracy backed by the FBI's support and resources.

"So, Mr. Finch," Keely asked, "are you in?"

He looked at her, then at Saxx. "One last question. So if I attend White Sphere as Joel Griffin—Brass Shoes—what's the cyber-name of the guy I need to ID?"

"Someone you already know," Keely said. "The Orange Man."

Finch felt his pulse quicken. "The Orange Man? He was behind the murders in Rapid City last year. He ran a syndicate right across the country. The Brothers of Vidar." At one time he imagined the Orange Man might be the past president of the USA. Not now.

"One and the same. White Sphere is the digital wing of The Brothers of Vidar. The brain trust. If we can crack it, we can bring the entire enterprise down." Keely sounded thoroughly convinced.

"You should've told me this before."

She gazed at him. "So. Are you in?"

*The Orange Man.* Finch gazed at the door and tried to calculate his odds. Was he ready for a new battle—for another fight in an old war? A struggle marked by stealth and cunning —but no less lethal than the combat in Iraq. He now realized the extent of the threat to him, Eve, and the baby. He had no choice.

"Yeah. I'm in. With both feet."

# CHAPTER FOUR

SAINT PETERSBURG — 12 OCTOBER, 1996

Joseph Tull woke with a start. Lost in a wandering nightmare, he'd plunged into the chaos of a city he couldn't name, at a time he could never remember. In the dream, he is always scouring the shops to find potable water. Hordes of citizens surround him, their faces gaunt, their eyes darting from the gray snowbanks to the pale clouds stacked above the city. Strangers who possess bottles or carafes, quickly tuck them away in their shoulder bags. The savvy, flat-faced babushkas have a way of hiding dozens of water containers under their billowing coats. If he and Zena can find fresh supplies by noon, they return to their apartment and set one liter aside for emergencies. If they manage to secure three or four liters at one time, they can dedicate the afternoon to their studies. But on rare occasions, they find no water at all. Those are the days that inspire his recurring nightmares. Then he and Zena compromise and fill their empty bottles with ditch water and snow, strain the water through a filter of cotton cloth stretched over an open pot, then boil the water for twenty minutes. From this, they make Dilmah tea in the samovar that Joseph brought with him from Tver after he'd completed high school. The samovar was a graduation gift from Uncle Valery and Aunt Tanya.

"Josef, ssshhh. It's okay. You're just dreaming." Zena jostled his shoulder and planted a kiss on his cheek.

When his eyes blinked open, he gasped for air and his shoulders bolted from the pillow. *"Srat,"* he moaned and ran his hands over his face.

"The same dream?" She lay beside him on their bed and rolled her hand over his chest.

"Yeah," he conceded. "It worries me."

"What? The days we have no water—or that the dream recurs again?"

"Both, I guess." He turned to her and ran his fingers over her shoulder. Her blonde hair was loose and fell across her face. She swept it away and drew herself closer to him. She was gorgeous, especially when she looked into his eyes like this. Her green eyes swimming in his blues. She liked to call his eyes the blues because of his affection for American blues singers.

"So okay," he said. "We don't say recurs *again*. Because recur means to happen again. It's redundant."

"Redundant?"

"Means repeated. It's unnecessary."

"Oh. Okay, got it." She nodded as if she'd snared another linguistic nuance in her steel-trap memory.

He never had to correct her more than once. Part of their

"program" called for him to instruct her in American English. He'd met Zena Smirnov at an "Our Home—Russia" political party rally in 1994, just a few months after they started classes at Saint Petersburg State University. Joseph, in computer science, Zena in microbiology. Until then, Joseph had zero interest in politics, until the student union presented a charismatic speaker, Dmitry Pushkin. A firm believer in what he called the new Russia, Pushkin was himself a graduate of Saint Petersburg State University, and since 1994, the First Deputy Chairman of the Government of Saint Petersburg. As a former Soviet KGB spy, he'd developed a reputation. Last year he'd been investigated for $93 million in foreign food aid that "vanished" under his administration. Consequently, certain people didn't like him. But others revered him. The recommendation to fire him was ignored and his political star began to rise. His resilience proved that Pushkin was a man whose career could influence his country's fate. And as the Soviet Union collapsed, Pushkin charted a path forward to the new Russian state.

"I have two eggs for us and some bread," Zena whispered and rolled her tongue under his ear. "And the jam from the market last week."

"Two eggs?"

"From Tania. You hungry?"

He chuckled a that. He was almost always hungry. They both were. "And some tea?"

She pointed to the samovar. "I made it already."

"Okay. Then we'll go to the American Club."

"Of course." She smiled as her hand traveled beneath the

blanket. "First we eat. Then make love. Then we go to club."

"To *the* club," he whispered and kissed her lips. "But remember, no sex before food."

"No. Never." She liked his humor and laughed at the way Joseph mocked the set of rules she'd proposed the week that she'd moved into his flat. She pulled herself from the bed and stepped over to the samovar to pour the tea. "I'm not the only one still learning. It's taken you a while, but now you know what it means to be Russian, too."

ON Saturday mornings the American Club met in one of the basement rooms of the Saint Petersburg State University Student Union building. At first Joseph had been amused by the name of the club. He assumed it hosted American students looking for companionship or seeking answers to common questions about the city. Where to find decent housing. Where to find friendly restaurants and clubs. And most importantly, where to find fresh water.

In fact, of the twenty-three students in the group, he was the only American citizen. Twelve students hailed from Moscow and Saint Petersburg. The others came from small towns and cities all over the country. From Murmansk just below the Arctic Ocean near Finland, to Yakutsk in Siberia. All of them had been recruited into the club. Or perhaps *drafted* was the better word, Joseph thought. They all shared a common goal. To master American English so that they could become a credible voice of the new Russia as it re-entered the global community.

After the Soviet collapse, a new attitude emerged. No more

ideology. No more political cant. The new pragmatism demanded that Russia engage the real world. The Germans had a word for it. "Realpolitik" became a buzzword across campus. And like the Germans, French, Japanese—the Russians had to speak the lingua franca. English, English, English. Somehow England, the little island to the west, had won all the wars of the last 200 years. At least all the wars that mattered. And now English—in all its varieties and strange accents—unlocked all the doors to the world.

The club was guided by one of Dmitry Pushkin's deputies, Professor Misha Sakharov, who strode over to the lectern and tapped his pen against the wooden frame. "Tutchhh, tutchhh, tutchhh," he called above the rumors and gossip. "I hear some of you, maybe all of you, speaking Russian. So"—he checked his watch—"it's five after eleven and now we speak English until we finish our tea. Understood?"

A wave of light laugher rippled through the room.

"First, I have some news. Perhaps some of you will think it sad. But it is not." He gazed at the students sitting in chairs around him. When he observed their looks of anticipation, he continued. "Dmitry Pushkin will soon be leaving us."

"Leaving us?" Anton Ilin, an ardent Pushkin supporter, sat two chairs along from Joseph.

"Yes, he's departing for the Third Rome. It's a huge promotion, I assure you."

Joseph had to smile. He'd never heard of the Third Rome until he joined the American Club. It was an old nickname for Moscow coined by the medieval monk Philotheus who said, "Two Romes fell, a third stands, and there will not be a fourth."

The reference was to the fall of Rome, then Constantinople.

Professor Sakharov paused to ensure everyone appreciated the weight of Pushkin's new appointment.

"Sadly, Pushkin regrets he can't make a farewell appearance here, but he asked me to pass on a message of encouragement to you all." Professor Sakharov stepped back from the lectern and walked to the side of the room as if he had to gain a fresh perspective on the club members.

"Now we will start discussions on the topic promised last week. The extent of American power in Europe. Josef Tull is our moderator." Sakharov waved to the lectern, a gesture to indicate that Joseph now had the floor. "Please. A warm welcome."

Sakharov clapped his hands. Everyone joined in the light applause as Joseph made his way to the stand. He stood to one side and nodded. He lifted the lectern in his hands and carried it over to the wall behind him. Then he returned to his chair next to Zena, sat down, and smiled.

"So, in America, students sit in circles. Just like this." He swept his arm in an arc. "It's a gesture to suggest equality. That's the foundation of American beliefs. The keystone to their democracy. And capitalism. They have a saying from the Declaration of Independence. 'All men are created equal.' Of course we all know this is a lie. Something to give the masses hope. Marx called religion the opiate of the masses. But today, in the English-speaking world the opiate is the myth of equality. Who among them is equal to Bill Clinton? Or even his wife, Hillary Clinton."

"What does this have with America in Europe?" Anton Ilin

asked.

Joseph paused and lifted his right hand above his knees. "So Anton, forgive me, but in English we say, what does this have *to do* with America in Europe."

"Yes. Thank you." Anton nodded with a look of appreciation.

To be corrected was to learn. They all embraced Joseph's corrections as a mark of friendship. Everyone in the club had approached Joseph to welcome him personally as an ally in their cause. And one by one, they'd invited him and Zena to their flats for tea. Or if they could afford it, vodka.

"So," Anton continued, "What does this have to do with America in Europe?"

Joseph glanced from face to face. "Anyone want to answer this question? An important question."

Zena raised her hand. "It follows directly from what we spoke last week—"

Joseph interrupted. *"Said* last week."

*"Said* last week." She nodded to him. "So, the collapse of the Berlin Wall created a political void. As they say in physics, Nature abhors a vacuum. In this case, when one of two world powers collapses, the other sweeps in."

"But not directly," Professor Sakharov put in. "The Americans are grand puppet masters. They create client states who appear to govern own affairs."

Joseph raised a hand. "To govern *their* own affairs."

"Yes. Their own affairs. The Americans pull the strings and the puppet jumps." Sakharov smiled at Joseph and continued. "I can predict what happens next. Now that Germany has reunified, one by one European Union will annex all former Soviet bloc states."

"*The* European Union."

"Of course. *The* European Union. Next they will join NATO. When it comes time for American client states to take over Ukraine, we"—his voice warmed with passion and his arm swept across the room—"all Russians must be prepared to resist."

"Yes. We must!" Anton exclaimed.

"Absolyutno!" Dimitri yelled.

"My vse brat'ya," one of the women said in a quiet but determined voice.

It meant *we are all brothers*. A more honest expression than all men are created equal, Joseph thought. He realized that everyone was speaking Russian again. He let the rant continue until they'd vented their rage. The anger of young men and women struggling to survive in a broken empire. When their fury subsided he raised his hand in the air.

"Back to Realpolitik," he said. "From now on, we speak *American* English. In a year I want everyone in this room to sound like they were born in Brooklyn, Queens, LA, Rapid City. No one will have Russian accents. And you will all become perfect spies."


ANTON Ilin locked the gate to the pistol range and walked with Joseph and Zena to the security desk next to the athletic field. As a cadet in the Reserve Officer Training program at the university, he had access to a range of resources that weren't available to his friends.

"I tell you, you both should join the ROT." He passed the gate key and three automatic pistols to the ROT commissioner behind the wire security screen. He turned to Joseph and said. "You see, membership has its privileges."

"Indeed." Joseph laughed at Anton's sarcasm as he rattled off the American Express tagline. For the past month, he'd encouraged everyone in the American Club to use American slang and idioms.

"It's so totally capitalist," Anton added.

"And now everyone says it," Zena said. She spun a hand around the side of her ear as if the words had become a cultural earworm.

"Srat!" Anton cursed. "They've taken over the world. And you expect us to play their game?" He flashed a critical look at Joseph. "You see, that's why we all need to join Reserve Officer Training. Professor Sakharov is right. One day we will have to fight. Best to prepare now."

"And lose," Joseph countered. "Look. If we fight, we have to fight smart. Smarter than anyone ever."

Anton led them through the exit and walked into the sunlight. The autumn sun felt warm on their faces, but the breeze surging above the Neva River carried a chill. Joseph tucked his hands into his jacket pockets.

"And learn to fire weapons," Anton said and hooked his thumb back toward the pistol range. "Did you like shooting the automatic pistol, Zena?"

"To be honest, I did." As she paused to consider what it felt like, she flicked up the collar of her jacket to cover the back of her neck. "It has a hard force. The way my hand kicked into the air revealed its power. Mmm-mmm. Like a good *soitiye.*"

Soitiye. Joseph smiled at that. Zena loved to screw. And she had a fondness for comparing sex to every novel experience under the sun. Eating caviar. Drinking vodka. A blistering hot sauna.

"Hah! Yeah, yeah!" Anton laughed. Zena's carnal zest seemed to lighten his mood. He continued in English. "I say we go back to my flat and take some shots." His eyebrows raised as if he wanted Joseph to confirm that he'd made a passable English pun. "Natalia and I have some vodka. We drink from shot glasses, right?"

"Yes, that's what they're called."

"So then firing a gun and drinking are the same in America. Both are taking shots. Well, come on then. Natalia's mother sent us some Stolichniya. And strawberry jam to go with it."

ANTON and Natalia's apartment was a little larger than the room Joseph and Zena shared. Anton's flat had a separate bedroom with a double bed. But the view looked onto a dingy alley strewn with rubbish. Only recently had the city been able to fund a new department to replace the waste disposal collective that had collapsed in 1993. Gradually they were getting around to clearing the alleys and cul-de-sacs. Until then, the residents tried to maintain some level of waste management on their own.

"So our view is not as good as yours," Anton said as he stood at his window.

"No? What do they see?" Since Natalia spoke no English, it was understood that they would speak Russian.

"We're on the second floor at 8 Ya Liniya," Zena said. "A busy street. Noisy all night."

Natalia tipped her head to one side. "Next to the Sokos Hotel?"

"Two doors down."

"My sister used to work there until...." Her voice trailed off. Her shoulders curled in the hopeless shrug that was all too common now. Her words hung in the silence as everyone imagined any one of dozens of situations that could force her sister to move on.

"So vodka for all," Anton said to dismiss their misgivings. He set four shot glasses on the little table that overlooked the back alley. "Natalia, do you want to offer your mother's Stolichniy and jam?"

"Of course." She stepped over to a narrow pantry that stood beside the sink and reached to the top shelf and lifted the loaf of rye bread into her hand. "She sent it from home last week, but it's still good."

"Where's home?" Zena asked.

"Kazan."

"A long way." Joseph knew that meant Natalia likely wouldn't visit her mother during Christmas. They'd probably settle for an exchange of cards or a small gift that could be delivered through the mail. "So she's a baker there?"

"She was. Before." She turned her wrist in the air, a reference to the years before the collapse. "Now she sells bread from her kitchen."

She set four plates and the jar of jam on the table while Anton retrieved a bread knife and cutting board from the sink.

He sliced off four thin pieces and placed them on side plates.

"Now we eat?" Zena asked. "Before grace?" She laughed at her little joke and skimmed a slick of jam over her bread.

Anton smirked. "In this house, there is no grace. Never."

"And no god," Natalia added.

Joseph raised his glass to propose a toast. "To the great void!"

"Which looks into our hearts." Zena clicked her shot glass with the others. They drank and began to eat the bread and jam.

"Do you really believe that old saying?" Anton asked Zena.

"What saying?"

"From Nietzsche. 'When you look into the abyss, the abyss looks into you.' The idea turns the void itself into God. This means Nietzsche's atheism is a fraud. Never forget, he was mad."

"I don't believe it," Natalia said. She poured another shot of vodka and tossed it down her throat. "There is nothing but this." Her hand swept across the room and then she thumped it against her heart. "We are animals with a few big ideas. Monkey ideas—and most of them are lies. The biggest lie of all is that God waits to embrace us after death. Or to bury us in hell. This is what happened to my father. He went to war believing in life after death."

She refilled everyone's glass. They drank again.

"In Chechen?" Joseph asked.

Natalia pouted and glanced away. After a pause, Anton spoke for her. "In Afghanistan."

A wave of silence flushed through the room. Joseph rotated his empty glass on the table. Two, three turns.

Anton leaned over to refill his glass. "He was guarding a perimeter outside Kabul—"

"Anton, don't." Natalia's eyes cut toward him with a sharp look.

He shrugged. "They should know." His chin notched up as if he were inviting her to take a punch at him. "Everyone should know."

"Please."

Anton turned to Joseph. "He was one of five men in a trench. Taken out by the Taliban using American mortars. Two weeks after the Americans started to supply them with Yankee weapons. State of the art," he said in English. He winked at Joseph, pleased to recite more American jargon.

Natalie narrowed her eyes and leaned toward her boyfriend. "I told you not to."

"What? Did you not hear the news?" He sneered at her. "The Soviet Empire is dead. Since Christmas Day in 1991. A gift to all Russians from Comrade Mikhail Gorbachev. A present without ribbons or bows. But now no one needs to hide the truth anymore."

"It's not about the truth." She stood up and leaned over him. "It's about my heart." Again her hand struck her chest. "Why do you have this contempt for me?"

Zena turned to Joseph. "Josef, we should go."

He studied her face, surprised to see her eyes brimming with tears. He nodded. "All right."

Zena rose from her chair. "Now," she whispered to him. *"Right now."*

Joseph stood.

"I'm sorry," Zena offered her hosts a wilting shrug. "I have to go."

She stepped over to the door and into the hallway. Joseph heard her feet tromping down the wooden staircase. He uttered an oblique apology—for what, he didn't quite understand—and followed her. By the time he caught up to her, she was standing near the street corner. When he reached out to touch her shoulder, she brushed his hand away and ran along the sidewalk toward their apartment on Ya Liniya.

JOSEPH found Zena laying face down on their bed, sobbing. He closed the apartment door and stepped over to the foot of the bed as her body trembled under the blanket. In the six months they'd lived together he'd never seen her shed a tear. Quite the opposite. Of all the women he'd met at the university, Zena was the most self-possessed. More than her good looks and her zest for life, it was her steely confidence that appealed to him.

After he'd revealed the personal tragedy that ended his childhood—the murder of his parents as they flew over the Persian Gulf—she'd said nothing. Not a word. In the silence that followed his confession, his eyes began to well with tears. Tears that he'd blocked behind a dam of pain for so many years. When they came flooding out, she'd brushed her fingers over his eyes and daubed them onto her face in two streaks across her cheeks.

"Your tears are mine, too," she'd whispered.

She'd drawn him into her arms and kissed him. After a slight hesitation, he returned her kiss. She murmured something he couldn't make out, unbuttoned his shirt, and began to peel off his clothes. When he was naked, she tugged off her sweater and jeans, her bra and underpants, then led him by the hand to her bed. That night they made love three times. Each encounter driven by an explosive passion that purged his grief. A blood-letting of his soul. In the morning he understood what she'd done for him.

"Promise me something," he said over breakfast.

Her eyes swept over his face. "Anything."

"Never tell anyone about my parents."

Her lips parted as if she were about to make a confession of her own, then decided against it. She looked away and shrugged to suggest the revelation about his past was over and done. Obliterated. "I won't. I promise."

"Good."

She waited a moment and forced a smile to her lips. "Do you like to make love like we did last night?"

"I don't know." He felt pleased that she'd changed the subject but wondered if he should hide what he was thinking. No, not from her. He'd told her everything the previous night. Why hide anything now? "I never met a girl who likes it so much."

She laughed at that, leaned over the table, and kissed his cheek. "Well, now you've met *me*. And if you like it so much too, then I think we should try to be together."

"Mmmm." He'd rolled his shoulders back in an easy stretch. "Yes, maybe we should."

Now, six months later, as he watched Zena shift on the mattress, he saw *her* eyes were wet. She tried to smile but instead choked in a breathless gasp. He knew she'd left something unsaid that night when they first made love. Now it was his turn to wipe her tears, but he didn't know how to do it without aggravating her pain.

"So," he began. "First me. Then Natalia. Now you?"

She nodded and held an edge of the wool blanket to her mouth like a child warding off a recurring nightmare.

He sat on the side of the bed. Her ankle slipped out of the covers and he caressed her foot.

"Was it something Natalia said?" He waited for her eyes to link with his before correcting himself. "Or what Anton said to her?"

She nodded. "He was a shit to say all that. Especially when she asked him not to."

"It was embarrassing."

"It was. Not like when you asked me not to say anything. That night after we met." She peered into his eyes to be certain he understood. "I've never said a word to anyone about your parents. And I never will."

He stared at her with a comforting look to acknowledge her renewed promise. "So do you want to tell me something?"

She blinked. He waited to see if her expression would change.

"It's all right. You don't have to." He shifted his legs to stand up, but she grabbed his wrist.

"Wait. I do." Her lips pursed together. Did she? Could she tell him?

"You sure?"

"No." She sat up and rested her back against the headboard.

"But I'll tell you anyway."

He stretched his left leg along the top of the bed and let the other foot swing down to the floor. "Okay. I'm listening."

She clutched a pillow to her chest and stared at him. When she gathered her resolve and was about to speak she stopped herself. It took her three tries before she could voice a complete sentence.

"My father was a helicopter pilot," she began. "During the Soviet war in Afghanistan. He flew an Mi-24 gunship." She closed her eyes to scan her memory for the exact details. "It was 1984. I'd just turned eight. I remember the parade on the airbase outside Moscow as my mother and I waved goodbye to him from the crowd. The day he left it was raining. The two of us clung together under this ratty, old umbrella that kept blowing inside-out." She inhaled a long breath then continued. "Somehow I knew—I just *knew*—I'd never see him again. And that started my crying. My mother kept shushing me. *'Shush-shush-shush.'* I could tell she felt embarrassed. No one was allowed to cry in front of the parade of heroes."

Zena continued her story about the parade, about losing sight of him as he led his crew inside the helicopter gunship. The whooshing sound as the rotor wash tore the umbrella apart, then the terrifying roar as all twelve choppers rose into the air. She remembered her hand waving as the rain dashed against her face. That made it so easy to cry. No one could hear her. Everyone would mistake her tears for the rain.

Then came the long absence during his tour of duty. And finally, the news that fulfilled her premonition. Her mother broke it to her after Zena returned from school. It was November 17, 1985.

" 'Your father is dead,' she announced. Her voice was hard. Totally impersonal, as if my mother had never met the man. Her husband. 'Somewhere outside a place called Kandahar. Who knows where it is.' She shrugged as if the place didn't really exist."

Zena paused to gauge the effect of her story on Joseph. Over the past two years, she'd gathered what information she could find about the circumstances of his death. Since the Soviet collapse, the archives were more accessible. She rattled off the information she'd discovered in a flat voice, the neutral tone all the TV newscasters used on *Russia Today*.

"In 1983, the United States Congress provided funding to the CIA for weapons in Afghanistan. Fifteen million dollars. Then they added another forty million specifically for anti-helicopter weapons. And that's what did it. A US-made stinger missile fired by the mujahideen." She released the pillow from her arms and it fell to the floor. "Click. Boom. Done." She spit the words out one at a time. "That's who killed him. The Americans. *I hate them.*"

Joseph drew a hand across his face as the image of his parents' death flashed through his mind. "I hate them, too," he murmured.

"What?"

"I said I hate them, too." He reached out to stroke her ankle but she shifted it back under the blanket.

"No, don't touch me." Her voice hardened. "Don't make me cry. It's done. Besides, that's still not the main thing."

"The main thing?"

"No." The skin on her face tightened from her chin up to her forehead. "A week later, after she gave me the news … she disappeared."

"Who? Your mother?"

"When I came home from school, she was gone. All her clothes. Her money. Completely gone." She braced her arms across her chest as if the chill of her abandonment descended on her once more.

"Did she leave a note? Anything?" Joseph's hand swept the air for something, anything, to grasp.

She shrugged off the question.

"My God, Zena, that's just—"

"No. Don't say anything." She shifted her head to one side. "It was for the best."

"For the best." Was it possible? "So you stayed in Moscow?"

"At the Dmitri Mendeleev School. If your grades are good, they take in boarders. It was the only advantage I had." She tapped the side of her head with a finger. "But being smart isn't good enough. You have to work. And that's all I did. When I was seventeen my academic advisor lined me up for a microbiology scholarship here at St. Pete's."

"You had no other family?"

"An uncle. Like you." She offered a vague shrug. "An uncle in Vladivostok. But his wife wouldn't have me. When I realized my old life was done—*completely finished*—that's when I changed my name."

A look of disbelief notched his face. "You changed your name," he repeated. It was the only response he could find.

"From Olga. A babushka's name. It made me feel dead before I found my own life. So I made up a name. The feminine form of Zen. Zena meant I would live in the moment. And make every moment my own."

Zena—but she pronounced it Zee-na. Regardless of where the name came from, he knew she was right. He'd never met another woman who lived so much in synch with her beating pulse.

"And your last name, too?"

"Yes, from Karavayev to Smirnov. With the original spelling," she said with a smirk. "Either way you spell it, Smirnoff is still everyone's favorite drink."

He had to smile at that. "I guess it is."

"You see. It was for the best," she repeated. She took his hand, then broke into a smile, too. "Now *you're* my family."

His family? Perhaps she was right. Yet he couldn't quite fathom what was happening. Was he making a choice, or were they simply flowing together, drawn by gravity, two rivers merging into one?

"I'm just like you. The past is over. And just like you I learned to start a second life and harden the old pain. Now it's steel. Nothing can break it." She gazed into his eyes, her self-possession more evident than ever. "I can see it in you, too."

"See what?"

"How pain is transformed. When a broken heart becomes a forge for revenge."

# CHAPTER FIVE

SAN FRANCISCO — 24 FEBRUARY, 2021

Will Finch marched along Sutter Street toward the parkade entrance of the Sir Francis Drake Hotel. Last summer when the pandemic ran out of control, most of the hotels—including the Drake—canceled their reservations and ceased operations indefinitely. That made the Drake both an ideal location for a rendezvous with White Sphere—and the worst choice he could imagine.

Finch loved the Drake and had spent more than a few pleasant evenings with Eve in the rooftop Starlight Room on the twenty-first floor. Built the year before the stock market crashed in 1929, the hotel evoked a European sensibility, and rumor had it that the architect, Benjamin Marshall, had constructed hidden cellars to store Canadian booze for hotel guests during Prohibition. Despite the economic crash, the Drake became a non-stop party venue through the dirty thirties. Herb Caen, the celebrated San Francisco columnist, called the

Drake's Persian Room, *The Snake Pit.* "You never heard such hissing or saw such writhing," he wrote. To protect their interests, the hotel owners drilled discrete spy holes in the ceiling above the lobby so they could lock up the cellar warehouse when the cops organized a booze raid. The record shows that every police bust on the Drake came up empty-handed. Eventually, they gave up trying. But if you know where to look for them, the spy holes are visible to this day.

On Monday Agent Sandra Keely told Finch the White Sphere meeting would take place at four o'clock on Wednesday afternoon, just before the Drake security team rotated through a shift change. Since the pandemic closure, the security staff had been pared to three people per shift. One maintained a constant vigilance in the basement control room which housed the computer systems and the video monitor array. Two "roamers" conducted walking surveillance of the lobby, hallways, and the 416 hotel rooms. Today the roamer positions were filled by two FBI agents. Jeremy Saxx and Sandra Keely.

Finch walked down the sloping parkade garage ramp into the shadows of the Drake's underbelly. The garage had been blocked with a pair of rising swing barriers controlled from the security station. Finch buzzed the control room and placed his face squarely in front of the camera. Seconds later he heard Keely's voice as one of the barrier arms rose above his head. "Down to your left. First door past the fire alarm box," she said, her voice barely audible under the electrical static sputtering through the speaker.

As he eased along the concrete ramp he noticed twin cameras anchored to the ceiling, one pointing up the ramp, the other down. When he reached the security station he tapped on the unmarked steel door. From where he stood, no one could see into the room. For all anyone knew, it was just another faceless portal in a labyrinth of closed doors.

He knocked and the door swung open into a room that looked about twenty feet long and wide. A concrete box. He stepped inside and followed Keely to where Saxx stood—next to a hotel security guard seated at a computer console. All three of them wore shirts with "DRAKE SECURITY" emblazoned in bold, yellow letters across their backs.

"Take off your mask, Finch. To White Sphere they're the mark of the devil." Saxx glanced at Finch and pointed to a table near the far wall. "You'll want to leave your shoulder bag, watch and phone here, too. Otherwise, they'll probably be confiscated."

"No doubt." Finch forced a chuckle. "I hope the meeting's in the Honeymoon Suite. I always wanted to see what the fuss is all about."

The guard at the console turned. "You'd be surprised at the number of celebs who book into that room. Fred Astaire and Ginger Rogers. Burt Lancaster. Robin Williams. Sinatra. Even Marilyn Monroe." He pronounced it Mun-Row. "Betting money says most of 'em took a tumble between the sheets."

"Gentlemen. Focus, please." Keely gave the men a wary look. "Finch, this is Troy Hammond."

They nodded a greeting and Finch peeled off his mask and tucked it in his pocket, reconsidered, and dropped it into his courier bag along with his watch and cell phone. Then he put the bag on the far table next to the door.

"Hammond's helping Agent Saxx and me navigate the hallways." She tapped an earphone under a wide strand of her blond hair. "Rest assured, we'll have you under surveillance the whole time."

"No earpiece for me?" A moot question. Finch understood that he wouldn't be supplied with an earpiece. Another dead giveaway to White Sphere. "So I'm playing this deaf and blind?"

"No worries. We'll be your eyes and ears." Her tone provided a little comfort.

"All right." He exhaled a long breath to suppress his doubts. "Where's the meet-up?"

"We just intercepted the latest message to Brass Shoes," she said. "Four o'clock. Room 505."

"Does 505 have a security camera?"

Hammond turned to him. "All the hallways, elevators, and stairways do. But none of the rooms. Hotel privacy policy."

"Don't worry, Finch," Saxx put in and tapped one of the monitors, "we can see everyone come and go into 505 from the hall camera." He chugged the remaining water from an Evian bottle and set the empty on the table next to Finch's courier bag.

"Speaking of which, here's a master key to all the rooms and elevators." Keely handed him a pass card. Apart from the Drake logo on the face, it looked identical to a typical credit card. "We all have one."

"In the unlikely case an elevator or door lock calls for a PIN code, use 1928," Hammond said. "The year the Drake opened its doors."

Saxx's phone buzzed and he pulled it from his pocket. He held up a hand to call for silence as he listened to the voice on the other end. He turned to Keely. "Okay. That was Agent Jacks." He glanced at Finch. "There's more agents positioned outside. Two near the lobby entrance, two at the rear exit."

Finch nodded.

"And if you get spooked, I'll be in 507," Saxx said.

"I'm in 510," Keely added. She checked her watch. "Meeting's in thirty minutes. We'll head up now. Follow us in twenty, okay?"

"507 and 510," he repeated. Finch studied her eyes. She seemed so sure of herself. Both of them did. "Just don't lock yourself in a box, okay? If things go south, we may need to improvise."

"Improvise? Hey, I'm known as the Dizzy Gillespie of the FBI." Saxx smiled again.

His expression made Finch nervous. The man didn't look like he could play a note. Let alone hum a tune.

FINCH opened the staircase door to the fifth floor and peered down the empty corridor. He checked his watch. 3:52. The overhead lamps were off. A narrow ray of sunshine from the far window tapered down the hallway. He turned left toward the window, saw that the room numbers ascended—520, 522, 524—then swung around and walked east along the plush carpet. As he approached 505, his shadow lengthened and then merged into the gathering darkness of the corridor. He passed 510 and 507. Keely and Saxx's hideouts. He imagined Hammond sitting at his station in the basement, watching him slip along the hallway.

He paused in front of the eyehole to 505. Apart from his breathing and the heavy pulse in his chest, he couldn't hear a sound. He tapped on the door with a knuckle. A light knock, three times. Tap. Tap. Tap.

Again silence. A string of doubts slipped through his mind. Wrong room. Wrong time. Wrong day. Wrong, wrong, wrong. He pulled the passkey from his pocket and swept it in front of the metal bar below the doorknob. One pass and he heard the door lock release. He turned the handle and walked into the room.

"Hello?" He glanced across the room. The bed was made, the desk clear, the TV off. "Anyone here?"

Nothing.

He dipped his head into the bathroom. Empty.

He walked to the mini-fridge and opened the door. Also empty. The drapes were open and the afternoon light cast a pallor through the window. He stood next to the glass and peered down to the sidewalk. He recognized all of the surrounding buildings on Sutter Street. He turned and glanced at the bed again. A haze of dust floated through the air.

What to do? He sat on the foot of the bed and tested his weight against the support of the mattress. Not bad. He flopped onto his back and stared at the ceiling. No one was here and they had no way of reaching him. Perhaps Saxx and Keely had misplayed their hand. He decided to give them ten minutes. By then they might realize they'd been duped, then knock on the door to relieve him of his role in their game. Brass Shoes? More like cement feet. Soon he'd be done with them.

The telephone rang. He sat up and watched it ring again, then picked up the handset.

"Brass Shoes?" A woman's voice.

"Yes?"

"Walk down to the elevator bay. There's two cars. Press both the up and down buttons. When the down car arrives, send it to the basement. Then take the up car to the twenty-first floor. Got it?"

"Yeah. But—"

The line went dead. He paused, then placed the handset back in the cradle. He stood up and pressed his fingers to the twitch in his belly. He slipped into the bathroom, tugged the sanitary sleeve from a glass, filled it with water, and took a drink. Barely a sip. He studied his face in the mirror. You ready? he asked himself and waited a moment as if the reply might come from the blank glare in his eyes. Finding no answer, he made his way out the door and walked past 507 and 510, along the corridor to the elevator bay.

He paused to consider where he stood. On a precipice. If he followed the instructions from the woman on the phone, he would plunge into the unknown. It reminded him of the two parachute jumps he'd made in Iraq. Each a test of his nerve. The hell with it, he told himself. *Jump*.

After he sent the first car to the basement he rode the second up to twenty-one. Up to Lizzie's Starlight on the top floor of the Drake. As the car shuddered to a halt he stared into the security camera on the ceiling. Again he imagined Hammond observing him on his monitor and waved with his right hand, a mock salute to his comrade in arms.

The steel doors slid open and he stepped onto the carpet and turned to his left. He immediately recalled the layout. Before the new management team took over the lounge two years ago, Lizzie's Starlight was known as the Starlight Room. If you knew who to ask, you could climb the inner staircase to the open rooftop and gaze into the heavens, or down onto the mass of humanity wandering through Union Square. Either way, Finch and Eve had enjoyed the view—and a romantic interlude on top of the tower.

But little of the glamor remained. Today Lizzie's Starlight radiated nothing but scant memories. Finch walked from the elevator bay past the reception desk and coat check station into the desert of dreams. He crossed the hardwood dance floor over to the west side, then along the bank of windows to the south. The view was every bit as good as it used to be, he thought. But where was White Sphere?

"Hello?" He directed his voice back towards the reception desk. Nothing. "Hello. Brass Shoes here," he added as if it might provide some clarification.

A woman appeared from the corridor which housed the toilets. That is, he assumed it was a woman. She was five-five or -six and had the curves—maybe—of a woman's body hidden under a beige kaftan that fell from her shoulders to her feet. She wore a face mask that caught his attention. Unlike most common ear-loop masks, this was a medical issue—N95 —with one strap tied over the top of her head and the second around her neck.

As she turned away, she gestured for him to follow. Finch crossed the dance floor. Next to the men's room, he discovered a small side table and a single chair.

"Sit," she said and pointed to the chair. A DNA swab kit lay on the table. A five-inch long probe sealed in a plastic sheath. Beside the stick stood a short vial with a snap-on lid.

He studied her, tried to capture her image. She didn't offer much to work with. Her eyes, green; hair, brunette; her skin—what he could see of it—pale, almost ghostly white. The thin lines stemming from her eyes and across her forehead suggested she could be in her early forties. Maybe if he could get her to talk, he could derive something from her voice.

"What's this?" he asked.

"Verification."

He shrugged. "What do you mean?"

She glared at him. "DNA testing."

He drew a breath. Now he had to assume the identity of Brass Shoes. Aggressive. Belligerent. Condescending to women.

"Fuck that," he growled. "You know who I am, but who the hell are you?"

She propped her hands on her hips. "Musk. You responded to a few of my posts on White Sphere."

"Yeah right. I remember." He put on an impatient expression. "So you're Musk? Who fuckin' cares? I'm supposed to meet with Orange Man."

Her shoulders stiffened a little, and Finch realized he had her on the defensive. "He's ready to meet you once we verify your identity. I'll do the swab. You'll go back to room 505 and wait for a call. We have a quick test. It won't take more than fifteen minutes to get results." When she saw him hesitate, she grew impatient. "Look. You were told to prepare for this."

Her voice carried a slight accent. Mid-western? Maybe she's a daughter or granddaughter of Ukrainian immigrants.

"All right," he said and sat in the chair.

She looked rattled as she tore the top end of the wrapper from the swabbing tool and pulled the test stick free. In her rush, the top of the wrapper fell to the floor. "Open wide. I'll take sample from both cheeks."

Take sample? Was she Russian? He opened his mouth and set his jaw. Her fingers trembled—a slight betrayal of nerves—as she leaned toward him. The brush on the end of the stick tickled the inside of his cheeks as she swabbed one side, then the other.

"Good," she said and snapped the brush tip into the vial and snapped the lid over it. She gathered the empty wrapper, the broken end of the swabbing tool and the vial containing his DNA in one hand and slipped them inside her kaftan.

"Wait here five minutes. Then take the elevator back to your room on fifth floor. I'll call when we're ready to meet."

*On fifth floor.* She had to be Russian. Maybe Ukrainian. He watched her turn the corner and walk back into the main hall. A moment later he heard the elevator bell chime. He waited a moment and then slipped off his shoes. No need to crush the evidence underfoot, he thought. In his sock feet he walked to the far side of the table and kneeled on the carpet where she'd stood. Was there something? Anything visible?

"Ahh," he whispered. "There you are, my friend." He plucked a one-inch square of plastic between his fingernails and held it up to the light. The end piece that she'd let slip away as she opened the swab wrapper. "And now *I* have a piece of you."

FINCH sat on the bed in room 505, tuned the TV to the weather station, and set the volume to mute. The one channel that always showed a digital clock blipping on the screen. It read 4:27. He could feel the blood thrumming in his heart. Adrenaline mixed with anticipation. Where would they meet? Who else would attend? He watched the clock tick onward, each passing minute another stroke from his life. 4:33, 4:41, 4:57. The meeting with Orange Man was running late. Something was off.

He decided to call room 510. Maybe Keely could bring him up to speed. He lifted the handset and punched in her room number. The line rang five, six times before he hung up and tried to call Saxx. Again no answer. Perplexed, he sat on the bed and ran a hand through his hair.

After another five minutes, he stepped into the hall and knocked on Keely's door. When she failed to answer, he swiped his card over the lock bar. A password alert appeared in red letters: PASSWORD. He keyed 1928 into the keypad and her door clicked open.

"Keely?" He stepped into her room. Someone had sat on the bed and left a shallow impression on the mattress cover. He walked toward the bathroom. "Keely, you here?"

He shook his head and walked down the hall to Saxx's room, knocked on the door. When no one responded he used the card and password to enter the room. Empty.

As he returned to his own room, he heard the telephone

ringing.

"Finch, get down here."

"Keely? What's going on? I'm supposed to meet—"

"It's all blown up. Get down here. *Now.*"

Finch stared at the TV monitor. The weather girl pointed to the five-day forecast. Sunny skies ahead. "Where's *down here?*"

"Fuck. *In the security office.*" She cut the call and he hung up the handset.

He clicked off the TV, locked the room, and made his way down the staircase to the basement. A few minutes later he reached the security office. The door was ajar. When he stepped into the room he counted Saxx, Keely, and four other men hovering over Hammond's computer keyboard. Their jackets all bore the bright yellow FBI letters. Keely traversed the narrow space behind Hammond's chair, her hand pressed to her mouth as if she were bottling up a scream.

"Keely, what happened?'

Her hand dropped from her lips as she turned to him. "It's Hammond."

He saw Hammond slumped over his control console. A splash of blood had sprayed across the computer monitor. "Omigod," Finch muttered and wrapped his arms around his chest. All of the video displays were fluttering in a haze of static. Apart from the bullet wound in the back of his head, Hammond looked as if he'd simply leaned forward, and laid his face on the table to enjoy a nap.

"Looks like he didn't even turn in his chair. One shot and done." She pointed to the blank monitors. "The shooter put a bullet into the computer, too. Then stole the memory drives."

"So it was the Orange Man?"

"Dunno. At this point, we've got no visuals. No audio." She shrugged. "Forensics should be here soon."

As she checked her watch they could hear a van slipping down the garage entrance as it approached the office.

"This'll be them. Forensics is here," she called to Saxx. "We're going to have to clear the room. Agent Jacks, string some tape across the top of the driveway. Then clear the block along the sidewalks outside and tape off both ends. Forbes, help him out."

"Will do." Marcus and Forbes left the room, marched past the forensics truck, and up the ramp to the street. Meanwhile, three more agents climbed out of the vehicle and walked into the office to examine the crime scene.

"All right, everyone out," barked the team leader. The name tag on his jacket read, VOLGER. "Who's the agent in charge?"

"Me." Saxx stepped forward with a sheepish look. The operation had failed under his watch and he knew a heavy fine would be charged to his account. "We've contained the scene. But there's a helluva lot more to do."

Volger stepped over to Hammond's corpse and shook his head with a look of remorse. When he noticed Finch, he swung around to Saxx. "This the catfish?"

"Will Finch. He's part of the operation."

"Right." Volger studied Finch. "The guy you put up to bait the hook."

Saxx frowned when he heard Volger's reaction. "Yeah. The stand-in for Brass Shoes. Look, we couldn't run the operation without him."

"Maybe. Maybe not. Either way, it's completely FUBAR." Volger tipped his head towards Finch with an unforgiving look.

FUBAR—fucked up beyond all recognition—the foot soldier's by-word for one more military boondoggle. Finch grimaced and averted his eyes.

Volger examined the bullet hole in the computer and turned to face Keely and Saxx. "So the security files are missing?"

"Looks like all of them. Yeah," Keely said. She pointed to the empty hard drive rack.

Finch took a step toward the computer console. "I'd be surprised if they didn't back up to the cloud." He waved a hand at the ceiling as if a digital cloud hovered above the building.

Volger studied Finch's face as though he needed to reassess what he might have to offer. He turned to Keely. "Does the Drake use a cloud backup?"

Her eyes swept across the floor. "I don't know."

"Saxx?"

He looked away and blew a long stream of air through his pinched lips.

Volger shook his head in disbelief. The operation had failed in every conceivable way.

"Okay. Take Brass Shoes up to the lobby. It should be quiet in the lounge." Volger crooked his thumb toward the ceiling as if he were familiar with the hotel facilities. "Debrief him while we try to figure the inside story down here." He leaned forward to study Hammond's corpse again. "By the way, Maitland wants to meet all three of us at HQ at nineteen hundred."

"Copy that," Saxx said and pointed a finger at Keely.

"You're with me. Finch, grab your bag. We're going upstairs."

Finch stepped over to the table where he'd stowed his courier bag. Beside the bag stood Saxx's empty water bottle. Finch drew his watch and cell phone from the outside pouch of his bag. As he strapped the watch to his wrist, an impulse struck him. A whim. He turned his back so that no one could observe him as he slipped Saxx's Evian bottle into his bag and zipped it shut.

It's a day for collecting cast-off plastics, he told himself. You never know where these things can lead. He followed Saxx and Keely up the staircase and into the empty lobby. They found a corner with a set of four plush chairs surrounding a circular glass coffee table.

When they sat down Saxx said, "Okay. You were up there for at least ten minutes. What'd you find out?"

Finch shrugged. Years ago he played a decent game of five-card stud. Today he knew he held a decent poker hand.

"WE were in constant contact with Hammond," Saxx said. "Right up until you moved from Lizzies Starlight into the hallway."

"He reported every move you made from when you left 505," Keely added. "The way you sent one elevator down, then took the second car up to the top."

"Why'd you send the first car down?" Saxx asked.

"I was told to."

"By who?"

"The woman who called. She fed me all the instructions."

"A woman?" Saxx extended an arm toward Finch, his palm

up, fingers curling in a gimme gesture. "So tell. We want every word."

Finch began to recount the phone conversation. He repeated the brief dialogue word for word.

"Then upstairs in Lizzie's Starlight. What'd she say?"

"Your turn." Finch had to smile. "You said you lost contact with Hammond. When? How?"

Saxx and Keely traded a look. When she nodded to him, he continued.

"When you met her in the bathroom corridor. Hammond said he lost visual contact. I guess the Drake didn't want any cameras in the hallway showing their guests coming and going to the can."

"So we waited," Keely continued. "What happened during that ten minutes?"

"As expected. She had me sit at a table in the hallway. She had a DNA swab kit and I let her take a sample. Mouth swab."

Saxx's eyebrows rose in surprise. "So you let her take it."

Finch realized that Saxx harbored some doubt that Finch would follow the script and allow her to sample his DNA. Maybe now the agent would finally concede that Finch was no toy soldier.

"Did you get her name?" he asked.

"Yeah. Musk. She said I'd come across her on White Sphere."

"Musk?" Keely looked at Saxx. A confused look crossed her face. "You heard of her?"

"No. That name never comes up in the transcripts." Saxx shrugged. He studied Finch's face. "Maybe she tried to deke you out. Did you acknowledge it?"

"Acknowledge what?"

"The name. *Musk.*"

Finch had to think. "Yeah. I did."

"That could've done it. Fucking hell. *There is no Musk in White Sphere.*" He waved both hands in the air. "You blew it, Finch. You jumped into her trap with both feet. Now Hammond's dead."

Finch looked up to the ceiling. Could it be? He recalled her body language at that point. How her shoulders tightened when he acknowledged the name Musk. That was when she dropped the top of the DNA wrapper. At the time he assumed it played to his advantage. Now he realized that he might have triggered Hammond's murder.

Keely clapped her hands over her ears as if she needed to block what she was hearing. After a moment she regained a sense of equanimity. "Okay. So what did she look like?"

"Green eyes. Five-five, or -six. Beyond that, hard to say."

"Give us a hint. What was she wearing?" Saxx snarled.

"An oversized beige kaftan. Almost head-to-toe. Covered everything but her face. And that was covered with an N95 mask."

Saxx and Keely exchanged a frown. They realized they were getting nowhere.

"What about her hair color?" Saxx asked.

"Brunette. But don't count on it. Most likely it was a wig."

"Her eyebrows?"

"Also brunette."

"Any facial marks? Moles?"

"Her skin—what I could see of it—was pale. The lines around her eyes and forehead made me think she was in her early forties." He shrugged and glanced away.

"Damnit, Finch, you got anything more for us to go on?"

He waited a moment to break the momentum of their rapid-fire interrogation.

"I do. But first, it's your turn again." His eyes shifted from Saxx to Keely. "How did you know Hammond was dead?"

She let out a heavy sigh. "When we didn't hear anything. Maybe ten minutes after you met Musk."

"So then what?"

"So I went down to the security room," she continued. "That's where I found Hammond, the computer with a bullet in it, and the backup drives stolen. The killer knew what he was doing."

"You know the rest," Saxx added. "Nothing more to tell."

Finch gazed at the ceiling again. Above them, he spotted the spy holes used to monitor the Prohibition raids. He wondered if anyone was watching them now.

"All right." He decided to disclose the rest of what he knew. "I can't be certain, but I think she's Russian or Ukrainian. Maybe second generation. Her English was flat, but with a slight accent. Midwest. Like North Dakota or Minnesota."

Keely leaned forward. "You sure?"

"I'm no linguist, but I have a decent ear."

Now Saxx angled forward as if he smelled a fresh scent. A tracker dog ready to run off-leash. "What else, Finch? I know you got more."

Finch ran his tongue over his lips as he contemplated how to present the evidence in his shirt pocket. "Do either of you have an evidence bag?"

Saxx shook his head as if Finch was leading them off on a tangent.

"I do." Keely tore open the velcro strip on a pouch inside her jacket and drew out a clear plastic envelope. "What've you got?"

"Maybe her fingerprints. *Maybe* her thumb and forefinger."

"What?" she gasped.

"You got a pair of tweezers in there, too?" He tipped his chin toward the compartment where she kept the evidence bag.

"Yeah. That, too."

She passed him the tweezers. He dipped them into his shirt pocket and after two attempts he pinched the tiny plastic wrapper between the steel tongs.

"Open the bag."

She opened the evidence bag and he dropped the tip of the wrapper inside. "You should get that down to your forensics unit. ASAP."

"What is it?" Saxx asked.

"The top strip from the DNA swab kit Musk—or whoever she is—used on me. She tore off the top and it fell to the floor. Turns out she didn't notice it. If we're lucky it could be a win."

FINCH had to wait for the traffic to clear a three-car collision on the Bay Bridge and consequently he didn't arrive at his sister-in-law's house until nine-thirty. Now that Eve had moved over to Berkeley Hills, he was getting used to the drive.

"You're running late," Eve said when he walked through the front door.

"Yeah. Bad day. A triple-x disaster actually," he muttered and dumped his courier bag beside the door.

"Oh? What happened."

"I'll tell you later." He waved a hand to dismiss the question. "Baby okay?"

"She's asleep." She checked her watch. "For over an hour now."

Just as well, he thought and made his way along the hall to where Eve had set up a temporary nursery. He opened the door to the bedroom and studied Casey's face as she slept in the crib.

Eve slipped an arm across his shoulders as they marveled at their beautiful child. He caressed Casey's cheek with his pinkie. One stroke so as not to wake her.

"Look what we made," he whispered.

"Yeah. She's prettier than either of us."

"Or both put together," he added. He turned toward the door. "Any food in the house?"

"You kidding? With Brock and Klare locked up here 24-7?"

Yesterday, Eve estimated that between them, the two students devoured eighty percent of the household edibles, "Including the plants," she'd added with a laugh.

She followed as he walked into the kitchen. He opened the refrigerator door and scanned the shelves. "Anyone got dibs on these chicken fingers?"

"All yours." Her tone suggested that any leftovers were nutritionally suspect. "God, I do miss eating out in North

Beach. Remember the pasta at DeLucchi's?"

"Barely."

He placed five chicken pieces on a plate and grabbed a paper towel to wipe his fingers. He sat at the table overlooking the backyard and began to eat. During the day the view swept down over the Berkeley campus and across San Francisco Bay to the ocean. But now it was obscured by the night clouds and the shadows cast by the towering redwoods that surrounded the house.

Eve prepared two decaf coffees and sat beside her husband. She set her hand on his knee. "So. Tell me about your triple-x disaster."

He shook his head and stared at the pieces of chicken on his plate. "The whole operation blew up. A security guard was shot."

Her hand slipped away from his leg. "Shot?"

"Yeah." He lifted the palm of one hand to his head. "Back of the head. He's dead. And all the surveillance videos destroyed. The backup drives stolen. No one has a clue how it happened."

"Oh my God." She glanced away as she recalled the FBI's main objective. "How close did you get to the Orange Man?"

"Not at all."

As he chewed on another chicken finger, Eve considered the crisis he'd endured. One more in the series of disasters he'd survived since they met six years ago.

"Okay, so walk me through it."

As Finch ate and sipped at his coffee, he revealed the moment-to-moment encounter in the Drake Hotel. When he told

the story he admitted that he'd blundered when he acknowledged meeting Musk online. She'd used it as a ruse. When he
stepped into her trap, Hammond had been executed. In all
likelihood, she was wearing a wire. Whoever listened to their
conversation killed Hammond and destroyed all evidence of
their encounter on the twenty-first floor.

"All right. But knowing you, you came up with
something." She placed her hand on his forearm. "Am I right?'

"Maybe a fingerprint. She might've left something on a
plastic tab from the DNA swab." He frowned. "If we're lucky."

"Well, luck is good. Sometimes essential." She smiled, a
hopeful expression that betrayed some doubt.

Then Finch remembered the bottle he'd taken from the
hotel security office. "Speaking of luck, I wonder if you can
ask Leanne Spratz to profile the DNA on a water bottle."

"Sure. I've got an open invitation from her." Eve's eyebrows rose across her forehead. "What bottle are we talking
about?"

He retrieved his courier bag from the front doorway and
returned to the kitchen. He opened the cutlery drawer and
found a pair of salad tongs. Then he carefully drew the container from his bag and set it on the table. "Agent Saxx was drinking from it. Before I left the hotel I grabbed it."

Finch tried to explain the impulse that inspired his theft.

"Those FBI bastards. *It's their attitude,*" he whined and
curled his lips. "It pisses me off that they've got *my* DNA on
record. And I've got nothing on them." He pointed to the
bottle. "So now—maybe I do."

# CHAPTER SIX

## ST. PETERSBURG — 20 JANUARY, 2001

Joseph Tull sat next to the phone in the new apartment that Zena found for them in December. The three-room flat on the top floor above their old unit on 8 Ya Liniya, was a prize neither of them expected. A gift—along with the telephone—from Ossip Vitvinin, the Saint Petersburg recruitment director at the "Academy"—their code word for the SVR, Russian Foreign Intelligence.

After Joseph heard the telephone voice message from Zena he mulled over the nuances and implications. Her absences were more frequent now and it worried him. She'd experienced three "flings" (as she called them) over the past year. Each one, part of her SVR training. What bothered Joseph was that she'd grown a little too fond of the training itself. He clicked the button on the recorder and listened to her message again.

*"Hey. Looks like I might be gone for the weekend. Sorry, but Anton managed to get an extra hour for practice at the*

*pistol range. Then Vitvinin wants me to take on some extra training at the Academy. Sounds like they have a center in the country somewhere that I haven't heard about. I'll tell you more later. I should be back by Monday. Don't forget to feed Mouse!"*

To end the message she added a kissing sound. A wet smooch that provided little comfort. On the other hand, her English was almost perfect now, the result of speaking English for the past five years to one another—and the entire team in the Academy. The local Academy recruits numbered almost thirty people now. All of them smart, dedicated, resourceful. He'd heard the rumors that the Kremlin had similar academies scattered across Russia. But of course, he was never privy to any detailed information.

He walked into the bedroom and found Mouse lying on the comforter. Her favorite nesting place.

"Hey, Mouse, ready for some dinner?" He scratched the cat under her chin. She responded with an affectionate purr, rose on her legs, posed in an elaborate stretch, jumped to the floor, and circulated between his ankles as he walked to her water bowl in the kitchen. She knew how to manipulate him. "Because you learned all your tricks from Zena," he whispered.

Mouse was a white Siamese cat with a beige face that framed her shocking blue eyes. A beauty. Zena enjoyed the looks of astonishment when she introduced the cat to her guests.

"Your cat's called Mouse?" or "Mouse is really a cat!" or "But I thought you had a mouse for a pet."

"Ah, fooled you!" Zena smiled broadly, amused again by

her small deceits.

And there were many of them.

ZENA had a new tattoo. Joseph noticed the three-word script written vertically below her left armpit. He'd finished a shower and when he pulled the shower curtain aside he watched as she shaved her armpits in the bathroom mirror. First the right, and then as she lifted her left arm, and began to shave the tuft of hair above the latest tattoo.

*Rhymes with Luck*

"A new tatt," he said. "What's that? The fifth?"

"No. Number four." She turned and patted both her inner thighs and her narrow pelvis. She had a man's narrow hips, but by any other measure she was all woman.

"I thought Vitvinin said no tattoos."

"Not exactly." She shrugged off the admonition. "No *visible* tatts."

Don't kid yourself, he mused. The way you live, they're all visible. "And has Vitvinin seen this one yet?"

She turned so that he could see her pouting in the mirror. "He might have. I'm not sure. Why don't you ask him?" she asked as if it were a dare.

"Don't play smoke and mirrors with me."

Her lips curled together as if she'd bitten into a lemon seed. "Smoke and mirrors? What about you? Your so-called *trust* from the Americans."

"All right. Not another word." He pointed a finger at her nose. Now she was digging too deep. Twelve years after flight 655 was destroyed, the American courts continued to dispute the compensation to the victims' families. Joseph's case was the last to near its final determination. His situation was complicated because his father was British, his mother Russian. While everything hung in limbo, his lawyers' fees consumed the vast majority of his expected indemnification. Joseph and Zena both knew his case had become a legal charade.

He wrapped the towel around his waist and took a step away from her. "Look, Zena. I've told you before. I don't care who you sleep with. Vitvinin, or anyone else in the Academy. But don't try to use it against me."

"Why do you say that? If we're going to be married in May I think we have to be honest with each other."

He laughed. "Get real. Neither of us believes in marriage vows. We both know I'm your ticket into the USA and so does Ossip Vitvinin. When—*if*—we move to the States I have to trust you. Completely."

"Of course you can. And I know that." Her voice carried a note of sincerity. She set her free hand on his shoulder and caressed the length of his arm. In her right hand, she held the razor, poised to shave another stroke from her armpit.

"When we get to California, it has to look right. I can't be seen as your third wheel."

She giggled. Third wheel, a new term for her. "Yeah, once we get there. But until we leave, let me have fun, for now, okay?"

He shrugged and made his way past her toward the bedroom. He swiveled back to her. "By the way, what does that mean? *Rhymes with luck.*"

She held a finger to the corner of her lip, turned it a little as if she had to guess. "Let's see. Run through the English alphabet with me. Mmm, *buck?* No. *Duck?* No. Hmmm... What comes after that?"

He rolled his eyes and glanced away. He'd make sure that Vitvinin talked with her. Somehow she had to straighten out before they departed for America. It wouldn't be easy even for a man like Vitvinin. Everyone knew Zena Smirnov was what Americans called an IED. An improvised explosive device. A homemade bomb, primed and ready to ignite. Who could cut her fuse?

OSSIP Vitvinin leaned against the bookcase that lined the wall behind his desk. As the head of the St. Petersburg Foreign Intelligence Service Recruitment Bureau, he managed to convey an intellectual demeanor. A floor-to-ceiling stack of books behind his tall, heavy frame supported the illusion. He could well pass for a professor of history. On the other hand, his massive chest and perpetual grimace reminded Joseph Tull of a mafia hitman, now all the rage in the American crime films that flooded through Russian theaters.

Along with a well-worn tweed jacket and his version of Leonid Brezhnev's thick, untamed eyebrows—he appeared smart, tough, self-assured. Brezhnev was no longer in favor, of course, but to old-school communists, he was the last competent Soviet leader. He was followed by two short-lived amateurs. Yuri Andropov and Konstantin Chernenko. Then came Mikhail Gorbachev. And with him, the collapse.

"Cut straight to your point, Josef." Vitvinin swept a hand toward the chair next to his desk and they sat down facing one another. "I have a call coming from the Kremlin in twenty minutes."

Joseph narrowed his eyes. So be it. "It's Zena Smirnov. She's screwing everyone in the Academy." He let Vitvinin absorb the accusation. "She's becoming a nymphomaniac."

The frank expression drew a smile to Vitvinin's lips. "Well, not everyone. But all the men, perhaps."

Joseph refused to be drawn in by a cynical joke. "If she cannot control herself, it presents a huge risk. One that neither of us can afford."

"You forget it's part of her training. Yours too, if I recall the curriculum."

*The curriculum.* It was all so clinical for Vitvinin. The art of seduction, manipulation, and betrayal. Scores of agents used sex to blackmail informants and recruit new agents. With persistence and a bit of luck, sometimes they could twist the game to turn foreign spies into double agents.

"Yes. But once my lessons were mastered, I closed the door to the classroom." He paused to prepare the question he knew he must ask. "Have you seen her latest tattoo?"

"I'm not sure."

"No?" He raised an eyebrow. "Well, perhaps that says something about you."

Vitvinin looked away and shook his head as if he'd fallen into a devious chess gambit. He nodded and returned his gaze to Joseph. "Bravo, Josef. Your audacity makes you one of our best recruits. If not the very best." He tipped his head from side to side as if debating a response. "Since you are unafraid to ask the hard question, I must respond with the hard answer. The answer is, yes. But since all her tattoos are written in English, once again, I don't know what they mean. They're posed as riddles, are they not?"

"More like Zen koans."

"Like what?"

"If you meet the Buddha, kill him." He waved a hand, searching the air. "Or, I am the sound of one hand clapping."

"What about this new one?"

"Under her left arm." He raised his arm and drew a line descending from his armpit. "Have you seen it?"

"Oh yes, that one." He nodded. "What does it mean?"

Joseph ignored the question. Vitvinin was trying to deflect the issue. And becoming impolite. "You—and the Academy—have forbidden body markings of any kind. The ban is understandable. The Russian obsession with tattooing is now a mania. Based on gang celebrities from the prison gulag."

Vitvinin tipped his head from side to side as if he had to choose between Joseph or Zena. "Granted, she may have this one flaw. Temporarily. But she has many other assets. Some invaluable."

Joseph knew Vitvinin meant her killer instincts. Which—like Joseph himself—she'd demonstrated on three condemned terrorists in a Caucasus jail.

"As you know, tattoos are forbidden not only because of the mafia affiliations." Vitvinin's rough voice hardened. Everyone feared his temper. His knife edge could cut deep in one thrust. Which was exactly how Joseph wanted him before he proposed a solution. "They also compromise our agents' ability to infiltrate our enemies. We all know—even Zena herself—not everyone likes tattoos," he added.

"So then. You will discipline her?"

The question brought a spiteful look to Vitvinin's eyes. No one told him what to do. Or even suggested it. "Audacity is one thing, but insubordination another. Be careful what you say next, Josef Tull. And more important, how you say it."

Joseph paused, a thoughtful hesitation to suggest his compliance. "Please, Ossip Vitvinin. This year I will return to America with our shared mission in my heart. As an American citizen, I will be your most valued asset in the USA since the Soviet collapse. And I will take Zena Smirnov with me as my wife. But"—he raised a finger in the air, a clear warning of his determination—"I will not be compromised by her. She must be disciplined."

Vitvinin pressed his lips together, a gesture to confirm that Joseph had responded with the necessary respect. "How do you suggest?"

"Instruct her to have all her tattoos removed before our marriage."

He cringed. "That will be painful."

"Discipline is necessarily painful. By definition." He leaned forward, his determination etched on his face. "She must be cleansed before the wedding. Otherwise, I will disavow her."

"You will disavow *her?*" His tone suggested there could be another option.

"We're to marry on May 15. In July we depart for America. You'll recall that we're both enrolled in graduate studies for the fall semester."

126

"Yes, yes. I know all this."

"My status is guaranteed. Her status depends on me." Perhaps, he thought, Ossip Vitvinin had forgotten this essential requirement.

"Josef, the marriage is one thing, but there is another." Vitvinin flattened his hands on the desk.

"Oh?" He leaned back in the chair. "And what is that?"

"The question of your loyalties."

A silence welled between them. Joseph decided to wait for Vitvinin to continue.

"The blue bloods harbor doubts." He waved a hand toward the door to suggest the cadre of officers in the SVR.

The blue bloods—Russians who tracked their heritage from the middle ages. Joseph shook his head. "What kind of doubts?"

"Doubts as to who you are. To be specific, *what* you are."

*"What* I am?"

"Yes." His eyes narrowed. "Are you Russian? Or American?"

Joseph felt his throat tighten. "They dare to ask me this?" His throat pinched tight as he struggled to continue. *"You* know who I am."

"I do. But others—"

"Do they know the Americans murdered my mother and father?"

"Yes. Some." His chin nodded to one side. "Probably all."

Joseph glanced away. So either Vitvinvin or Zena had broken her pledge to him. Perhaps it had been a mistake to discuss his parents' fate. But his pain still lingered. The passing years had sharpened the sting. He knew it always would.

"Then let me say this. No one—*no one*—in the SVR bears the hatred of America as I do."

Vitvinin waited for Joseph's anger to cool. While he favored his young disciple, he knew the SVR blue bloods would banish him without remorse.

"All right. Let me say one final thing, then our discussion is closed."

Joseph nodded, a gesture to acknowledge Vitvinin's power over him.

"I still support your mission. Enthusiastically," he added. "But others want to test you. The test may not come tomorrow. Or next year. But one day it will come and I might not be able to block it. In fact, I may have to support it. You must understand it's not a betrayal. It is a simple inevitability." He held up his arm and turned it slightly as if a handful of sand slipped from his open fingers.

Joseph blinked. Here was the twisted logic of the Russian mind. The contradiction of self-sabotage and unfettered control. He understood that he had to embrace it or be dismissed. But the question of Zena lingered.

"And what about Zena?"

"Enough." He drew a deep breath and puffed out his cheeks as he exhaled. "Don't worry. I will resolve this."

Joseph smiled to acknowledge the favor.

"Send her to me. Tomorrow. Eleven a.m." Vitvinin stood and reached across his desk, his big hand extended to his apprentice. "Remember one thing, Josef. Soon you'll be our best hope in America. To you, my door is always open."

Joseph stood and shook Vitvinin's hand. Then Joseph turned and left the office, wondering if Vitvinin offered any hope at all.

AFTER she met with Ossip Vitvinin, Zena Smirnov flew into a rage that tore open the depth of her anger. When she screamed that she would never forgive Joseph, he calmly replied that Vitvinin should be the object of her fury. Not Joseph. After all, he still intended to marry her.

"Marry me? You *still* want that?" she cried. The idea threw her off balance. "Would you marry me for love?"

"For our mission," he allowed. "But love could follow. It's your choice."

"My choice? Vitvinin says unless I remove the tattoos I'll be dismissed from the Academy."

He shrugged. "You knew the rules."

She stood beside him, her hands knotted in fists. He could see the rising blood pressure blooming on her face.

*"FUCK!"*

He walked over to the kitchen and picked up the business card that she'd thumped onto the table with such rancor when she'd returned from her meeting with Vitvinin. A plastic surgeon's name, address, and telephone number were inscribed on the card in Cyrillic letters—as well as his specialty, laser surgery. Joseph read the name aloud.

"Dr. Matveyev. I suggest you call him soon. The wedding is still set for May. Or not. As I said, it's your choice."

Following her treatments, Zena refused to speak to Joseph for four weeks. They avoided one another in the kitchen and living room and she slept on the sofa every night. Each morning and evening she endured a silent ritual of nursing her skin with an antibacterial ointment. In a way, he admired her stoicism. She'd had to swallow her resentment—and her ego—to restore her credibility with Vitvinin. Eventually, she recognized that she'd endured a test of will that changed her for the better. Her sexual desire was now a useful tool under her command and control. Hardened by iron determination.

"You want to see?" She emerged from the bathroom and confronted Joseph as he flicked through the Stanford University graduate orientation guide in the living room.

"See what?"

"What Matveyev did to me." She dropped her bathrobe and stood naked, a hand poised on her hip. It was more of her than he'd seen in a month.

"All right."

She lifted her arm. The calligraphy that had been inked into her flesh in a narrow strip—*Rhymes with Luck*—had been eradicated. She turned her leg so that he could see the smooth flesh of her inner thighs. She ran a hand across the narrow band of skin above her pelvis. All of the tattoos were eliminated.

"They're gone," he said. "I can barely remember them." He lied to diminish her feelings of regret. Not that she would reveal any remorse to him.

"Which? You can't remember what they said, or you can't see any traces?

"Both."

She pouted a little but was pleased to hear his approval. She swept a foot back and forth across the carpet and stepped toward him. After a hesitant pause, she dropped into his lap and slung an arm around his shoulders so that her breasts rolled against his chest. "I've missed this."

"You have?" He needed some convincing. Could they ever recover what they once had? Despite his uncertainty, he ran his hand along the top of her thigh.

"I'm sorry, Josef." She kissed his cheek. "Did I hurt you?"

He withdrew his hand. "Better not to ask a question like that."

"Okay. No more questions." She put his hand on her leg again. "I want to marry you and go to California. Then we'll focus on our mission. But tonight, let's go to bed, okay? I feel so empty inside. I can't tell you how empty I feel." She kissed his mouth again. "I need you to fill me up. Completely."

He responded to her kisses, wound his arms around her, and caressed her until her breathing became a long, continuous purring. As he led her to the bedroom, he thought how empty he felt, too. Was it a sickness they shared? A psychological infection? Or just the way that each person lived in this world, inhabiting a transparent bubble that revealed the void inside everyone.

# CHAPTER SEVEN

SAN FRANCISCO — 26 FEBRUARY, 2021

As Will Finch entered the board room in the FBI regional headquarters, he paused to study his surroundings. Not much had changed since his last visit when Agents Jeremy Saxx and Sandra Keely recruited him to penetrate White Sphere. This was his third visit within ten days and he hoped it would be his last.

Keely slipped through the door behind him, followed by Saxx. They all wore masks and respected the pandemic six-foot social distancing protocol. Saxx told Finch to sit on the far side of the plexiglass divider and plodded to the front of the room, his thick bulk swaying from side to side. He stood beneath a mid-size TV monitor which hung from the ceiling. Despite the bright look in her eyes, Keely's body language revealed signs of exhaustion. She swept her hair over one shoulder and turned to Saxx.

"Ready to begin?" she asked.

Saxx nodded.

"Looks like we caught a break. Turns out we did recover some of the Drake surveillance videos from the cloud." She tipped her head towards Finch, a concession that he'd been correct—the hotel surveillance systems were configured to backup straight to the cloud.

Finch leaned forward. "So whoever murdered Troy Hammond failed to disable the cloud video?"

"That's why we needed you to come in," Keely said. "Especially if you can tell us more about the woman you met."

"You mean Musk?"

"Well, whoever she is."

Finch wondered if he could add anything substantive to his statement during their debriefing in the hotel lobby. Determined to give it his best shot he said, "Whatever I can do to help."

"All right." Her head swiveled back to Saxx. "Run the tape, Jeremy."

Saxx pointed a remote at the TV, clicked a button, and sat three chairs away from Keely. The screen lit up with a wide-angle view of the basement ramp that led down to the security office. Then an edited sequence showed Troy Hammond entering the office and moments later, the day-shift guard closing the door and walking up the ramp to Sutter Street. Next, Saxx and Keely entered the room. Then Finch. Each clip showed a digital date and time stamp in the top right corner. Finch joined the team at 3:23 p.m.

The scene cut to reveal Saxx and Keely walking along the fifth-floor hall and entering rooms 507 and 510. Then the video showed Finch climbing the staircase from the basement to the fifth floor where he entered room 505. After twenty minutes, Finch walked down the hall to the elevator bay and sent one car to the lobby. He entered the second car. The elevator camera seemed to hold him in a freeze-frame as he rode to the twenty-first floor. Then a series of cameras tracked him when he turned through the reception area in Lizzie's Starlight, walked through the main hall, then over to the bathroom corridor. At that point, the surveillance stream ended.

Ten minutes later the video cut to the woman in the kaftan —Musk—striding past the reception desk toward the elevator bay.

"That's her," Finch said.

Saxx glanced at Finch. "The woman you call Musk."

"Yeah, Musk," he repeated. "But where the hell is she going?"

"To the service elevator," Keely said.

They watched Musk stride past the public elevators where she tapped an elevator call button. A *ping* sounded immediately —the sound Finch had heard as he waited the extra five minutes in Lizzie's Starlight.

At the far end of the hall she swung open a heavy wood door. A new camera showed her as she stepped into a window-less space that reminded Finch of a storage locker. Facing her stood a single-bay elevator. Instead of housing the standard up-down call buttons, the elevator required a key. The camera showed her draw something from her pocket and insert it into the elevator lock. After a moment, the steel door slipped open, she stepped inside and disappeared.

Finch said, "She had a service key."

"Yes," Keely said with a heavy moan. "They had every-thing covered."

Finch turned his head as a new thought struck him. Now he understood. "Maybe that's how they shut the elevators down on me."

"What do you mean?" Saxx tapped the pause button on the video. For once he appeared interested in what Finch might have to offer.

"On my way back to 505, I couldn't get an elevator. That's when I remembered Hammond saying I might need to use the hotel PIN code. 1928."

"And that worked?" Saxx leaned forward in his chair.

"Without a hitch." Finch nodded. "And I used the code to open 507 and 510. By then you must've gone down to the basement."

Saxx touched the play button and the video stream contin-ued. The fifth-floor camera now showed Finch using his card and passcode to enter his room, and after a few moments, rooms 507 and 510 where he searched for Keely and Saxx. Saxx paused the tape again and the three of them reflected on the situation.

"Okay. So show him the rest of the video," she said.

Over the next five minutes, Finch watched the disaster unfold as the cameras revealed two people entering the base-ment security office. Musk wore her kaftan, with a hood that covered most of her head. The second figure wore jeans, a fleece hoodie, and a ski mask pulled over his face below his chin. They appeared to swipe the lock with a security card followed by a four-digit PIN.

Saxx paused the tape again. "The forensic report says the PIN is the same one you used, Finch. 1928. One PIN for the entire building." He clicked the remote and the video continued.

Next, Musk drew a pistol from under her kaftan and led the way into the security room. Hammond never bothered to turn around. She fired once into the back of his head. He died without knowing he was gone. Then she held her weapon six inches above the computer and fired a bullet into the hard drive. The second figure took control of the security console. He shut down the cameras, detached the backup drives, and stashed them in a shoulder bag. Finch guessed the raid took less than two minutes.

"What the hell?" Finch held up a hand. "Stop a sec. What's the time signature there? From when they open the door, shoot Hammond, and then exit?"

Saxx paused the tape.

Keely studied Finch's eyes so she could consider his reaction to what she was about to say. "One minute and forty-one seconds."

"Unbelievable," he whispered. "Strictly professional."

"Yeah. We know."

Saxx clicked the play button and the video sequence came to an end. After a few seconds, a series of grainy clips showed the exterior of the Drake as two figures emerged from the basement ramp and turned onto Sutter Street, then crossed over to Powell.

"These shots are from the street cameras," she said. "Once

they hit Powell, we lost track of them."

Saxx stood up and began to pace across the carpet. He pointed the remote at the video monitor and clicked off the TV. A tormented look filled his eyes. An expression that refused to acknowledge he'd been outplayed in every inning of the game.

Finch swiveled his chair so that he faced the center of the room. He glanced at Keely through the plexiglass shield. "Okay, so the security tapes confirm that the woman I met— Musk—is the same person who murdered Hammond."

"Maybe. Most likely, I guess. Whoever she is." Her voice revealed her doubts. What could anyone prove based on the videos? More important, could Finch convince a jury of any- thing—let alone Musk's identity.

He paused to collect his thoughts. "All right. Two questions. Does the slug that killed Hammond match the bullet that took out Myfanwy Thomas?"

Saxx sat down in his chair. His eyes narrowed with an impatient gaze. "And your second question, Finch?"

He sensed something unexpected was about to hit him.

"What about the fingerprints from the swatch of plastic I gave you. Any match in your database?"

"So the answers are, one, we can't tell you that," Saxx said. "And two, that information is privileged."

Finch felt as though he'd taken a soft punch to his chest. He leaned back in the chair. "What do you mean?"

Keely offered a sympathetic smile. "Operation Brass Shoes is done."

"And so are you, Finch." He tipped his head to one side. "But thank you for your services."

Finch was dumbstruck. "… So…?"

"So you need to recall the terms of our agreement. Everything you've learned through the investigation remains confidential. That means you have no first amendment rights to publish anything about this until the case is publicly disclosed by our office." Saxx's hand swung between his chest and Keely, a finger extended to demonstrate only the two of them could release him from jeopardy. He waited a beat to ensure Finch understood.

Finch realized more was coming.

"And you should bear in mind your ongoing liability regarding the shoot-out in South Dakota last year. You shot a man with a weapon that you illegally transported across state lines. A gun that did not belong to you."

Finch closed his eyes. Once again, they had him cornered.

Saxx prodded him. "Do you understand?"

He refused to respond. Instead, he leaned over the side of his chair, clutched his courier bag in his right hand, and walked out of the room. As he marched along the hallway to the elevator bay, he heard Keely call after him.

"Finch, wait. You need me to sign you out of the building."

He kept walking. When he reached the security gate, she caught up to him and made a gesture to the guard as Finch handed over his visitor pass.

"He's free to go," she said.

Finch swung around to glare at her—the steel in his eyes sharp enough to cut her. Better not to say a word, he warned himself and entered an elevator car and descended to the lobby.

As he walked onto Golden Gate Avenue a dense fog rolled

across the street. It admitted no sunshine, no shadows, no color. Yet the bleak air suited his mood. A dark funk infused with deceit and betrayal flushed through his belly and chest.

"The hell with you," he muttered as he walked straight ahead and let the fog slip around his face and shoulders as if it belonged to him alone.

D. F. Bailey

# CHAPTER EIGHT

SAN FRANCISCO — 1 AUGUST, 2001

Joseph and Zena arrived in California and moved into the married graduate student housing complex on Comstock Circle in the Stanford University campus. They spent their first week in an orientation program to guide them through the complexities that confront every international student. Banking, health insurance, employment, student affairs. They met their thesis advisors—Computer Science for Joseph, Microbiology for Zena—and confirmed the academic requirements for the fall term.

Zena quickly adapted to American English with little trouble. Both of them began to absorb the current colloquialisms which introduced them to new ways of thinking. Language shapes consciousness, Joseph claimed. Zena didn't dispute it for a minute. They both understood that they'd entered a world that could completely change them. Unless they maintained their allegiance to Russia—and each other.

140

By the end of August, they'd visited all nine counties that comprised the Bay Area. Above all others, Zena loved San Francisco—The Golden City—and together they explored the most acclaimed attractions. Fisherman's Wharf, Coit Tower, Alcatraz, Golden Gate Park, The Embarcadero, The Presidio. The city offered endless distractions. It reminded her of the title of Neil Postman's book, *Amusing Ourselves to Death.* One day, she felt certain, America would implode. But until then, her infatuation blossomed.

"It's more intense than I imagined," she confessed as they sat in a Starbucks two blocks off Union Square. "Their wealth. Okay, back home, we all heard about it. But when you actually *see* the money. The people on the street, the clothes, the cars"—her hand swept across the window overlooking Sutter Street—"you can *witness* the American cultural compulsion. Buy, buy, buy."

"Not everyone has it all." Joseph pointed to three down-and-out men squatting on the sidewalk, passing a flask from hand to hand.

"They're no worse in Russia. At least these tramps all have shoes." She said with a hint of remorse. She knew the homeless in Russia and America shared a common bond. They may not speak the same language, but they were brothers.

"Zena, it could be easy for us to forget why we're here. Keep these same men in your mind. Forget the Cadillacs and Macy stores. We're not here just for Russia"—he pointed at the most grizzled of the three men as he vomited into the gutter—"but for him, too."

She smiled. "Now you sound like an old Soviet

apparatchik. At the ripe old age of twenty-five. What do the Americans say? *'You drank the Kool-Aid.'* I don't even remember their names anymore."

"Whose names?" He took another sip of his coffee, frowned, and pushed it aside. A Caramel Macchiato. Liquid candy.

"The communists. The leaders. It's taken me years to purge their names from my memory."

"Your father was a communist."

"No." She glared at him. "He was a *soldier.*"

"Yes, you're right. And so are we. Let's not forget that either."

AT 5:50 a.m. on September 11, Joseph left Zena sleeping in their apartment and walked along Comstock Circle toward the Gates Computer Science Building. There he met Dr. Jerry Gonzales, Joseph's thesis advisor, who held a fellowship at the California Academy of Sciences. The position—Advisory Chair in the Information Technology Department—required Gonzales to spend one morning each week in the Academy building in Golden Gate Park. A month after meeting Joseph and discussing his thesis proposal on cyber security, Gonzales invited Joseph to accompany him so that he could familiarize himself with the Academy's IT program.

"You might be a good fit," he suggested. "No promises, but over the past five years, they hired two of my grad students."

However, Gonzales's early morning schedule meant that if Joseph wanted a ride to the Academy, he had to meet Gonzales at six a.m. Joseph admired Gonzales's work ethic. It seemed that everyone he met at Stanford shared a commitment to learning. And to self-discipline. He knew both he and Zena would fit in if they could mimic the Americans' unlimited belief in manifest destiny.

When he saw his thesis advisor's Jeep parked outside the Gates Building, he noticed Gonzales's bearded face hunched over the steering wheel as he studied something on his phone. Joseph tapped on the passenger window. Gonzales glanced up as if he'd been roused from a dream.

"Hey. Sorry." He released the door lock. "Just trying to keep up with the email."

Joseph climbed into the passenger seat and Gonzales started the ignition. Ten minutes later the car barreled along the 280 towards San Francisco. "Depending on the traffic," Gonzales said, "the drive takes about an hour."

The sky was clear, the air crisp from the morning wind coursing off the Pacific Ocean. Joseph lowered his window to absorb it all. This new life in America. His first visit to the Academy. So amusing that it had the same nickname as the Russian SVR training program. A good omen? Perhaps.

Gonzales drove through the south entrance into Golden Gate Park, parked his car, and led the way to the front entrance of the Academy. By the time they walked into the staff office quarters, the south tower of the World Trade Center in New York City had already collapsed.

"Over here!" one of the secretaries called from the far end of the corridor. Her voice sounded the alarm as people streamed past her into the staffroom.

"What is it?" Gonzales asked.

"The World Trade Center." She held her hands to her face. "We're under attack!"

Joseph followed Gonzales into the staff room. About twenty people stood scattered in front of a TV. The heavy silence was broken by cries of horror as the video stream replayed the images of two airplanes dashing into the concrete towers at full speed. Then the Pentagon was attacked. Joseph braced himself against the door as a flood of energy coursed through him. His arms and chest flooded with adrenalin. Could it be? Someone striking a blow against the empire in broad daylight. So audacious, yet so simple. The attack required no neutron bombs. No biotech. All it took was imagination and the blind dedication of suicidal warriors. In World War Two, they were called Kamikaze. Now, Jihadi.

IN August, 2005, Joseph and Zena marked their fourth anniversary in America. Zena had secured a three-year endowment that covered her tuition and the rent for their off-campus loft apartment. Joseph's scholarship was a five-year full ride, intended to cover all his food, accommodation, and tuition. But their combined income didn't provide for many extras, so Zena took a job at the campus childcare center and Joseph worked an afternoon shift at the Academy of Sciences in Golden Gate Park. In an emergency, Joseph could transfer funds from a stipend that Ossip Vitvinin funneled into Joseph's numbered account in the Grand Cayman Islands. But so far he let the money accumulate without drawing a penny for himself.

"So how much money do we have in the Caymans?" She could read the tension on his face as soon as she asked this always delicate question. She paused to correct herself. "Sorry, I meant how much *do you* have?"

"Enough," he answered and began to stack the dinner dishes in the dishwasher. "Why do you ask?"

"Because, dear husband, we forgot to celebrate our fourth anniversary." She wound an arm around his waist. "And our arrival in Amer-*ika*."

Although she still bore a slight accent, her American English was adept enough to twist her pronunciation of America to suggest a Kafkaesque hell. Turn the sound of a 'c' into a hard 'k' he'd told the students in the American Club, and it shows the American dream is a nightmare.

He returned her smile. "So. You want to celebrate?"

"Yes, I do." She stood on her toes to kiss his lips. "I want you to take me to the club on top of The Drake Hotel and dance with me."

He set the cutlery aside and let his hands travel over her breasts. She always loved his caresses, could never get enough of them. She began to unbutton his shirt.

"Not right now," he whispered. "Wait until tonight, okay."

"Why? You have another woman to meet?"

He laughed. "No. There is no other woman. And you know that."

"All right. I guess I do." She let his fingers toy with her. "So what is it that's so important?"

His hands fell away. "Rome3."

A broad smirk crossed her face. Rome3 meant he would make his way to the computer lab where somehow—and she never knew exactly how it worked—he would communicate with Ossip Vitvinin who'd been promoted to SVR headquarters in Moscow. The Third Rome as Vitvinin called it, or Rome3, the SVR code name.

An hour later Joseph settled at one of the computer terminals in the grad library and logged into the Hotmail account he shared with Ossip Vitvinin. Their method was simple, a trick that Joseph had adapted from a Stanford undergrad who arranged secret dates with his girlfriend. Because Joseph and Vitvinin used a single account with the same login ID and password, they could write messages to one another—but never send them. When Joseph checked into the joint account, he could read the most recent entry from Vitvinin where it sat in the Drafts folder. To respond, Joseph simply added to the draft message. Vitvinin would add his reply, and so the thread continued—without ever traveling through the internet. To heighten the security, all messages were written in Russian using the Cyrillic alphabet. A simple set of commands in the computer control panel enabled the switch from the American keyboard layout. Vitvinin was so impressed that he used their method as a template to communicate with all his global operatives.

Joseph opened the draft folder and saw two recent entries. The first was a typical update about his Grand Cayman account. *"Postcard sent today. Check your mailbox."* Postcard referred to a cash deposit. The mailbox was his Cayman numbered account. The amounts varied and averaged about five thousand US dollars a month. The money—his war chest—now amounted to almost two hundred and forty thousand. Not bad for four years' effort. He smiled, amused that he'd convinced Zena that the total amounted to little more than pocket change.

The second entry in the draft folder was considerably longer. And intriguing.

*Rome3 has an opportunity to work with a rising underground movement known as The Defense. Their network is building across the USA. Contact Samuel Weems in Frankfort, Kentucky. Arrange a meeting. Offer financial assistance from an "anonymous supporter" in the Grand Caymans. $100k installments each quarter. Over the next five years, your goal is to become their chief financial officer. Work your way in. Encourage Zena to utilize her training. Target Weems for her charms.*

BY February, 2008, Joseph successfully penetrated Samuel Weems's cabal of associates known as The Defense. His infiltration introduced him to the key players in a network determined to transform America. Some were small-town politicians and businessmen like Weems who vowed to restore the USA to the pre-911 status quo. "The good ole days run by good ole boys" as Weems liked to say.

Weems himself represented a living model of the group. He was a one-time mayor of a small town in Indiana. Following his second-term election loss, his wife divorced him and he moved to Kentucky. With the money he received from his divorce settlement—after his income dropped to zero, and she inherited over $2,500,000—he bought a five-vehicle trucking company that shipped corn, potatoes, and tomatoes from Midwest farms to city grocers. He styled himself as a self-made entrepreneur and bought an upscale condo in the downtown core of Frankfort, the state capital. When his operation ran headlong into a federal tax audit, he liquidated the trucks and condo, paid off his taxes, and turned his attention to what he called "radical libertarianism."

"Radical libertarianism," Joseph repeated the phrase to Zena as they sat at the bar in the graduate student lounge at Stanford. "Two very big words for someone like Weems."

"You mean Worms," she countered. Zena drank the last of her Bloody Mary and rolled her eyes.

She loathed the afternoon she'd spent with Weems in January. As part of their honey-trap, Joseph had installed a spy-cam in a room at the Travelers Motel in Frankfort and recorded Zena's theatrical sexcapade with Weems. Joseph had to swallow his bitterness as he watched his wife's enthusiastic performance. He scanned the video once, then sent a copy to Ossip Vitvinin. Six weeks later, Zena could still feel her skin crawl from the memory of Weems's fingers worming along her thighs.

"Don't ever ask me to do that again," she warned Joseph in Russian. "Not with him, anyway," she added.

"Believe me, I don't want to." For his part, Joseph felt relieved as she unburdened herself of the loathing she felt. "But it may be necessary. Remember, the order came from Vitvinin. And stop speaking in Russian. Especially *here*." He jabbed a finger at the polished bar top. "You understand?"

She glanced around the graduate student lounge to determine if anyone might be watching them. She waved at two women wandering through the cafeteria. Students from her microbiology seminar. "And don't *you* ever show that tape to anyone." Her lips pinched into a tight frown.

Joseph suppressed his feeling of bewilderment. "Vitvinin insisted I send him a copy."

"And did you?"

He shrugged.

"Fuck…" Her voice trailed off in a whisper. She knew Joseph had to do it. Had to betray her to Vitvinin once again. "Well, I guess it's nothing he hasn't seen before. I hope he enjoys it," she added.

When she said this, Joseph glanced away again. The memory of their confrontation over her tattoos had almost vanished. Since then, they rarely talked about her promiscuity. Or her tatts. Now that her "training" had come into play with Weems, he wondered where it would lead.

"Look. You know this is business. If we have to threaten Weems to serve our cause, then we will do whatever is needed. And thanks to you, Weems is in my back pocket."

Her lips twisted into a frown of bitterness. "Worms! Worms!" she repeated to ensure his nickname stuck.

"All right." He reached across the table to hold her hand. "Worms, then," he said with a laugh.

"Thank you." Knowing their balance was almost level again, she returned his smile and blew him a kiss. "Now let's go back to the apartment. I have something to show you."

"Oh?"

She squeezed his fingers, released his hand, and stood up. "Yes. Something someone like Worms will never see. Something no one but *you* will ever experience."

He knew this was her way of restoring his faith in her. Her magic, her obsessions erupting within her psyche. She had to release them and he felt compelled to participate in all her acts of passion and desire. Otherwise, what would become of them?

OVER the following years, Joseph reported weekly to Vitvinin about The Defense and their growing organization. With the steady flow of financial support, Joseph assured his handler that they'd become essential to The Defense operations. Without Joseph and Zena, The Defense would collapse. His exchange of notes on their shared Hotmail account detailed the growth of his network.

Joseph Tull to Rome3: *Samuel Weems from The Defense introduced me to Right Flank, a decentralized, underground group based in Oregon and Washington states. Their leader, Franklin Delacroix, wants us to fund weapons training and a summer recruitment program. Suggest we support them using the model established with Weems and The Defense.*

Rome3 to Tull: *Approval granted. Offer quarterly investments of $100K.*

Rome3 to Tull: *The Global Stock market crash presents a once-in-a-lifetime opportunity. Identify new partners for our program. IF Obama wins the election in Nov., expect deep grass-roots opposition. The next 5 - 10 years are critical.*

Tull to Rome3: *Right Flank and The Defense identified three new opposition groups dedicated to destroying the Obama government in DC. Request funds to supply them using The Defense model for all three. Would need additional $300k per* *quarter. Can Rome3 support?*

Rome3 to Tull: *Approval granted. Allocate $100K each per quarter to all three. Maintain current funding to The Defense and Right Flank. Total allocation is now $5 million annually. Offer annual bonus of $1m to groups that achieve program goals. Rome3 assigns the highest priority to your initiatives. You are instructed to identify, penetrate and fund all viable dissident groups. Technical and financial support are yours to command. Our strategic goal remains unchanged. Spread chaos throughout America.*

During the next decade, Joseph recognized the prescient policies flowing from the Kremlin. A Russian chess master—Pushkin—now dominated world politics. Not only did their leader foresee what lay ahead, he drove his opponents from his path as if they were mere pawns. Joseph and Zena drew new courage as Russia crawled out from under the ruins of the Soviet Union. The "Great Bear" had grasped the oil and gas fields in the east. When the oligarchs were unleashed to exploit the nation's vast resources they generated the wealth to rebuild the military foundation of the country. Then the oligarchs' assets were expropriated—or "restructured" as Vitvinin put it—and the Kremlin regained control of its territorial resources from the Baltic Sea to the Arctic Circle and across Siberia to the Pacific Ocean. With Russian pride restored, the foreign policy now focussed on an overriding objective. Uncouple the USA from Europe and NATO. Disrupt the American electorate. Unhinge democracy from the people.

IN 2006 Joseph and Zena completed their PhD programs at
Stanford—Joseph in computer science, Zena in microbiology.
Two months later Zena surrendered her green card and swore
her oath of allegiance to the USA as a naturalized citizen.
Joseph, as a native-born American, never surrendered his
citizenship even after he immigrated to Russia. Ossip Vitvinin
claimed their cover would be bullet-proof once they became
tax-paying citizens with respectable jobs. Consequently, both
secured full-time employment in the USA and pursued the
strategy mapped out by the Kremlin.

In 2011, to the horror of the university IT community, Dr.
Jerry Gonzales, his wife, and two children drowned when his
car veered off a ferry loading ramp into the ocean during a
vacation in the San Juan Islands. Joseph accepted the offer to
fill Gonzales's shoes as the acting IT Chair at the California
Academy of Sciences—on one condition. His once-a-week
volunteer post became a halftime, paid position. A year later,
the Academy Board extended his employment for five years—
and renewed him for a second five-year term in 2017. Meanwhile, Zena started her own company, Zena BioTechnologies,
to capitalize on her knowledge of virology. By 2016 she had a
roster of three start-up clients with big ambitions—but shoe-
string budgets.

And all of it a mirage. Two elaborate disguises to mask
their only purpose in life. All that was missing was a weapon to
strike a fatal blow to the heart of the beast—the animal Zena
called Amerika. What could it be? Something simple but dev-
astating. A new version of the 9-11 attack.

IN February 2018, Samuel Weems introduced Joseph and Zena to a new ally. Vince Mathews, the Governor of Kentucky. The couple flew to Nashville, rented a Mercedes SUV, and drove across the Tennessee border to the governor's private lodge on Lake Barkley in rural Kentucky. The ninety-minute trip was uneventful and they used the time to review their plans.

By now Joseph had infiltrated five right-wing groups that challenged the federal—and several state—governments. Together all five comprised over two hundred thousand members. Some focussed on political lobbying while others maintained militias that ran monthly weapons and battle training. They all shared two goals: expand personal liberty and eliminate government controls. However, the very principles that drove their activism prevented them from forming alliances. The last thing they wanted was a governing council.

"And that's where we come in," Joseph said as he drove the car along Lakeside Road.

"But they're all crazies. Right Flank and The Defense. Bringing them together will be like herding cats."

"I know. But we hold the whip hand."

She smiled when he said this. Always the same magic. "You mean money?"

"Yes, Comrade Wife. Always the money."

He spotted the sign on the roadside—Vidar's Glory—and turned onto a long gravel driveway. The car passed under a lodgepole entrance gate that supported a wood carving of a creature that neither Zena nor Joseph could identify.

"Looks like a sea monster," she said. She took a final sip of the soda she'd been drinking over the past hour and tossed the empty can into the back seat footwell.

"Or maybe it's a lake fish of some kind. The yellow bass are supposed to be huge here."

The driveway curled through a dense stand of trees. In the winter chill, they looked barren, forbidding. Not unlike the countryside surrounding Uncle Valery's home back in Russia. When they approached the lodge, they noticed Samuel Weems step onto the covered porch. He wore a well-worn, brown leather jacket and clapped his hands together for warmth.

"Oh my God," Zena whispered. "There's Worms."

"I told you he'd be here. Just be nice to him. Remember, boys like him respond better to promises than threats. What do they say on Madison Avenue? Sell the sizzle, not the steak."

"Maybe I'll smile, but he's not going to touch me."

"Let him kiss your cheek. Then stay beside me. He won't bite."

"*Sidet,*" she whispered in Russian.

Joseph pulled the SUV into a spot next to a Cadillac. They stepped out of the car and approached the verandah. Another man—tall, swarthy, his dark hair groomed to perfection—stepped beside Weems. He wore a cable-knit sweater and brushed a hand over a tidy mustache. He reminded Joseph of Clark Gable in *Gone With The Wind.*

"Joseph!" Weems called as he waved a hand. "Good to see you again."

Joseph stepped onto the porch and shook Weems's out-stretched hand. "And you."

"And here we have the very beautiful Zena Smirnov." He made a move to hug her but she braced her hands on his shoulders and offered her right cheek to him. A gift.

"Ahh," he whispered as if he'd misread a subtle message. He planted his lips on her cheek and sighed. "So sweet."

He turned to Joseph. "Let me introduce you to Governor Vince Mathews. Governor, meet Joseph Tull and Zena Smirnov."

"Smirnov?" The governor's smile exposed a set of perfect teeth. "Like the vodka?"

"Almost. But the vodka is spelled o-f-f. I'm spelled o-v. Sadly, I'm not part of the family fortune." Her face wrinkled into an expression of mock disappointment. "Still, it's a good drink, don't you think?"

He laughed and led them through the front door into the great room which overlooked the lake. Adjacent to the row of picture windows stood a two-story-high stone fireplace. Above the mantel, a curved sword balanced between two ornamental railroad spikes set in the chimney mortar. The surrounding timber walls were adorned with deer, moose, and elk antlers. A U-shape arrangement of overstuffed chairs and sofas faced the fireplace hearth. On the plank floorboards lay a bear rug with its arms and legs outstretched, chin on the floor, teeth bared in one final bellow of contempt.

"Beautiful home," Joseph said as sat on the loveseat next to the fire. Zena snuggled next to him, clasped his hand in her fingers, and smiled at Weems.

"Thanks." The governor beamed his perfect smile and shrugged with a suggestion that Joseph's compliment was a routine expectation. "The family cottage," he added. "Since 1858. The colonel acquired it a few years before the war broke out."

Joseph notched his chin to one side. So Mathews's roots reached back to the Civil War. "And the sword?"

"The Colonel's own." He stared at the weapon as he continued. "Colonel Mathews led the 4th Special Cavalry Battalion. For the Confederates." He turned to see if Joseph might be surprised. When he detected no reaction, he said, "Not everyone recalls that Kentucky had troops fighting for both sides. Caused a fair bit of division at the time." He turned away and stood next to Weems.

"It's fair to say that division continues to this day," Weems put in.

"True enough!" The governor smiled again. His teeth seemed unable to hide behind his generous lips for more than a few moments. "Before we dive into that, let's talk about drinks. Sam and I drink Bird Dog. The local Kentucky screech. How about you, Zena? Joseph?"

"Sparkling water if you have it," she said. "I'm the designated driver."

"Leaving so soon?"

"This afternoon." She checked her watch. "We booked the 5:10 flight out of Nashville."

"Ohhh. Too bad." His face swiveled toward Joseph. "How about you, sir?"

"Sure. I'll join you in some screech."

"Ha-ha! Enjoy a good slug, do you?" Governor Mathews chuckled and waved his hand as if he might be campaigning for another term in office. "Okay, coming up."

He turned to Weems. "Sam, can you get the sandwich

platter from the kitchen while I fix the drinks?"

"You got it, boss." Weems wheeled across the floor and into the kitchen.

Five minutes later they clinked glasses in a toast. "To our shared ideals and goals," Weems pronounced with a flourish. They sat facing one another next to the warm winter fire. Everyone placed a sandwich or two (egg, chicken, or salmon) on their side plates along with a few pickles and olives.

"Since our time is short, we oughta cut to the chase," Weems said as everyone began to eat. "Governor, you're aware that Joseph has been supportive of our national cause."

"So I've heard." Mathews's eyes settled on Joseph as if he were only now assessing what his guest could offer. "And if what I hear is true, I am also impressed."

"Let me say that I'm always willing to support a just cause." Joseph swallowed a dill pickle and set his bourbon on the glass side table. "But as Sam knows, I consider my options like investment properties, so to speak. I like to know where my dollars are going and interview the management team."

The governor swirled his glass from side to side. The bourbon sparkled in the light of the fireplace. "That's good to hear. I wouldn't have it any other way. On the other hand, I like to do my due diligence, too. No one gets into the Brotherhood without my say-so."

The Brotherhood. Joseph knew he meant the Brothers of Vidar, a clandestine organization that spanned the entire country. He also knew that no one spoke the full name aloud until the day of their initiation. Weems had warned Joseph to refer to the organization as a single entity. The Brotherhood.

Joseph smiled. "And I appreciate the security that provides."

"Exactly." Mathews set his hands on his knees and leaned forward. "Sam tells me that you provide financial support to some like-minded organizations. So who's in your stable?"

Joseph tried to block his laughter. "Like you, governor, discretion is my by-word. I would never reveal that. And you can rest assured that if we form a partnership, the Brotherhood's identity will never be revealed."

The governor nodded with a look of respect. He took a bite from an egg sandwich and chewed quietly as if he had to test its flavor. "So how many so-called properties are in your portfolio?"

Joseph glanced at Zena.

"Even I don't know." She rippled her shoulders up and down in a sexy shimmy-shally.

"Really?" Weems let out a chuckle. "Not even *you,* Zena?"

She waved a dismissive hand and then speared a pickle on the end of a toothpick. "Joseph tells me nothing about business. As you know, Sam, I'm all about the people. Bringing us all together." Her free hand clasped the air and tightened in a loose fist. "There's hundreds of us. I consider most of them my friends."

Mathews sensed some frisson between Zena and Weems. What was it? He turned back to Joseph.

"So what are you offering, exactly?"

Now Joseph put on the high-beam smile. Once his prospects asked this question, he knew an alliance was at hand. "I invest an initial one hundred thousand dollars. Then I examine the investment value after three months. If I'm happy, I commit to depositing one hundred thousand dollars each quarter for one year. After a year, we conduct a review to determine if the program's goals are achieved. Just you and me." His hand pivoted between them. "If your program is successful, I award a one million dollar bonus. Then we decide if we want to continue the arrangement. So far," he added, "all parties have renewed our arrangements without a single default."

"Default?" Mathews seemed surprised. "So who decides how the money is spent?"

This was the second most important question. Joseph referred to it as *the teaser.* "You do."

*"I* do." He slipped the last of his sandwich into his mouth and chewed thoughtfully. "I like the sound of that."

"Some organizations spend it on recruitment. Some on community awareness. Others use the funds for field training. Each property is at a different stage in its growth. I don't pretend to get involved." He laughed. "Hell, I don't want to!"

They all broke into laughter and Joseph drank off the last of his bourbon. The meeting was going well. He could almost smell the governor's appetite. His greed. Then the governor held up a hand as if he wanted to block everything he'd heard so far. Soon he'd ask the final question. The clincher.

"And what do you expect in return for your investment?"

"I thought you'd never ask." He grinned and shifted his gaze from the governor to Weems and back.

"I host an organization called White Sphere."

"White Sphere," the governor repeated. "Never heard of it."

"Good. You're not supposed to. It's a group of like-minded leaders who meet in what outsiders refer to as the dark web. The leaders of all my affiliates meet in the Sphere."

"You meet in the Sphere? What—so the FBI can listen in?" He coughed up a cynical laugh.

"Not gonna happen." A supercilious grin on Zena's mouth melted into a forgiving smile. "Joseph's specialty is dark web communications. He rarely tells anyone, but he's the IT Fellow at the Academy of Science. His PhD is in cyber security."

Vince Mathews crossed his arms over his chest and sat back in his chair to study the fire crackling over the wood in the fireplace. He looked subdued. A rare mood for a man who believed he shaped his own destiny and carried the world on his coattails. He turned back to Joseph with a weak smile. Perhaps now was the time for a well-worn joke. "So who has the most brains? A rocket scientist or a brain surgeon?"

Weems laughed. Zena winked at him knowing she could reel him in any time she wanted.

"Neither." Joseph shook his head. A gesture of toleration. "It's all about Artificial Intelligence now. AI engineers are the new masters of the universe."

"Ha-ha. Yes, I guess you're right." The governor realized his joke fell flat. He shrugged and topped up his glass of bourbon. "All right. So how does someone join the White Sphere?"

Joseph leaned in. The deal was virtually done. "The day before I make my first cash installment, I will text you a message. It will contain the first part of the White Sphere URL. I'll send a second text to Sam. It contains the second part. You need to piece them together and log into White Sphere. You'll be blocked of course, but when I recognize your login ID, I will text you a password. You'll have no control over passwords. Furthermore, I change them once a month. You'll need to stay current on the changes."

The governor glanced at Weems. "All right. Paste the parts of the URL together, try to log in, and wait for a password from you."

"Right. And be sure you use a VPN."

"A virtual private network." The governor's mood had shifted again. His sober expression revealed that he'd followed the instructions so far. "Don't worry. I already use one."

"Good. You'll need to start the login process with a user ID I already know. Something to ensure your anonymity." Joseph studied the governor's face. "Do you have one?"

He nodded. "Vidar One."

"Spell it."

He did and then Joseph asked, "Who's Vidar?"

"You might have noticed a wood carving suspended above the gate as you drove up to the cottage. It's a replica of W. G. Collingwood's original drawing of Vidar and the monster Fenrir."

"Oh. So who are Vidar and Fenrir?" Zena asked.

Weems appeared amused by her curiosity. "Vidar was a son of the Nordic god, Odin. Odin was killed in the Battle of Ragnarök by the monster Fenrir. In turn, Vidar killed Fenrir."

"Ragnarök was a battle to end the world," the governor added. "Those of us in the Brotherhood believe that the war continues to this day."

Joseph's face acknowledged the governor's solemn belief.

Despite the cult liturgy, he knew that many Americans bound their lives to occult mysteries and rituals. Who was he to dispute their philosophies? The more radical the better. They were all welcome in the White Sphere.

"Perfect. Vidar One it is," Joseph said and stood up. He checked his watch. "Zena, shall we? We have a flight to catch."

"Right." She wrapped her purse strap over her shoulder. "May I use the bathroom?"

The governor pointed to the corridor on the left. "Second door on the right," he said and turned back to Joseph. He leaned close to his ear and asked, "Is she part of it?"

"White Sphere? No. Strictly a boy's club."

"Good. That's smart." The governor smiled. "So how will I know you once I get into White Sphere?"

"I'm known as the Orange Man."

"The Orange Man. A codename that matches your hair." The governor smiled at his cleverness and let out a friendly laugh. "Like the talk show host. Conan O'Brien. You know him?"

"Uh, no."

The governor's lips curled with a look of disappointment. "Oh. Did they call you Red as a kid? Or Rusty?"

It was an insult, but Joseph knew he needed to embrace it. For now. He chuckled and tapped the governor's shoulder with an open hand. "Except for a few close friends, no one else got away with it."

"Ha-ha! Good to be a close friend, then."

When Zena returned from the bathroom, Joseph guided her to the front door. "My turn," he said. "I'll meet you in the car."

As he relieved himself in the bathroom, Joseph noticed a large pen-and-ink drawing of a battle scene hung next to the mirror. Monsters swinging through massive clouds, thunderbolts cast into the wings of flying beasts, the Mouth of Hell consuming the fallen. Below the image, the artist had inscribed the title. *The Battle of Ragnarök.*

A war still raging in the minds of The Brotherhood, he mused. Yet none of them know of the coming battle. Maybe they'll learn. But by then it will be too late.

JOSEPH gunned the Honda CBR650R as he turned onto Stanyan Street. After he reached Parnassus, he rode onto Shrader and up the road to the third house on the left. He slipped the bike onto the driveway, cut the ignition, kicked down the stand, and slipped off his helmet.

"You okay?"

"Better than okay. Much, much better," Zena replied. She unclipped her helmet and swung it against her hip. "Any time I can beat you is a good day."

Joseph smiled at that. Nine times out of ten she outmatched him at the pistol range. Once a month they drove over to Tru-Site Pistol Club, an indoor gun range in Lower Pacific Heights. During their years in St. Petersburg, she'd kept up her target practice with a variety of weapons and continued her training once she found a club that suited her in San Francisco. Her current favorite: a Ruger LC-9 which fits perfectly into her purse. She'd purchased it at a gun show for just under $400. "Worth every penny," she claimed. It was "light, tight, and bright."

Always a poet, now a Hip-hop artist, Joseph thought as he led the way up the staircase and into their home. The house had a living room, kitchen, den, three bedrooms, two bathrooms, and a full basement. It represented a huge step up after the years they'd spent in the off-campus apartment near Stanford.

Each chose a bedroom and transformed them into home offices. But most important to Zena was their master bedroom. It became a personal project. A wanton obsession. Decorated with art from Freida Kahlo, photos from Russian female photographers, sculptures of nude men and women, fresh flowers arranged in glass vases, a Japanese Shoji screen behind which she draped her various costumes and toys. She fashioned their bedroom into a constantly shifting psycho-sexual playground. Joseph encouraged her in all this, knowing it was essential to her, and therefore to their marriage. More often than not, it amused him, too.

"Did I tell you I bought champagne?" He called over his shoulder as he opened the front door.

"No, but we definitely should celebrate, yes?"

"Yes. For the two of us." He set his helmet on the rack next to the door and peeled off his leather jacket. "Vitvinin sent a bonus. So we could celebrate our eighteen years in America."

"How much?"

He put on a frown. She'd never been part of their financial arrangements.

"A thousand," he said. He'd deceived her about the money for so long that now the lies always came with a wink or a smile.

"Then we can go dancing!" she squealed and wrapped her

arm around his waist and led him on a two-step along the hallway to the kitchen. She opened the refrigerator door. "So where's this champagne? Ah here!" she seized the bottle by the neck and passed it to him. "Wahoo. Dom Perignon. You do the honors, darling."

She passed the bottle to him then pulled two flutes from the cupboard as he unspooled the wire top from the cork.

Before he could pour the champagne, his phone chimed. He glanced at the screen and frowned. "Sorry, looks like I have to take this."

He walked into the living room and leaned a shoulder against the window frame overlooking Shrader Street. As Samuel Weems delivered the news, he ambled across the room, mumbled one- and two-word replies, then dropped onto the sofa cushions and stared into the blackened hearth of the fire-place. Ten minutes later he returned to the kitchen where Zena leafed through a bioscience journal.

"Must be serious," she offered.

"Yeah. It is." He sat at the table where they ate breakfast each morning. He took a moment to consider what Weems had said. "You know, maybe this will lock everything into place," he mumbled as if a few puzzle pieces began to align in his mind.

"What?" she put the magazine aside and sat beside him.

"Vince Mathews is dead."

"The governor?"

"Ex-governor," he reminded her. He shook his head with dismay. Since Vince Mathews lost the recent election, his utility to White Sphere had diminished. "Yeah. Last night.

Apparently he was killed in a gunfight in South Dakota. Just under Mount Rushmore."

She braced her elbows on the table. "The monument with the presidents?"

He nodded.

"In a gunfight? What the hell was he doing up there?"

"No idea. Weems doesn't know either. He just wants to ensure my quarterly installment is deposited with the Brothers of Vidar next week."

Her lips curled with a look of spite. As if she and Joseph were only good for the money they provided to all the affiliates in White Sphere. Since Governor Mathews joined the Sphere, the Brotherhood had become a greedy dependent. The "high hog" she called them.

"Maybe this is our chance, Zena. With Mathews dead, we can take the lead hand. Weems might become the token head, but the Brothers are addicted to the cash we funnel into them."

"Maybe," she allowed, "but what about the others? Right Flank. The Defense."

"Same play." Joseph was sure now. All the pieces aligned, pointed in one direction. "They're all on our hook. We can drag them any way we want. And I can run it all through White Sphere. All of it online."

"Yeah." She smiled. "I know you can." She wrapped her arm around his shoulder. "So all the more reason to celebrate, right?"

He nodded and returned her smile. "You know, until now I never imagined it. But his death is the best thing that could happen. And look"—he snapped his fingers—"it just fell into our laps."

"Meant to be." She offered him another smile. He knew the look. "All right, darling," she whispered. "So back to our little celebration."

He poured the bubbly and they clinked glasses. She put a hand on his chest. "So here's my idea. We take this bottle from Vitvinin up to bed. Drink, make love, then go dancing in the Starlight Room."

"That's your plan is it?" He rolled his free hand over her hip.

She giggled. "No it's yours, remember? Back in St. Petersburg? You said drink first, then sex."

Despite everything—her occasional bouts of promiscuity, her racist rants against Jews, Blacks, and Asians—she still knew how to make him laugh. The truth was, he admired her flaws. They marked her authenticity. The real Zena lived in a lawless realm, one that continued to lure him into its depths. "No. It was always *eat* first."

"Sure, but now we have the good times. Now we drink Dom Perignon instead of eating."

"Comrade Zena, I'm sorry to say it, but I may have to report you to the Kremlin. You've become a pétit bourgeois."

Comrade. The running joke had carried them through more than two decades together. The only reason it still made them laugh was because that old world—the Soviet world—seemed sadder with every passing year.

"Me? Come on, Comrade Citizen." She smiled as she unbuttoned her blouse. "What do the pétit bourgeois really know about sex?"

"Quite a bit, I suspect."

AFTER they showered, they took a taxi downtown to the Drake Hotel and rode the elevator up to the Starlight Room. They sat next to a window and gazed at the midsummer scene on Sutter Street. The street pulsed with the masses of tourists and party animals weaving through the lines of cars crawling along the asphalt.

"Life is short and the night is young," he mused.

"So what do you suggest?" she asked. "A little more champagne?

"Of course," he said with a chuckle. He waved to the waitress and ordered a new bottle of Dom Perignon.

"Mmmm. *Two* bottles. You *are* in a good mood tonight."

I am, he thought and turned his attention to the delicacies on the menu.

As she studied the specials list she tipped her head from side to side in a struggle to choose from the most expensive options. "So, I can eat scampi tonight? Ossip Vitvinin allows it?"

"He does."

"Hmmm. After all these years you know him well."

"We both know him."

"Yes, but with men it's different."

"Well, he trusts me."

"What does he say about me these days?"

He ignored her question and smiled at the server when she brought the champagne to the table. "And we'll have two scampi linguini, please," he said.

"And a Caesar salad for me."

"Good idea." He returned the menus to the server and said, "So make it two of both. Two scampi linguini and two Caesars."

After they ate, Zena began to turn her shoulders to the beat of the music thrumming from the stage. "Look at them." She nodded to a couple whose dance moves looked like a prelude to sex.

"Can't miss them," he said. "Who can?"

"Our turn. Let's show them." She waved her fingers in a come-on gesture and pulled him from his chair.

When it came to dancing, Joseph wasn't naturally gifted. But the combination of the scampi, Dom Perignon, and Zena's determination uncovered a latent talent. After ten minutes on the dance floor, her infectious enthusiasm generated a new spontaneity in him. Soon their smiles and laughter had them both churning around the floor, spinning and whirling among dozens of couples, gays, straights, men, and women all infected by the music, the joy, the alcohol, the food, the money, their clothes and the warm tans radiating from their smiling faces. This was the pulse of California and the drumbeat of San Francisco.

All of it surging through their blood.

A little after two-thirty, as they gathered their belongings from the coat check girl, Zena's mood slipped into a somber reflection. "You know, it's one thing to enjoy this madness for one night. It's another to remember why we're here."

"I know. It's the one thing we always agree on." Joseph led

the way to the elevator bay, where the revelers queued for the elevators to carry them down to the hotel lobby.

She squeezed his hand as the elevator door slid open. "Maybe we should take the antidote."

"The antidote? To what, the Affluent American Virus?"

"Yes, AAV." She let out a chuckle. He often teased her when she spoke in microbiology metaphors. Viruses, bacteria, antivirals, vaccines. How could she help herself? This was her training. Her career. Sometimes her work obsessions exceeded her craving for sex. She doubted she could find a cure for any of it.

"Okay, so I think the antidote for AAV is to take a walk down Turk Street," she said and pulled him by the arm just as he was about to flag down a taxi.

"No. Let's go home."

"We can go home after we visit The Tenderloin."

"Zena, you're crazy."

"No. We both need to cleanse."

"A cleanse. In The Tenderloin?" Had she lost her mind? "You've had too much to drink."

"We've both had too much to drink. But that shouldn't stop us, Comrade. It's just ten minutes up the street." She tugged on his sleeve and pulled him two steps away from the taxi stand. Another couple jumped into the waiting cab's open door.

Her sense of timing was precise. Ten minutes later they turned right off Taylor Street and entered the gauntlet of despair and desolation known as The Tenderloin. Within ten paces, Joseph had to steer them around two drunks sprawled across the sidewalk in front of Richland Pawn Shop.

"You sure you want to do this?"

"It's not what I want, it's what we need." She drew a breath as the stench of vomit stung her nostrils. She tried to spit it out. "Just two blocks. Then home."

They walked on, trying to discern if the destitution matched the worst of what they witnessed in Russia.

"No. It's worse here," Zena insisted.

"I don't know. Back home they'd toss these men on a train to Siberia." He was surprised—but pleased to hear himself refer to Russia as home.

From across the street, they heard someone call out in a heavy Latino accent. "Hey, jefe. Can you give some chicos a hand?"

When Zena turned, she saw two men stumble across Turk Street toward them. "They've followed us since we left the Drake."

"What?"

"I'm sure of it."

He pushed Zena behind him with his hand. The men were fifteen yards away. As they stepped over the curb onto the sidewalk, they seemed to find their feet and adopt a muscular swagger.

"Oye, amigo." Joseph knew less than ten words of Spanish. And nothing of the local Latino vernacular. "Nice night. We're good. You?"

One man had a round face with a patchy mustache and goatee. The other bore an old scar that crossed from his forehead over his right eye to the top of his cheek.

"Amigo?" Round Face let out a tired chuckle. "Not so

good, Amigo. Not so good as you, jefe."

Joseph felt Zena tug his elbow. "Yeah, they followed us. Definitely," she murmured. "Cross the street. There's a park."

Two doors along, on the corner of Hyde Street he saw an empty children's playground. Without a backward glance, he let her lead the way across the quiet street. As soon as they slipped through the park gate the two men closed in on them. Joseph tried to shake the boozy feeling in his head.

"Jefe, no hiding in this leetle park," Round Face said and swept an open arm to confirm they had nowhere to run. "We just need a leetle dinero. Five dollar. For food."

"Five dollars?" Joseph guided Zena behind him again with his arm.

"Si. I know you have it, jefe."

Round Face shifted his weight from one foot to the other. Hard to tell if he was preparing to fight, or trying to find his balance after an overdose of booze. Both men stood about his height but looked twenty pounds lighter. Joseph could smell the despair on the man who did all the talking. A desperado, half-drunk—with a mean-looking amigo who now circled to Joseph's right, as his eyes swept over Zena's body. Two street fighters. Out of money and amped up. Maybe he could talk his way out of this.

"All right. Hey, let's keep this friendly. My name's Joseph. What do they call you?"

Round Face blinked with a look of surprise. "Joseph? They should call you Rojo. For your hair." He gestured to his head.

"My friends call me Joseph."

"Really? I surprise they don't call you Rojo. Or maybe

Naranja. Is better. Means orange." He held an imaginary orange in one hand and bit into it. His tongue slurped up the juice.

"No. It's Joseph. What do they call you?"

"Me?" He thought for a moment, a pause to invent a new name. "Bufón. This is Zurdo." He crooked his thumb toward his friend.

"Bufón. Good." Joseph held up both hands, palms forward. "Look. I can give you five dollars. Ten. But we'll all be good amigos tonight, si?"

Bufón grinned. "Si, of course. Todos somos amigos." He opened his hand, curled his fingers. A gesture that said, show me your money.

As Joseph drew his wallet from his jacket pocket he noticed the time on his watch. 2:54. The streets were empty. The city mute. The silence felt too quiet. He shook his head with a shrug of anxiety, and pulled two fives from the wallet flap and offered them to Bufón.

"Oye, Naranja. I see more there. How 'bout we take all." His eyes narrowed.

"No, no. We need money for a bus."

"No. I don't think you need a bus tonight." He glanced at Zurdo.

Zurdo pulled a barber's straight razor into his hand. His thumb pressed down on the tang and the three-inch blade pivoted out of the handle and clicked into place.

"Hey, no need for that." Joseph felt his heart leap and raised his arm. Suddenly he felt stone sober.

In one deft move, Zurdo gripped Joseph's wrist, swung him

around in an armlock, and held the blade to his carotid artery. He could feel the steel edge pressed against his skin. One slice of the blade and he'd be finished. He began to pant for air.

"Let him go!" Zena yelled as she tugged her hand from her purse.

Zurdo and Bufón froze when they saw her pointing at Zurdo. Her Ruger LC-9 was aimed at Zurdo's face. She shook her head. A warning.

Behind Bufón's dilated eyes she could see him making a series of calculations.

"Don't even think about it. You try to cut him and I will kill you both." Her voice ice cold. She shifted her weight to her left foot, lifted her right heel, ready to absorb the shock of the recoil.

"No, no. This is bad for you, senora. Bad for everyone." Bufón paused as if he felt unsure. Could the woman do this? No, not this whore. Go on, roll the dice. "No, I don't think so, perra. No tienes estómago para esto. You got no guts." He sneered at her and nodded at Zurdo.

She watched Zurdo draw a breath, saw the resolve in his mouth as he pinched his lips together. Before he could make a cut, she fired one shot into his nose. His razor fell away from Joseph's throat. Then she pivoted and shot Bufón in the forehead. Both men flew backward and dropped to the ground.

"My God." Joseph shuddered as he stared at her. "I didn't know you—"

He couldn't finish his thought. Then he had no thoughts. Just feelings: the pumping of his heart. His throat flooding with hate. His arms heavy at his sides, energy streaming from his hands into the summer night.

"Give me your gun," he muttered, the raw anger now surging through every cell in his body.

"What?"

"*Just give it.*" He wrenched the pistol from her hand and looked down at the two men. He fired one shot into Zurdo's chest, then spat on his face. He took a step to one side and fired a second bullet into Bufón's belly.

Zena leaned toward the two corpses. She examined the cadavers to assure herself they were dead. She felt disgust but no pity. She lifted the barber's razor, pushed the tang down, eased the blade into the handle, and dropped the prize into her purse. Then she held out her hand and studied Joseph's face. He passed the pistol to her with a shrug. She slipped it into her purse next to the razor and turned back to him. She took a moment to adjust to his blind stupor. She knew she had to think for both of them now.

"Take off your jacket."

"What?"

"You've got blood on your face."

She stepped behind him, yanked the jacket off his shoulders, and tugged the sleeves from his arms. Next, she wiped his face and hair with the sleeves. When the splatter was swept away she dragged the sleeves inside out so that the blood smears were hidden. She folded the jacket over his left arm and wrapped his right hand around the back of her waist.

"Come on," she whispered in Russian. "Hold me tight. There's nobody watching. No witnesses. We walk down to Market Street, two lovers on a stroll. Then we take a taxi home."

*"Blyad."*

"Shhh. Don't say another word. In ten minutes it's forgotten."

She guided him through the park gate and across Turk Street. When they were walking at a steady pace along Market Street, she spotted a cab and waved her free hand in the air.

"Someone sent them to kill us," she said as the taxi veered toward them. "I'm sure of it."

"What?"

She silenced him with an iron glare and climbed into the backseat of the taxi. He sat beside her. Mute. The heat from the pistol still warm in his fingers.

"I don't know who sent them," she whispered in Russian. "Not yet. But I'll figure it out. Whoever did this is already dead. Soon they will pay with their blood."

# CHAPTER NINE

SAN FRANCISCO — 24 FEBRUARY, 2021

In the six years that he'd known Eve Noon, Will Finch had never met one of her oldest friends, a colleague from their days on the SFPD, Leanne Spratz. So when Eve told Finch that Leanne wanted to meet him in person, he felt a mix of anticipation and anxiety.

He set his reading tablet aside and looked at his wife. "When?"

"This morning. She can be here at eleven. That work for you?"

"It does. What's up?"

"She knows enough not to say anything on the phone."

"Maybe it's got something to do with the Evian bottle."

"Maybe," she said with an uncertain look. "You never know with Leanne."

Eve took a sip of her coffee and gazed out the kitchen window across the gentle slope that fell from her sister's house in Berkeley Hills to the university campus below. Like everyone else in the family, she loved the view across San Francisco Bay, past Alcatraz Island, and beyond to the open Pacific Ocean. Over the past week she'd fantasized about moving to the east side of the bay from their cottage on Telegraph Hill. Much better to raise Casey here compared to the city, she thought. They could keep the cottage *and* buy a house a few blocks away from her sister.

Besides, she knew Megan would prefer to have her, Casey, and Will closer at hand. Megan loved little Casey and often volunteered to babysit while Eve tended to the never-ending challenges of running *The Post*. Furthermore, when the pandemic subsided, Megan's son Brock planned to move out with Klare. That would leave Megan ghosting through the house on her own—a home still haunted by the murder of her husband. In so many ways a move to Berkeley Hills made perfect sense. She decided to discuss it with Will. But not yet. He was still wrestling with the murder of Myfanwy Thomas and the ensuing FBI investigation.

"So what's the news?" Finch asked Leanne after they settled in the living room chairs next to the fireplace. The gas-burner element seared the cast iron logs which radiated a warm stream of air into the room.

"You know, normally I frame forensic results with statistical probabilities," Leanne said. "You both know how it works so I won't belabor you with the nuances."

Finch studied her heavily freckled face. A woman in her late thirties who'd worked as a police forensics officer then moved on to a tech startup that specialized in DNA typing,

Leanne's features revealed an intelligence shaped by street-tough experience. Except for a sheen of lipstick, she wore no makeup. Her rusty red hair was swept over her ears and bound by a green scrunchy at the nape of her neck. A camel-colored blouse was buttoned up to her chin and tucked into pin-striped navy pants. The matching jacket fell open across her chest. She radiated the determination of a savvy businesswoman thriving in an industry dominated by San Francisco's geek tech-bros.

She turned her attention to Finch. "What I found goes back to the first materials you gave me."

"You mean that letter and the bullet casing?" Eve asked.

"Those and the wrapper," Leanne said.

Finch leaned forward. "So this doesn't have anything to do with the Evian bottle that Eve gave you?"

"Oh yeah." She nodded with a grave look. "It's got everything to do with the bottle."

"All right." Eve swept her hand through the air as if she were trying to catch a few raindrops. "So connect the dots for us, Leanne."

"First things first. Remember neither the brass nor the letter itself had any trace of DNA or fingerprints."

"Right. But the sealing tape did," Finch said, impatient that Leanne was taking a long way around. If they were lost in the woods, she'd be guiding them along the scenic route.

"Correct. And now the Evian bottle. It also collected fingerprints and DNA. Both clear signatures." She nodded to Eve. "And they match the sealing tape from the envelope you gave me."

Everyone paused to consider the connections. Finch knew

it was up to him to state the obvious.

"So it comes down to Saxx," he said.

"The FBI cop?" Leanne turned back to Finch.

He nodded. "FBI Special Agent, Jeremy Saxx."

"Which means Saxx sent you the bullet casing," Eve whispered. "And the note."

"And the note." Finch glanced at the ceiling. A wayward cobweb rippled in the convection draft from the fireplace. He repeated the rhyme for Leanne's benefit. *"Play the game, or you'll end the same."*

"All right. Okay." Eve held up a hand as if she needed to slow the rush of mid-town traffic. "What are the chances that the forensics are inaccurate?"

"Less than one percent. But from my experience, I'd say there aren't even *nuances* of an error." Again she turned to Finch. "Look, I know this means you're at risk. At the very least you've been manipulated by the FBI. Into what, I don't know."

He could feel his pulse thrumming in a low, heavy beat. He narrowed his eyes. "Into being their patsy, that's what."

Leanne glanced away with a guilty air. She'd brought the dreaded news into their home, now what could she do? "I'm sorry." She seemed unable to continue, then asked, "What do you want me to do with this?"

Eve studied the distant expression on her husband's face. "Give us a day to think on it, okay."

"No," Finch put in. "This is my chance to turn things around. Leanne, can you make a certified finding based on this evidence? Something that would hold up in court. Even years after we're all dead and gone, some kind of bullet-proof testimonial that links Saxx to the letter, the brass shell, and the Evian bottle."

She pondered the options for a moment. "I can. I've done it before. Twice now, the court has accepted sealed documents similar to this from me."

"Okay. Can you get a copy to me?"

"Yes, but if you publish it, it will lose its certified status."

"Don't worry about that. When can you get me a copy?"

She checked the calendar on her phone. "Thursday."

Finch nodded. He felt a renewed sense of mission. He could see the fight taking a new turn. A struggle on a completely different front. "And can you trigger the public release of your testimony *if and when* I die."

The implications were stark. The women glanced at one another as the weight of his request dragged through them.

Leanne turned back to Finch. "Yes. I can do that, too."

He held up a finger to signal one more request. "And it should also be released if and when either Eve or Casey dies."

Eve held a hand to her mouth. "Will, are you sure about that?"

He nodded. "Dead certain. If anything happens to any of us, Saxx goes to jail. And there—as he well knows—he will die, too."


ON Friday at nine a.m., Finch walked along the wide concourse in front of the Civic Center to Fulton Street. Whenever he crossed the plaza he recalled the murder of his brother-in-law, Daniel Rivers. Before the pandemic struck, Daniel's son

181

Brock had persuaded Finch to join them in a massive New Years' Day Extinction Rebellion Rally. Finch had stood in the freezing plaza beside Daniel and his wife Megan while Klare spoke from a raised platform in front of the city hall dome. When the protestors began to storm the front gates, Brock and Klare returned to where Finch waited with his in-laws. A rapid turn of events ended in a shooting. The bullet meant for Klare hit Daniel as he and Finch tackled the gunman. The shooter was cuffed and taken away by the police. Daniel died on the pavement in Megan's arms.

Now, as Finch approached the Pioneer Monument he scanned the area for Special Agent, Jeremy Saxx. He checked his watch. Finch was five minutes early and grateful to be first on the scene. It offered a slight advantage. The illusion of home turf. While he waited, he studied the elaborate granite monument next to him. Atop the central column stood a bronze statue of Minerva, the Roman goddess of wisdom and war. An odd combination, Finch mused. A series of historic medallions were fixed to the base of her pillar, memorials to Francis Drake, John Sutter, John Fremont, Father Junipero Serra, and the millionaire who paid for it all, James Lick. Another three figures alluding to California's founding traditions surrounded the centerpiece: Commence, Plenty, and "49", which referred to the boom launched by the California Gold Rush in 1849. At one time a fourth pier of statues called "Early Days" touted the trinity of California's genesis: a Mexican vaquero, a missionary, and a Native American. For better or for worse— Finch could never decide—the last three had been removed in 2018 to eradicate the stigma of colonial glorification.

"Finch."

He broke from his reverie and turned to see the burly form of Agent Saxx approaching from Hyde Street. When they first met, Finch likened Saxx's physique to a baseball catcher, but now he took a different view. Perhaps in his salad days, Saxx had played varsity football. A tackle. But as he strode toward Finch, it appeared as if some of the muscle around his neck had melted into a slurry of fat and gristle.

"This better be good, Finch. I got an in-box stuffed with ninja-shit."

Ninja-shit? Finch shook his head with contempt. Now that Saxx pressed toward him he could almost smell the BS wafting from his open mouth. Neither of them wore masks. Maybe a mistake, Finch thought.

"Oh, it's good," he replied. "Let's find a place to talk."

They sat at opposite ends of a bench facing the monument. Finch knew that the shorter the meeting, the better. There'd be no time for debate. No bargaining. To that end he drew the manilla envelope from his courier bag and clutched it in his hand. He wouldn't allow Saxx to touch his copy of Leanne's file. All he needed to do was reveal the notary seal next to her signature.

"What's that, Finch?"

Finch stared into Saxx's face. "This is a certified forensic report that governs our new relationship." He opened the folder to show the seal and signatures on each of the nine pages. When he noticed Saxx's features shift from an expression of annoyance to deepening concern, he slipped the file back into the envelope and tucked it securely in his courier bag.

"All right. So what the hell?"

"Relax, *Jeremy.*" He emphasized Saxx's first name, a test to see if he would bridle at the informality. "It's nothing you need to worry about. Unless something goes wrong."

"Goes wrong? Okay, just get on with it." Saxx's eyes narrowed. "Otherwise, I'm outta here."

"All right. DNA and fingerprint analysis shows that the note and brass you and Keely used to extort me into impersonating Joel Griffin belongs to you. It's your DNA. Your prints, Jeremy."

"What?" His feet seem to bolt into the ground. He leaned toward Finch. "What the fuck are you talking about?" His voice a whisper.

"I'm talking about a mistake you made. A tiny error, really. But wow, a totally rookie move. Let me paint the picture for you. You put the brass in the envelope. You wrote the note. The one that said, 'Play the game or you'll end the same.' Remember that?"

Finch paused to gauge Saxx's reaction. His feet shifted under the bench. His jawline tightened as he set his teeth.

"I imagine you wore latex gloves for that. Smart. But when you sealed the envelope with sticky tape, the tape bunched up. You know, the way it clumps together? So to get it right, you peeled off your gloves to straighten things out. That's the mistake I'm talking about. Your prints and DNA stuck to the tape, Jeremy. Big time."

Saxx's face erupted. *"Bullshit!"*

Finch held up a hand as if he were testifying on a Bible. "God's truth. The match came from your Evian water bottle. At the Drake. You left it on the table in the basement security room after Hammond was murdered."

"What?"

"I took the bottle, Jeremy. And just like you, I've got friends in high places, too. Forensic specialists."

Saxx stood and paced out a tight circle in front of the bench. After a moment, he bunched his hands in front of his chest as if it helped to concentrate his thinking. "So where's the bottle now?"

"Safely stored away. But the bottle doesn't really matter does it? It's about your prints and DNA on the package." Finch shrugged. "What's important now is how we go forward with this."

Now Saxx's expression shifted to something new. A tossed salad of fear, dread, anxiety, and looming catastrophe. "Wha'd'ya mean?"

"Sit down again and I'll explain." Finch pointed to the end of the bench.

Saxx turned another narrow circle, then settled on the far end of the bench and set his hands on his knees. He let out a puff of air. A whiff of defeat.

"First, put your mind at rest. Neither of us wants to see this document opened in a court of law. And if I have my way, it never will." He gazed at Saxx's profile as the cop stared at the concrete below the bench. "Do you understand me?"

"What?"

"Saxx—*you're safe.* I've instructed my attorney that this document will only be revealed on my death."

"Your death?" Saxx turned his head toward his tormentor.

"Or that of my wife, Eve—or our daughter." He caught Saxx's eyes and for a few seconds they gazed at one another. Long enough for Finch to see the cop's pending surrender. "Do you understand me?"

His lips fluttered as if he were about to reply, then he waved away his thoughts with a hand and his mouth collapsed into a grim slit.

"Is that a 'yes?' "

Saxx nodded mutely.

"Say it."

"Fuck. Yes, I understand."

"Furthermore, you will ensure the FBI never prosecutes me for the charges stemming from the shootings in South Dakota. The charges you used to manipulate me. You see? It cuts both ways. Both of us are better off if we bury the past and move on."

"Okay." Saxx nodded. His energy deflated, and his face seemed to dissolve into a glob of thick, pale flesh. "I see that."

"And one more thing." He held up a finger. "White Sphere. After the screw-up in the Drake, I know they're targeting me. I want you to arrange protection for me and my family until you lock them up."

"I'll have to make a case—"

"Then make it. I want 24-7 protection at Eve's sister's place in Berkeley Hills. Effective today. Otherwise, the deal's off."

It took a moment for him to respond. "Okay. Text me the address."

Finch pulled out his phone, clicked on Saxx's name, and

typed in the address. A second later they heard Saxx's phone ping. Finch waited to see if Saxx had any questions. It took a moment for him to consider the ripple effects. The ramifications of his failed scheme could still entrap him. He lifted his arms from his lap and crossed them over his chest.

"What about Keely?" His voice stuttered in a brittle whisper. "I want her left out of this."

"Of course. This is between you and me. No reason for anyone else to hear about it. Ever."

He nodded and shifted his gaze toward Hyde Street. "Okay. We done?"

"I'll call you if I need you." Finch stood up and pressed his lips between his teeth. He took a moment to study Saxx's hands fidgeting at his chest. His jaw shifted from side to side as if he were working off a punch to his face.

"Yeah, that's it, Jeremy. We're done."

# Chapter Ten

SAN FRANCISCO — 2 FEBRUARY, 2021

Joseph Tull tapped on the half-open door to Sheila Griffin's office in the California Academy of Sciences. He leaned on the door frame as she peered into her computer monitor. He knew she had a deadline to meet for the annual Information Technologies department review. But as the IT Chair, he also knew he could preempt her to-do list with his own priorities.

However, Sheila's fascination for the clairvoyant genius of computer geeks—Steve Jobs, Bill Gates, Mark Zuckerberg—ended with Joseph Tull. Yes, he was brilliant. And yes, he possessed an uncanny vision of where digital technology was heading. His specialty, using artificial intelligence to ferret out criminals in the dark web, had elevated him to a prestigious consulting gig with the FBI. A remarkable triumph that bonded the Academy to the nation's power center. Because he "walked on water," the Academy Board loved the distinction Tull brought to the institution.

However, over the past year, his assertive personality had morphed into nothing less than the office bully. When his term as the IT Director was renewed for five years, the front-line staff in the office cringed. Unless she established some boundaries, Sheila knew she'd be in for a bruising. But Joseph Tull— *Dr. Tull*, as he insisted—seemed indifferent to limits of any kind.

Almost every day he would drag her into his office to review some dimension of his research into anti-vaxxer forums in the dark web. Although he was a national authority on the topic, she'd demonstrated her knowledge about anti-vaxxers. When Joseph discovered that her father Joel Griffin had died of anaphylactic shock following a routine vaccination, he pressed her to join him in his research.

Appalled by the prospect, she took up the issue with HR. A mistake as it turned out. Dr. James Higgins, the head of HR, admired Dr. Tull above all other Academy Fellows.

"But he asks me to investigate issues that have nothing to do with the Academy," she said once she had Higgins's attention. "Or anything to do with natural science, for that matter."

Higgins adjusted his glasses and peered at her as if he might be studying a small, diseased fish. She knew limnology was his specialty. Freshwater eels, his delight.

"Embrace your good fortune, Sheila," Higgins advised her. "Half the junior employees in the Academy would kill to work with Dr. Tull."

Are you kidding me? she thought. No one likes him. No one! She had to counter with something. What? Focus on the job mandate, she decided.

"But it's completely … off-task." Was off-task the correct phrase? What she wanted to say was *treason.*

"Sheila," his voice dropped to a paternalistic baritone. Patient, yet demanding. "We both know who Dr. Tull is. And the recognition he brings to the Academy. If you want me to update your job description I will. It would say something like, 'other duties as assigned by Dr. Tull.' Can you live with that?"

Her lips tightened into a thin line. What a bunch of mansplaining BS. But she realized that if she said "no," his next offer would be to re-assign her. Or fire her.

"Yes." Her voice was barely audible.

"Yes?"

"Of course. I know it's a privilege to work with him."

"Good. Then, that's the end of it." He smiled, swung a hand toward the door, then lifted the handset to his desk phone and whispered, "Sorry, but I have to make a few calls."

She nodded and left the meeting, hoping Higgins would never share her dread of Joseph Tull with the man himself. Another worry to add to all the other stresses of her job.

Twenty minutes later Tull appeared at her office door.

"Sheila. Got a minute?" He snugged his mask over his face. Office protocol.

Her fingers continued to type as her head swiveled from the screen. She'd once told him that her typing speed clocked in at just under one hundred words a minute. She had him beat by a mile, but after all, he was a research fellow. He'd didn't have to be faster. Just smarter.

"Sorry, Dr. Tull, but I've got to send the annual report to Jerry by four." Her flying fingers came to a rest. She pulled her mask over her nose. "But sure ... what do you need?"

"Take a look at my screen. Something is bothering me on my research hub." He tipped his head toward his office, three doors along the corridor.

Sheila pulled herself out of her chair and followed her red-headed boss along the hallway.

"I've been tracking someone on Twitter and a closed Face-book group," Joseph said as he settled into his chair and re-freshed his computer screen. "One of the more vehement acolytes," he added. "But I can't nail him down. Who is he?"

He brought up the Twitter feed of someone called Brass Shoes. "I've been in touch with my contacts in the FBI. They've tried to ID him for over a month now. Nothing." He lifted both hands, palms up, a gesture to reveal his amusement with their failures.

*Brass Shoes.* Sheila stood behind him and shuddered. Her father's nickname as a child entertainer. In the 1970s he'd been a star performer in Tampa's "Tap & Toes" ensemble. She could feel herself teetering and sat in the chair opposite Joseph's desk.

Joseph turned to face her. "Feeling okay?"

"A little dizzy for some reason." She shook her head with a weary look, then held a hand over her mask and let out a light cough.

He adjusted his face mask, pressed the noseband to form a tighter seal. "Have you been tested lately?"

She glanced at the ceiling, a ploy to suggest she couldn't quite remember. "Maybe three weeks ago."

He blinked. With his feet braced on the carpet, he pushed

his chair back toward the mirror behind his desk. "Why don't you get a test? Just to be sure," he offered. "I know some days there's a shortage, so if it's a problem, my wife can get you to the front of the line."

An easy out, she thought. "Maybe I should." She stood up and stepped away from the desk. "Okay, I'll call you if I need any help."

"Good." He raised his hand in a forgiving wave. "And when you have time, dive into this thing with Brass Shoes."

SHEILA Griffin studied the strawberry birthmark on her housemate's forehead. Over the past year, Sheila noticed that the color of Myfanwy's blemish grew brighter whenever she was stressed. Now, even in the evening dusk in Myfanwy's bedroom, it seemed to glow.

"You've crossed a line," Sheila repeated. No need to let up the confrontation now. "Your Brass Shoes Twitter and Facebook rants have caught the attention of Dr. Tull." She clutched her cell phone in one fist and glared down at Myfanwy as she closed the cover to her computer.

"Well, that's the point, isn't it? To get some attention. That's what you said."

"When you started, maybe."

Sheila shook her head and paced along the foot of Myfanwy's bed. Myfanwy leaned back into the pile of pillows under the headboard. Her favorite perch where she waged her nightly anti-vaxx campaign on her laptop.

"But this—*this* is going to backfire on you. And if it hits you, it'll hit me."

For a moment the still air in Myfanwy's room seemed to stifle them as they considered their options. But Myfanwy knew she had to respond.

"So Tull is following Brass Shoes. How is that not a good thing?"

"Because he's got the FBI dogging you. I told you before. He's a consultant with them. He told me they're trying to hack into you."

Myfanwy's lips creased into a dismissive smirk. Her hand stroked the cover of her computer. "Don't you remember? The Brass Shoes account is registered to *my* Joel Griffin. It's my Rapid City Joel Griffin whose ID is registered for the accounts. *He's* not your father."

"Okay, that's enough." Sheila held up her phone as if she wanted to smash it into Myfanwy's nose. "I want you to move out of my house. You've got to the end of the month. And until then—"

"No, no, no. Sheila, come on." Her voice was soft. Pleading. "Look, I'm sorry about your father. You know I am. I never should have used Brass Shoes for a Twitter handle."

"No, you shouldn't have. Not for the hate you're spreading around the world. *In his name.*" Again she raised her hand. "And don't mention my father again. Not in front of me. Or his nickname."

"Really?" Her voice softened. "You mean all this? About me moving out?"

Sheila took a step toward her. "You've got 'til the end of the month. The sooner the better."

"This is unbelievable."

Sheila shook her head. "Unbelievable? You know what? You should be asking yourself what this is really about. All this anti-vaxx shit." She waved her arms across the room to suggest Myfanwy's entire world was a fraud. Should she say it? Yes. Definitely. "Know what you need? A boyfriend."

"A boyfriend? Jesus, if anyone needs a boyfriend it's you. When was the last time you had"—she broke off, then decided to continue. "Oh, hell. Just go out and get laid, okay."

Sheila's head tipped backward in disbelief. How had the conversation turned this corner? "This is fuckin' nuts. *You* need to find a new hobby, girl. Find something new. Anything."

As she marched out of Myfanwy's bedroom, she slammed the door. Then she climbed up the stairs to her loft and changed the password to the internet router. That would stop the bitch. At least for tonight.

When she regained her equilibrium she felt pleased that she hadn't revealed everything to Myfanwy. Nothing about hacking Tull's computer. Nothing about his treason. Maybe she'd have to warn her one day. But not yet.

THE day that Sheila hacked into Joseph's computer at the Academy she discovered a world of deception beyond her worst nightmares.

The mechanics of the hack itself couldn't have been more simple. A gift from the cyber gods, she told herself. All she had to do was watch him log into his account during one of her visits to his office.

His bullying demands for her assistance had become so predictable that she wondered if he had a hidden sexual fascination for her. But he never flirted with her. Perhaps he was enslaved to his wife, Zena—a nymphomaniac, according to the rumor mill. A Nympho. The word made her gasp. The ultimate 1950s slut-shamer.

With his icy veneer, Sheila wondered if Joseph was an asexual genius trapped in a marriage to a sexual extravert. Why not? In the ever-evolving gender culture of San Francisco, sexual relationships often looked more like corporate mergers and acquisitions than traditional marriages. Now a new, distinct species had emerged. Asexuals. A new stripe in the Pride flag. Color it invisible. And the perfect flavor of the year during the pandemic lockdown, she thought. Indeed, she completely embraced the notion. She had no boyfriends, no girlfriends. She had no interest either way. She'd tried—a few times with men, once with a woman—but sex inevitably felt ... so empty. Her only truly intimate companion was herself, Sheila Griffin, flying solo.

"Sheila, get over here." As he leaned against her office doorframe, Joseph crooked his thumb towards his office. "Take a look at this."

Joseph led the way to his office, slid into his chair, and tapped a key to refresh his computer monitor. Whenever he did so, the machine prompted him to sign into the Academy's server. As he'd once instructed her, Sheila stood on the far side of his desk and waited for him to complete the procedure. Then he wagged a finger—a gesture to a dog—that brought her around the desk so that she could peer over his shoulder to consider his latest demand. She knew that if she had a tail, he'd expect her to wag it happily for his pleasure.

However, one day—the day of her breakthrough hack—she realized that she could observe his keystrokes in the mirror hanging on the wall behind him. Many times she'd watched him standing at the mirror, brushing his orange hair before he hustled off to an Academy Fellows meeting on the top floor of the building. But on her breakthrough day, she witnessed something new.

The evening after she gazed into the mirror and watched his fingers slowly typing—one key at a time—his ID and password, she walked home, opened her laptop, and launched Operation Open Mirror. Her codename for the hack. A joke to lighten her feeling of dread. She knew she'd be fired on the spot if Joseph discovered her treachery. And her dismissal would ruin her career prospects anywhere in the world that required computer security. Which was approximately everywhere, she figured. But it was a risk worth taking. Her contempt for Joseph's treatment of her was now unbearable. The bullying had to stop. What she might discover on his computer could give her the ammunition to destroy him. Despite her better angel, she found herself praying to find a demon hiding inside Joseph Tull's world.

While her typing skills were superior, memorizing what she saw in the mirror—then optically reversing them on her keyboard at home—took an hour of trial and error. Once she mastered the turn-about, she waited to make her move. She knew the best opportunity would come when Joseph departed for one of his junkets to FBI headquarters in DC. Then she could take all the time she needed to scan his computer. Fortunately, he'd given her the push-button passcode to his office door lock. A necessity after he'd asked her to forward some files he'd forgotten during a trip to Kentucky.

She entered his office, locked his door, and sat at his desk. She drew a shallow breath. She keyed in his ID and password. OrangeMan and Flight655. His computer desktop blinked, then came to life. Her heart fluttered and she stared at the screen, wondering what to do first. A quick scan for the obvious. Child porn, Tinder profiles, files labeled with obscure names. Nothing turned up. Then she recognized a familiar app on his menu bar. KeePassX. The same open-source password manager that she used at home. When the application presented the password screen she entered OrangeMan. Declined. Then she tried Flight655. Bingo! The door to the universe of Tull's internet accounts, login IDs, and passwords opened before her. She whispered a silent cry of delight.

"Guess what, Dr. Tull. Now I *own you,"* she murmured as she began to dig through his files. Dozens of folders held information about his bank records, social media, and email accounts. There she found one of the pioneer email applications. Hotmail. An antique. She clicked the icon and when it presented the log-in screen she entered the password scripts from KeePassX. The Hotmail home screen opened and all his correspondence flashed across the monitor.

As she read the long series of draft messages her surprise turned into dread. Then something like panic. Every word written in Cyrillic letters. *Russian.* An inner voice screamed at her, "Shut it down, shut it down." Then the cool voice of control began to whisper, "No, no. Wait. You came here for this. Now do it."

She tugged a thumb drive from her pocket and slipped it into a USB slot. She exported the complete database of login IDs and passwords to her thumb drive. Next, she copied all the Hotmail files and tucked the device back into her pants.

Now what? She stared at the keyboard and tried to think. Okay, *now* shut it all down. First, shut down the computer. Then eliminate any trace of your crime. Your crime? Yes, *your* treason. She balled a wad of tissues in her hand and wiped it over the keyboard. She wiped the chair, the desk, anywhere her fingerprints might have touched. Then she cleaned the door handle and listened for passing footsteps in the corridor. After two—was it three minutes?—she slipped back to her own office and shut the door.

What next? First, translate the Russian text into English. Then warn Myfanwy.

BACK in March 2020, Zena turned her attention to something new when she discovered that a team of biotech researchers had devised a breast cancer therapy paired with DNA targeting technology. The new approach could detect breast cancer DNA signatures and deliver the treatment exclusively to the patient's cancer cells. So clever. But what are the implications, she wondered. Especially if an old bug like H5N1 bird flu is paired with unique DNA targets. Perhaps targeting people with brown eyes. Or blond hair. Or black skin.

She decided to discuss the possibilities with Spiro Ratzman, a colleague from Stanford. After considerable debate, they weighed the options. Could DNA targeting be adapted to a virus? Perhaps. These days—with a little ingenuity, a middling amount of cash, and focused determination—if a biotech instrument can be conceived, it can be manufactured. And most of it could be produced in a university microbiology lab.

When Joseph returned from another week-long round of consultations in Washington she knew she had to bring it to his attention. His junkets to FBI headquarters in DC had become routine. And tiresome. At least for her. She didn't like the loneliness. Her remedy—to pour her energy into her research —provided only a partial cure. It helped when she doubled her target practice at Tru-Site Pistol Club to twice a week, along with an occasional romp with Hans Brinkmann, the club manager. However, her love of handguns and casual sex didn't displace her gnawing anxieties.

It was during these weeks alone that she unraveled the mystery that plagued her every day. Who sent the Chicanos to kill her and Joseph? Following Vince Mathew's murder in South Dakota, new tensions appeared in the ranks of White Sphere. The ex-governor had become a champion of Joseph and Zena's support—and their financial generosity. But following his death, the leaders of Right Flank, The Defense, and The Brothers of Vidar asserted the one thing they cherished above all else. Their independence. Many viewed White Sphere's control as a reverse takeover—"A coup," as Samuel Weems put it in a whispered conversation that Zena overheard at Vince Mathew's funeral. Yes, they were the sole entity with motive, means, and opportunity to execute Zena and Joseph.

The conspiracy against them bound her loneliness in a knot of sleepless misery. She needed immediate relief. And something to reinforce her survival instincts. A new tattoo. The pain of the tat needle etching the narrow script over her forearm provided the remedy. Then she needed Joseph to break out of the mirage of their existence. They'd worn their masks for far too long. It was time to act.

After she picked Joseph up at the San Francisco International Airport and drove them back to their house, she prepared egg sandwiches and set them on a plate along with gherkin pickles, Moroccan olives, and baby carrots. His favorites.

"Here. Time to eat, Comrade," she said and set the food on the table.

"Perfect." He glanced at her with a grateful look. "I'm starved."

As they ate he grumbled about the hotel restaurants and government cafeterias in DC, but she dismissed his complaints with a wave of her hand and leaned forward in her chair. She set her bare arms on the kitchen table and waited until they caught his attention. Finally he returned her gaze with a serious expression.

"All right. So what's that?"

She put on a look of mock surprise and examined her tattoo. "I got it when you were gone. Something to break the boredom."

Joseph read the elaborate calligraphy. *My Life, My Fate.* "What's that supposed to mean?"

"That I've got my mojo back." She chuckled. Mojo. So American. "It's on my side again."

He shook his head. "It's happening all over, isn't it?"

"What?"

"You're running out of control."

She scoffed and leaned back in her chair. "Out of control?"

"Yeah. First you think you've found some special meaning in simple words. So special you have to turn them into tattoos. Then abracadabra"—he spun a hand in the air as if he could conjure up some magic—"you run off into your crazy zone."

Her eyes narrowed and she set her jaw with determination. "No. It's the exact opposite. I have complete control now. And you need to listen to me. Very carefully."

"Listen to what?"

"I've come across something new."

"Something new?"

She paused to consider the best way to approach him. "Last year a biotech company in Palo Alto synthesized a new cancer therapy."

"Okay." His eyes widened in expectation. "And?"

"And I think it might be the answer."

*The answer.* He knew what she meant. The answer to the question they discussed month after month. How to bring America to its knees? The Covid-19 pandemic had exposed the country's vulnerability, but not broken its back.

"Yes," she said. "It's simple, clean, unstoppable." She tipped her head to one side and added, "If it works."

"There's always that. The big *if.*" He rubbed a hand over his face and felt a wave of exhaustion ripple through his chest. A week in DC always tore a piece out of him. Working in the intelligence community forced him to heighten his vigilance. His double-life always vulnerable to unknown threats.

Vitvinin had warned Joseph that his infiltration of the FBI

made him vulnerable. If he was caught out, Joseph would spend decades in prison. Possibly die in solitary confinement. As a safeguard, Vitvinin opened a Hotmail link with Zena. Joseph, disheartened by the shift of focus, knew he had to accept Vitvinin and Zena's collaboration without complaint.

"I talked to Spiro Ratzman last month," Zena continued. "He says what I'm thinking of can definitely work."

She studied his face for a reaction. When Joseph raised a hand, she pushed on before he could object. "In fact, he's started to work on it. You know him. Once he bites into something he can't stop chewing."

"You talked to Psycho Rats?"

"Nobody calls him that anymore."

Spiro Ratzman had placed first in Zena's grad class at Stanford. He'd been dubbed "Psycho Rats" when his talent in gene editing inspired dread in his peers. Simply because he wanted to grow a human ear on top of a rat's head. Was he serious? To everyone's dismay, he never quite understood their umbrage.

Joseph drew a long breath. "All right. So what are we talking about?"

"I don't mean to sound pretentious," she said and leaned toward him again, "but this is *really* new. Completely. Like the nuclear fission of uranium-235 during World War Two. And we both know where that led."

"Go on."

"A targeted bioweapon. Remember what the British did to the Indians? Back in the 1700s, they traded beaver pelts for blankets."

"Supposedly a clean trade. Except they smeared smallpox on the blankets. When the blankets made it back to the Indian villages, the tribes were devastated."

"Right. But what made it a tactical success was the broad immunity of white people developed over the generations who survived smallpox in Europe. Not all Europeans were immune, of course. Hardly. But enough to entice the Brits to roll the dice and launch the world's first biological weapon."

"So you're proposing a biotech version of what? Smallpox attached to DNA targeting?"

"No. Not smallpox. The Marburg virus."

A blank expression crossed his face. "Which is what?"

"A hemorrhagic fever virus. It causes severe watery diarrhea, abdominal pain and cramping. Something like Ebola."

"Ebola? My God. And what's the DNA target?"

"Two genes on chromosome 15. OCA2 and HERC2."

"Come on, Zena." He shook his head. "Let's pretend I don't know the genome map by heart." The sarcasm oozed through every word. "Who are you talking about?"

"People with genetic heterochromia."

"Should I Google that, or are you going to tell me?"

She smiled. She was enjoying the air of superiority the dialogue provided. Once again she held the whip hand.

"People with two different eye colors. Less than one percent of the population. But it will serve as a useful sample for the human trials. Once we know it works we can target other demographics. Say, skin color." An icy smile froze on her lips. "Think about it. This will sow chaos across the country. It will take months for the CDC to understand what they're dealing with. Let alone identify the source. And everyone in White Sphere will be chomping at the bit to target a specific, hmmm"—her voice hummed with amusement—"non-western demographic."

He let out a gasp of disbelief and held up a hand as if he needed to stop an impending train wreck. "Wait, wait, wait. What's Marburg's fatality rate?"

"Varies. Up to sixty percent."

*"Sixty percent?"* Jesus, Zena. What if the DNA targeting fails? What if the virus mutates? If there's a global breakout?"

She smiled. "Can't happen. The virus is ineffective if the DNA targeting falters. Besides, Spiro doesn't know it, but I've developed a vaccine."

"To counter the virus?"

"Yes."

He stood up and walked toward the kitchen sink, turned, and leaned against the counter. He looked at her as if he'd discovered something new in her. *Madness.* "Zena, I don't know."

Still sitting at the table, she swiveled to him. "I knew you'd say that. But Rome3 has a different view."

He blinked. "You've talked to Vitvinin?"

"On our private channel." Her lips pursed together as she considered how to prepare him for the news. "The same way you communicate with him. Draft messages in Hotmail."

He felt a light shock roll through his chest.

"Don't look so surprised. I know he told you this already. It began just after you started at the FBI. Now Vitvinin communicates with me almost every day." Her hand swept across the room to suggest that Ossip Vitvinin held the world within his grasp.

She read the sense of betrayal in his face. "Josef, you should know that people in the Kremlin are talking about your collaboration with the FBI. About the millions you've funneled into White Sphere. And the gossip's not all friendly."

"What?" His arms flew into the air. "Vitvinin himself certified the operation. Operation Dove Cove. That's *his* code-name for it!"

"I know. He told me that." A lie, but a needful one. Anything to suggest Vitvinin's confidence had shifted in her favor. "Vitvinin says we have to move into high gear. We've waited twenty years. It's too long, Josef. Some are saying that we've gone native. That you've bought into the American Dream. You can imagine the pressure on Vitvinin to turn things around."

Joseph crossed his arms and glanced away as he expelled a gush of air. This was the test. Vitvinin had warned him that one day it would come. A day when Vitvinin couldn't restrain the blue bloods.

"He wants me to put together a trial of the Marburg virus. Like I said, Spiro's been working with me since Vitvinin provided the research funds."

Joseph's eyebrows knit together. "This is madness, Zena."

"No," she countered. "It's science."

He stared at her with a venomous look. She'd never seen such anger in him.

"Look, we already started animal trials. If we succeed, then we follow with a human trial."

"You're saying that animals have heterochromia, too?"

"Some, yes. You often see it in dogs. Spiro's caught over twenty strays with heterochromia. Enough to complete the trial." She paused. "So Josef, now you only have to decide one thing. To support me with this. We need your answer. Yes or no?"

He leaned against the sink. Speechless.

"I'll take that as a yes," she said. As for a human trial, she knew it would never happen. The human strain would either succeed or fail completely. Should it succeed, there would be no stopping it. The genie would be out of the bottle.

"Oh, one final thing. I know who sent the two Chicanos to kill us."

"Oh? Who?" He stared at her, eyes half-closed.

"White Sphere. Or what's left of it without Vince Mathews."

"White Sphere?" His hands flew into the air as if they had to escape from his body. "Jeezus, Zena. Have you lost your mind? Those two bums were just homeless drunks."

"A perfect disguise," she countered.

"No. That's completely insane. How can you ever prove something like that?" He studied her face a moment then realized she'd gone one step too far. "Don't tell me. Have you told this to Vitvinin?"

She paused a moment to ensure that he'd absorb the final blow. "Rome3 has already authorized it. Before we return to Russia, we're to take down White Sphere."

SHEILA met Myfanwy at Flywheel Coffee Roasters on Stanyan Street. Paper cups in hand, the two women crossed the street into Golden Gate Park, made their way across Robin Williams Meadow, and sat on a bench overlooking the park lawn.

"So what's the deal?" Myfanwy asked. "First you kick me out, then you phone me and go all under-cover with '*we can't talk on the phone.*'"

Sheila sipped her coffee, rolled her tongue over her lips, and gazed at the people strolling along the path toward Hippie Hill. How to explain everything? "Just listen," she began. "You're better off living down on Carl Street. Believe me. Maybe they won't find you there."

"Find me? Who wants to find me?"

"You remember my boss? Joseph Tull."

"Yeah, the bully boss. A day doesn't go by that you don't dump new dirt on him."

"Yeah, right. Well, he's onto you. At least he's onto Brass Shoes."

"How do you know that?"

She watched a couple walking hand-in-hand along the path toward the Hill. "Okay, so what I'm going to tell you will mean the end of my job if you tell anyone else."

"So now you sound a little strange."

"Just promise me you'll keep this to yourself. Then you'll see what strange really looks like."

"All right. Go," she said with an impatient pout. "I promise." She smirked and crossed two fingers over her heart.

"Let's say I got access to his computer files—"

"You hacked his machine?" Her voice rose with a trace of disbelief. "How?"

"Just listen. Joseph Tull was twelve when his parents died in an airline crash. In 1988 the US shot down Iran Air Flight 655 over the Persian Gulf. Everyone on board died. Including his parents."

Sheila paused to study Myfanwy's response. For once she appeared speechless.

"A month later he moved to Russia to live with an uncle."

"How do you know this?"

"Google Iranian Flight 655 and follow the links to Joseph Tull. The Russians turned him into a poster boy against American aggression."

"My God."

"I know. Then, over the next ten years, he was recruited into SVR."

"What's that?"

"Think Russian CIA. Except where the CIA have no morals whatsoever, the SVR is the devil incarnate."

A lazy smile crossed Myfanwy's face. "I doubt it." She took a long sip of coffee, pressed the plastic lid on the rim, and set the cup on the edge of the bench. Her lips softened into a frown that revealed she might be reconsidering her judgment. "So what makes you say that?"

"Tull and his wife, Zena. They're a sleeper cell."

"Oh please." Her mouth curled in a sneer. "You've been locked up too long, girl. The pandemic's turned you into a Netflix spinoff." She glanced up at the clouds and let out a throaty laugh. "You said Zena was a sex bomb timed to blow off twice a month."

"Maybe. But she's also a PhD in microbiology. The last

message I downloaded said she's running tests to create a bio-weapon."

"And it's in Russian?"

Sheila nodded.

"And you're Russian's good enough—"

"Good enough," she cut in. "Enough to know what's going down."

Sheila decided to add a kicker, the one element guaranteed to draw Myfanwy's ire. "They're testing on animals. Dogs. Dozens a day in a lab somewhere in Santa Rosa. They all die. I mean, *that's the goal*. To kill them all."

"Who the fuck are you talking about?" her voice hardened. "*Who's they?*"

"Something called White Sphere."

"White Sphere?"

"Yeah. And so here's the connection to you. They're investigating Brass Shoes. I think they want to recruit him. Or silence him. Whoever he is. 'Course I don't know that. Only you do."

Myfanwy shrugged. "But we both know—"

"No. Not my father. They know *he's* dead. They want your version. *Your* Joel Griffin. The one you met in Rapid City last year."

They both took a moment to ponder Myfanwy's elaborate deception.

"All right. So maybe we should warn him," she said.

"We? This was your fucking idea. Not mine. *You stole my father's life to play this game.*" Sheila's voice cracked with indignation. "Now some innocent guy—some other Joel Griffin—is being targeted by the SV-fuckin'-R."

Neither of them could speak. Sheila's pain—her fury—was too much for either of them to absorb.

Finally Myfanwy found her voice.

"All right. Okay. Yeah, it's on me." She lifted her coffee cup, snapped off the lid, and turned the cup upside down so the coffee dregs dribbled onto the lawn.

Sheila watched her, wondered what she could be thinking.

"Do you even know who he is?"

"Yeah. I know who he is. Will Finch. A reporter at *The Post.*"

"Will Finch." She made a mental note to Google him when she returned to her house. "And you can find him?"

"Shouldn't be too hard," she whispered and slipped the lid on the cup again. "I already know where he lives. On Telegraph Hill. Him and his wife and kid. Maybe I can track him down tonight."

# Chapter Eleven

SAN FRANCISCO — 2 MARCH, 2021

During the weeks following the murder of Myfanwy Thomas, Will Finch began to vary his evening routines. He spent every fourth or fifth night visiting his ailing mentor, Wally Gimbel. Wally, now crippled by Parkinson's Disease, offered his spare room to Finch for as long as he wanted it. "Believe me, I love the company," he said.

Every second or third night he slept alone at the cottage he and Eve had renovated just below Coit Tower on Telegraph Hill. The other nights he spent with Eve in her sister's home in Berkeley Hills where she remained hunkered down with their daughter.

The reason for these checker-board maneuvers was simple. Paranoia. Or in more rational terms, an abundance of caution. Whoever had duped Finch at the Drake Hotel and taken Myfanwy's life was certainly capable of tracking his movements throughout the city. The more he could frustrate those efforts, the more likely he could challenge them on his terms. He could apply the guerrilla fighting tactics he'd witnessed in Iraq to his situation. *Take shelter, hide, then bring the fight to the enemy when he's exposed.*

Checking in with *The Post* headquarters provided another move that might keep his trackers off balance. As he climbed the staircase to the third floor of *The Post's* office on Mission Street, he slipped his gaiter mask over his nose and ears. When he reached the reception area he paused and scanned the empty corridors. Shortly after the pandemic hit California, most of the in-house reporting, sales, and production duties were suspended. Fiona Page, the managing editor, was an exception. As a single mom with a bright, demanding daughter, she found that she couldn't do her job from the kitchen table in her condo on Russian Hill. Eve agreed to pay for the nanny and a housekeeper to free Fiona from her domestic life.

"The wheelhouse is just too small," she'd said over the phone to Finch. "Besides, I love the half-hour walk to the downtown office. It keeps me real. And a sense of reality is the one thing I need every day."

Finch recalled their phone conversation as he walked along the hall toward her office. He was pleased to see her door ajar. He tapped on the door frame and eased his head through the opening. "So you're the only one who works here now?"

She let out a laugh. Even under her mask, he detected her broad smile.

"Good to see you, Will." She stood and embraced the empty air with a sweeping bear hug. "I'd squeeze you—maybe even try for a kiss—but I guess we can't do either anymore.

Sit." She pointed to the chair opposite her desk.

"Good to see you, too. It's been"—he glanced at the ceiling as he searched his memory—"what? Two Christmases ago since I saw you."

"I know. I used to dread staff parties." She waved a hand as if she were dismissing a tiresome memory. "Now? I can hardly wait."

Finch realized that he'd like to see the old gang too. It had been years since he held down a desk in the writers' pool —"The Bog," as they called it—where he made his name as a crime reporter.

"You said on the phone that you had a package for me?"

"Mmm-hmm." She opened a drawer and placed a brown envelope on her desk. "Someone dropped it off yesterday. It was addressed to me, but inside I found a second envelope addressed to you."

She passed the packages to Finch. A typed label affixed to the outer envelope read, *Fiona Paige, Managing Editor, San Francisco Post. Personal and Confidential.* He opened the flap. Inside lay a slightly smaller bubble-wrapped envelope. The typed label said, *To Will Finch. Hand deliver ONLY."* He squeezed the package between his fingers.

"Feels like a TV clicker."

He studied Fiona's face. Her eyes confirmed the mystery. She had no idea who it could be from—or what it might contain. He dragged his index finger under the seal and peered into the package.

"It's an old Samsung." He tipped the package on an angle and slid the cell phone into his hand. He opened the swing hinge. "A clamshell."

He checked the wrapper again. Inside he found a message typed onto a slip of paper. He read it aloud. *"Wednesday, noon. I'll call you on this phone. Urgent."*

"What? Read that again."

He re-read the message and held it above the desk so that she could read it for herself.

She nodded with an uncertain look. "Okay. So what have you got yourself into this time?"

"Honestly? I have no idea. I've been caught in some kind of deep-fake disaster. It could be the biggest mess we've ever seen."

"We?" She paused. "You mean *us?"*

"Yeah. I need some help, Fiona." He narrowed his eyes and studied her reaction.

"What for?"

"I can't tell you that."

She let out a weak cough and closed her eyes as if she needed to block what was coming. "So this involves either the CIA or the FBI."

"And you know what that means. I can't say anything."

"Shit."

"Yeah. Stinks, and I'm waist-deep in it."

She understood his predicament. It wasn't the first time they had to work on a story half-buried in legal restrictions due to the feds. "Does Eve know about this?"

He could feel the tension rising in his body. He nodded but refused to acknowledge anything more than the bare bones of his struggle.

"All right. Don't say another word. I'm here any time you need me." She lay her left hand on the desk and pointed to the Samsung phone. "And if you want to tell me how your conversation goes tomorrow, I'm here for you."

ON Wednesday afternoon, Finch sat with Eve at his side in Berkeley Hills when the Samsung cell phone rang. He checked his watch. Exactly noon.

"Run the recorder," he said to Eve.

She nodded and clicked the icon on her cell to record the call. He let the phone buzz three times, then clicked the speakerphone button to answer.

"Will Finch," he said.

After a brief pause, he heard a woman's voice. "Are you alone?"

He glanced at Eve. She gave him a thumb's up. The recorder was capturing the call.

"Yes."

"All right." She drew a long breath. "I assume the only reason you answered is because you know you've been manipulated by White Sphere."

"What's White Sphere?"

"Look. Mr. Finch, don't pretend you don't know what's going on. You were completely duped by them in the Drake Hotel. And your mistakes cost the security guard his life."

Finch cast a penetrating look at Eve. She shook her head to dismiss his guilt. *Not your fault,* she mouthed.

"Listen to me. Now they know who you are. Where you work. Where you live."

"If they knew all that, then why did they try to meet with me?"

"They had to be sure. When you fumbled, they had to react. Now the thing about Joel Griffin and Brass Shoes is a joke to them. And the FBI are almost as laughable."

He stared through the window. The mid-winter view over the university campus and down to San Francisco Bay was undimmed. Not a trace of fog in the air. Unlike his own situation. Everyone else had a crisp, microscopic view of their life —but he had no clear perspective of his own.

"All right. You seem to know more about me than I do. So who are you?" He could tell from her voice that this was not Musk. If she had any accent at all, it was softened with an Atlantic seaboard tinge. Was she from Miami? Tampa Bay?

"Not now," she replied. "Maybe never."

"Okay then, *Maybe Never*—if that's your name. You know what? I think you're just as nervous as me."

"Yeah. That's your first correct guess."

"So why are you reaching out to me?"

"Look. We're on the edge of catastrophe. And it has nothing to do with anti-vaxxers and the Covid pandemic."

He turned to Eve with a look that said, what's going on? She raised her eyebrows in skeptical disbelief. She whispered three words. "I don't know."

"Oh really?" he scoffed. "That sounds a little alarmist, Maybe Never. It's going to take some convincing for me to think you're nothing but a crank caller who stumbled on my name and number."

She paused as if the conversation had taken a wrong turn.

Something she hadn't anticipated.

"Look. I'm going to give you one day. I want you to research three terms. The Marburg virus, DNA targeting, and Syn-bio."

Again Finch turned to Eve. In her left hand she still held her cell next to the Samsung as she continued to record the conversation. She raised her free hand in the air and shrugged. She looked as mystified as her husband.

"Okay. I've never heard of the Marburg virus." He paused to think. "You said Syn-bio? What's that?"

"Synthetic biology."

"What about DNA targeting?"

"Look it up." Her voice acquired a harder, impatient edge. "Then put the first two together with DNA targeting and you'll see what we're dealing with."

"Wait a sec—"

"I'll call you tomorrow, same time," she interrupted. "Tell me if you're in or out. That's all that matters."

"Listen—"

When he heard the line go dead he looked at Eve once more and clicked off his phone.

LATER that evening Eve brought Gabe Finkleman into a Zoom meeting to discuss the research they'd found about the Marburg virus, synthetic biology, and DNA targeting. Even before their online meeting, Finch became concerned after he determined the implications on his own. However, he knew that *The Post's* research genius would help him and Eve decide if Maybe Never was credible.

"Well, depending on who's behind all this, it could mean trouble," Finkleman said. "Real trouble."

Even on Eve's laptop screen, Finkleman looked like a lanky beanpole. Finch, at six foot three inches, always felt dwarfed standing beside the tech guru. Despite his height, the man was perpetually deferential. Since the day they met, he addressed Finch as Mr. Finch. Only in the past year had Gabe embraced the forename, Will. However, he continued to refer to Eve—the owner of *The Post* and therefore his boss—as Ms. Noon. Finch doubted that would ever change.

"Trouble is one word for it," Eve replied. "But give us your overall impression. It could be a fantastic hoax. Or a catastrophe. What are you thinking?"

Finkleman adjusted his glasses. "So let's talk about possible catastrophe first. If it's a hoax, then it's just a five-inch story in tomorrow's *Post*. But the possible catastrophe, if it happens, will be front-page news for five years. Minimum."

"Okay, worst things first," Finch said. "What do you see?"

"Let's start with the virus. The Marburg virus disease— MVD—used to be called Marburg hemorrhagic fever. It made the jump to humans from fruit bats in Africa. On the face of it, it's not very transmissible and requires human-to-human contact via bodily secretions. Severity and fatality increases if it's transmitted by injections or prick injuries. It usually crops up in clusters of two to eight people. On the other hand, the human mortality rate averages fifty to sixty percent."

"Sixty?" Eve gasped. "Six-zero?"

"Yeah. Think of the Bubonic plague. That bad. Actually, worse. But because MVD has infected less than a thousand people so far, it's no longer front-page news. Until you take into account recent trends in synthetic biology."

"Like the mRNA vaccine?" Eve asked.

Last year, both Pfizer and Moderna had synthesized vaccines to combat the Covid-19 pandemic using mRNA technology. The results were so promising that the two vaccines formed the backbone of the president's push to vaccinate 100,000,000 Americans within his first 100 days in office. Eve and Finch hoped to receive their first jabs next month.

"Exactly." Finkleman nudged his glasses up to the bridge of his nose. "But let's imagine what might happen when microbiologists start to experiment with Marburg mutations."

"What? Why would they do that?" Finch asked.

"It's called Gain-of-Function research. The idea is to purposefully change pathogens in a lab so we can understand them —and develop vaccines in the off-chance the viruses mutate in the natural world."

"And someone is actually doing this?"

"Indeed. Our very own National Institutes of Health do this with the H5N1 virus." Finkleman smirked as if he couldn't believe it either.

"Bird flu," Eve whispered.

"Right. But Gain-of-Function research isn't a problem, provided the labs are one hundred percent secure." He tipped his chin to one side, a subtle gesture, but obvious enough to reveal his skepticism.

Finch fluttered his lips as he let out a long sigh. Everything Finkleman had said only multiplied his fears. "So what happens if this falls into the wrong hands?"

"Same problem as the six US nuclear weapons that have disappeared since 1950. The so-called 'broken arrows.' No one knows who has them. Most people don't even know about them." Finkleman shrugged. "They're not a problem until one goes off."

"All right. Okay." Eve's voice rose with a note of impatience. "So what about DNA targeting? What is it, exactly? How do you see them fitting together?"

"Honestly, I don't see how it fits with the Marburg virus. But with synthetic biology? Yeah, that could present a hiccup. DNA targeting is on the bleeding edge of cancer treatment research. Cancer therapists can now target specific cancer DNA in individual patients to attack the cancer cells only, so all the healthy cells are spared."

Finch thought of his first wife, Cecily. She'd died of breast cancer and suffered through the agonies of surgery and chemo —and left him alone to care for their son Buddy.

"All right, Gabe," Eve continued, "so what's your sci-fi speculation on all this? That some evil genius has synthetically manipulated Marburg so it transmits from human to human— but then what?"

"That maybe"—Finkleman scratched his narrow chin —"maybe they rejig the new virus so that it infects only specific people."

"Specific people?" Finch asked.

"You mean like Muslims?" Eve asked, then quickly dismissed the idea. "Except religious groups don't necessarily share unique DNA markers."

The array of possibilities floated in momentary silence.

Then Finkleman continued.

"It's more like people with blue eyes. Or maybe blue eyes *and* red hair." He glanced away. "Honestly, I shouldn't say more. At this point, I'm just guessing."

"All right, Gabe," Finch said. "Look, you've been a huge help. I'll get back to you if I need more info, okay?"

"You bet." Finkleman nudged his glasses up the length of his nose again, waved a hand, and then vanished from the screen.

THE woman Finch referred to as Maybe Never kept her word. When she ended her call to Finch she'd pledged to phone him the next day. Years of working at *The Post* had hardened his skepticism about anonymous tips and insider scoops. However, a few passed what he called "the stink test." And two or three of those led to the biggest stories to hit the front pages across the country.

Which meant that he could never afford to completely ignore any of them. That was the case when Maybe Never called him as he opened the living room curtains in Megan Rivers's house in Berkeley Hills.

"Well, well," he said. "Maybe Never strikes again."

No reply.

He waited and then tried again. "Hello. Who's calling?"

"It's me," she said. "Look, you've got a right to doubt everything I said. I get that."

"Yeah. I do."

"But now everything's worse than I imagined."

"Okay." He sat in a chair facing the window. "Tell me

more."

"Not on the phone. I want you to meet me. The sooner the better. Can you get down to Pier 23 by two?"

"This afternoon?"

"Yes."

"All right," he sighed. "Where?"

"Go to the tall palm tree on the south side of the dock," she said. "Sit on one of the benches facing the harbor. Two o'clock. Then wait ten more minutes."

"You know, I think you're over-playing this."

"Am I? Do you think Myfanwy was over-playing it, too?"

Finch closed his eyes as the image of Myfanwy's murder flashed through his mind. Maybe Never was right. Over-playing a game like this was impossible.

"Okay," he said. "See you then."

As Finch drove his RAV4 out of the driveway onto the street a smile crossed his face. Next to the curb, across the road, and two doors along, he could see a gray Chevy Camaro parked under the shade of a heavy limbed tree. Behind the wheel sat a clean-cut agent, half-hidden under the shade of the car's sun visor. Saxx had pulled the strings necessary to provide the surveillance Finch demanded. Score a point for the home team, he whispered to himself.

Forty minutes later Finch strolled along the sidewalk of The Embarcadero toward Pier 23. Even in the late winter months, the piers inside San Francisco Bay would normally be awash with tourists shopping, drinking, and dining—or climbing on and off the cruise ships and harbor ferries. But not today. Not while Covid-19 haunted the city.

When he reached the Pier 23 Café he paused to get his bearings. The café was a local landmark, a one-story, white-washed stucco building that looked like it had been teleported from a lonely Greek island. The row of wide window frames lining the front of the restaurant—all painted Aegean blue—confirmed the illusion. A year ago a queue of hungry patrons waited outside the door all day long. But today, the place was closed. Shuttered by the pandemic.

Finch sat on the bench overlooking San Francisco Bay. A few people strolled along the waterfront alone or in pairs, stopping to study the cityscape, the harbor seals, the wharves moaning as the rising tides ground their skids against the pilings. The still afternoon air held a lacy fog that skirted above the water. A place of mysteries and dreams. A beacon to anyone pondering the world's endless churn.

Behind him, he heard the smush of rubber-soled shoes padding across the walkway. As he turned, he heard her speak.

"Don't make it too obvious," she said and sat on the bench, three feet to his left. She wore a black mask and a gray duffle coat buttoned up to her chin.

"All right. So you're here." He adjusted his mask over his nose. "So you're Maybe Never. In the flesh."

"Don't play dumb. You know who I am."

She turned toward him. A flood of unkempt brown hair cascaded from under a French beret down to her shoulders. Her gray eyes caught his attention. She looked familiar, but he couldn't quite place her. Then she pulled her mask under her chin. He glanced at the rash of acne scars on her cheeks and shifted his attention to her eyes.

"Sheila Griffin."

A feeling of bewilderment welled through him. He hesitated. Her father, Joel Griffin—Finch's alias—was Brass Shoes, the revered leader of the anti-vaxx movement. Could he trust her?

"You look surprised." A cynical smile dipped across her face. "I know you followed me to work at the Academy."

He slipped the gaiter mask below his chin and stared at the scene beyond the waterfront railing. The haze hovering above the water sent a chill through him. He wondered if he was about to step into another trap.

"Well … I guess you got me. Like everybody else these days." He lifted both hands in a gesture of surrender. "But you're wrong. I wasn't expecting *you.*"

"No? I'm not so sure." She paused as she considered how to continue. "Let's get one thing out of the way. My father—"

"I know," he interrupted but immediately regretted breaking in. Nonetheless, he pressed on. "This whole thing"—his hand swept toward the bay—"it all got out of hand. I didn't know anything about your father. Joel Griffin was a name I made up. I pulled it out of thin air. And when Myfanwy—"

Now she cut in. "Myfanwy was an idiot. I loved my father. But *she* turned him into a cartoon character."

Finch nodded. "So you weren't part of it. After he passed, I mean. The anti-vaxx crusade?"

"No, that wasn't me. It was all Myfanwy. At first I might've encouraged her. After all, Dad died from anaphylaxis shock following a routine vaccination. But when I read the vile she generated on Twitter and Facebook? No way. I told her it was enough. But she continued to stir the pot."

*Anaphylaxis. Generated.* Finch considered her ten-dollar-a-word vocabulary. Sheila was certainly no cartoon character. But was she credible?

"She knew my dad had a nickname as a kid. Brass Shoes. She used that when she got involved with the anti-vaxx thing. But it took her down to a deeper level. Much deeper." Her eyes revealed a nagging fear, something bordering on horror. "They're completely irrational."

Finch believed her. "So why're we here, Sheila? My guess is I'm the last person you want to see right now."

Her lips rolled into a pout as she considered this. She was not a good-looking woman, Finch decided. But she was smart, with a challenging job at the Academy. And she had the confidence to reach out to him, her father's doppelgänger.

"Because we need to get the word out. If White Sphere releases a synthetic Marburg virus using DNA targeting it could lead to genocide. And I use that word literally."

She crossed her hand over her pock-marked cheek. One side, then the other. Was she trying to hide it, or had this deft gesture become a nervous tic to deflect the teasing she probably endured during adolescence?

"As a reporter you've got first amendment protections," she continued. "You could publish this in *The Post* tomorrow."

Finch let out a puff of air. Maybe she wasn't as bright as he imagined. "Publish what? That some evil genius is about to unleash a syn-bio cocktail on the world? I need facts. Evidence. Expert testimonials. Damn it, you should know all that." He leaned toward her and heard the anger rising in his voice. Easy, he told himself. No need to scold her. "Besides, the FBI has blocked me from reporting any of this."

"So what? I know you invoked the first amendment on stories you've covered before. That's the main reason I'm bringing this to you. You're the only person close enough to the facts who can report them."

"Look, you need to take this to the FBI yourself. Directly. Talk to Agents Keely and Saxx, the ones investigating Myfanwy's murder. It's their case."

"Directly? Fuck that," she groaned. "After Myfanwy was shot, they took her computer. The laptop that Myfanwy used for Brass Shoes. It probably took less than an hour to break her VPN password. So then they got her IP address. So now they know it all came through my home router."

Finch offered a sympathetic look. Without a VPN mask, her computer ID was visible to anyone who knew how to look for it.

"Any day now they can indict me on a co-conspiracy charge. Saxx made it crystal clear that's gonna be his next step."

He studied her face as she wiped a tear from her eye. Maybe she was under more pressure than he was. That's how they played ball. The FBI can run over anyone standing in their way.

"All right. I get it," he said. "Maybe there's another way forward."

"Like what?" she sniffed.

"Do you know who murdered Myfanwy?"

"Maybe." She glanced away. "Hell. No, I don't know for

sure."

"What's that mean? You either know or you don't."

"Or you guess. I'm just guessing."

"All right. So who're you guessing about?"

She brushed the back of her hands over her eyes again. "At work. We have Academy Fellows. Dozens of PhDs who guide research and programming. Because of my job, I work with the Information Technology Fellow. He's my boss. He and his wife are Russians. For whatever reason, he treats me like his personal assistant. *Download this. Double-check that.*"

"His go-fer."

She let out an icy chuckle. "Right. That's why I never told him I spent a year on student exchange in Moscow. He'd use that to drag me deeper into his world."

"You speak Russian?"

"Enough to interpret the messages between him and the SVR."

"What?" Finch couldn't disguise his surprise.

"The Russian version of the CIA."

"Yeah, I know what the SVR is." Finch held up a hand as if he wanted her to step back. "So what messages are you talking about?"

"Hotmail messages from someone in the Kremlin named Ossip Vitvinin."

"How did you see these messages?"

She shook her head as if she couldn't quite believe what she was telling him. No going back now, she thought. "I hacked his computer at the Academy."

Finch's eyes narrowed as if he needed to filter out the glare from a set of lights that flashed in his face. Time for an important question. "Did you by any chance keep a copy?"

A slight nod. "On a thumb drive."

Finch let out a sigh of relief. "Sheila, that could be the one thing I need to make this work. Tell me something. Is the thumb drive secured?"

"Yes."

"Okay. So you need to make me a copy."

She hesitated.

"Look, from this point on, once you give me the thumb drive, we are in this together. You have to trust me. Completely. Do you understand?"

"I know what you're saying, but I don't know how far I can go with this. I mean physically." She swept a hand across both cheeks and looked away.

"Yeah, it's hard. I understand that. But we either go all the way or no way. There's an old saying. When you challenge the king, you must kill him."

Her chest, neck, and face appeared to lock into place, rigid with fear.

Finch knew he couldn't placate her. The only option was to press forward. "And you can't hide anything from me. Okay?"

Her neck loosened up and she nodded. "I know. There aren't any other choices."

"Yes, there are. Like I said, you can go to Saxx and Keely."

"No."

"All right then. Once you give me a copy of the Hotmail files, I have to verify what's on them. Then I'll tell you if I can report the story in *The Post*. It'll be either *no-go* or *all-go*. Do you understand?"

"Yes. All right." Her voice softened as if she were making a concession. "I can get a copy to you today if you want."

"The sooner the better." Once again he glanced around the promenade. Not a soul to be seen. "But first, what's the Russian's name? Your boss."

"Dr. Joseph Tull."

"And he's got a PhD in what?"

"Computer Science. From Stanford."

"And his wife?"

"Zena Smirnov. Also a Stanford PhD. Microbiology. They live in a house on Shrader Street."

"Shrader Street," he repeated.

"Yeah." Her voice faltered.

She was behaving like many of the sources Finch interviewed for complex stories. Convinced their knowledge of a crime would implicate them. He knew he had to coax the facts from her one at a time. Word by word.

"Ok. So tell me about them."

"He's born American. But when he was a kid, his parents were killed when the US Navy shot down Iran Air Flight 655 over Iraq. All 290 passengers and crew died. Tull was left on his own, then moved to Russia to live with his uncle. It's all in the *New York Times* archives."

Finch paused to reflect. "In the mid-80s?"

"1988. He lived in Russia until 2001, then he moved here with his wife. A few years ago she became a citizen, too."

Finch held up a hand to slow her down. He had to stay focused.

"All right. That's all background. Let's get back to Myfanwy."

"Where do I start?"

"Do the files mention Myfanwy by name?"

She frowned with an uncertain expression. "No. But just like the FBI, they probably cracked her VPN, and computer IP address. From there they could track her social media. Once they did that, they'd know her name, what she looks like, her new address. Everything." She waved a hand in disgust. "She basically lived on Facebook and Instagram."

"You think they could trace all that?"

"Look, Tull's a computer genius. The FBI hired him as a consultant."

Finch ran his tongue over his lips. "He works for the FBI, too?"

"Yes. *Look, he's playing everyone.*" Her voice rang with a dizzy fear.

Finch paused to consider her claim. Was it possible? He worked for the FBI *and* the SVR. He didn't know how to continue. Best to prompt her with an open question. "All right. So let's get back to Myfanwy."

She nodded and glanced across the bay. "Myfanwy was scared. Two weeks ago when I told her everything, she realized she was in trouble. And so were you. That's why she decided to tell you what she'd done."

"And when was this?"

"The same day she was shot. February sixteenth. We had coffee together. She said she knew where you lived. That was the last time I saw her."

He now understood how all the pieces fell into a grid defined by a timeline that extended before and beyond the evening when Myfanwy stopped him on the top of the hill on Vallejo Street. There was one story right here in San Francisco. His story. And another that played out over decades in Russia.

"My God, Sheila. Look, you've got to talk to Keely and Saxx."

*"No. I won't."* Her face contorted into a hard grimace. "I hate what they're doing to me. This can only make it worse."

Finch realized she wasn't thinking straight. But with the thumb drive as evidence, he could break the story in a day. The evidence could save her, but only if it became public knowledge. Then the FBI would have to pounce before another victim fell to Tull and Smirnov. His timing was critical—the sooner, the better. As he considered what else he needed to know a new thought came to him.

"Have you ever heard of the Brothers of Vidar?"

"Who?" She squinted as if she'd lost sight of a boat slipping into the fog. "No. Never."

"What about a woman named Musk. Ever heard of her?"

"No."

"How about someone called the Orange Man?"

"The Orange Man? That's Tull's computer login ID." Her head turned and she looked into Finch's eyes.

Finch ran his tongue over his lips. Finally, a second confirmation of the FBI's claim.

"You know something about the Orange Man?"

"Maybe. But for now, let's focus on White Sphere. I can't do anything about them until I verify the files on the thumb drive." He checked his watch. "When can you get it to me?"

"I don't know. It's in a safety box in my bank in The Haight."

"When does it close?"

"Six."

"All right. Let's meet back here at seven. That gives you enough time?"

"I think so."

"Meanwhile, I'll call Saxx and Keely about Joseph Tull and Zena Smirnov. They'll want to know how I got their names. But I'll hold back on that until I give them the evidence on the drive."

"Without saying it came from me."

He nodded. "Meanwhile, if you hear anything more about them—or the Marburg virus—you know how to reach me."

He pulled the Samsung phone from his pocket. That was smart of her. Her first move, to open a private link to him.

"And don't worry. I'll keep this on me twenty-four-seven."

AFTER he met with Sheila, Finch drove from Pier 23 towards Coit Tower on the top of Telegraph Hill. He hadn't been to his cottage for a while and wanted to check if anyone had been monitoring his house.

As he wheeled around the corners to the top of the hill he set Sheila's revelations in the context of Saxx's extortion. No doubt Saxx was a bent cop. Finch decided his best option would be to reach out to Sandra Keely. Ask to meet her alone. As he unlocked the door to the cottage he called her and left a message to phone him ASAP. He was pleased when she returned the call within five minutes. That meant she still considered him a trusted player. They agreed to meet in an hour at the Caffé Trieste on the west side of Telegraph Hill in North Beach.

After he ended the call he inspected the cottage, pleased to see that nothing was out of place. He rang Eve to bring her up to date.

"Hey. How was your meeting?"

He responded with a bleak laugh. "Believe me, this thing goes way deeper than we imagined."

"Really? What's going on?"

He could hear the concern in her voice. "Nothing to worry about right now."

"You always say that."

He tried to laugh, but only managed a shallow gasp. "Look, I'll be back in Berkeley around nine or so. I need you to find a Russian translator. Somebody *The Post* can trust. Someone who can guarantee confidentiality."

"For an in-person interview?"

"No, someone who can transcribe a file. And we'll need it done tonight."

She held a hand to her face as she considered the possibilities. "Hmmm. You know, Daniel had a friend in the Russian Studies Department at Berkeley."

"Daniel?" Finch recalled some mention of the academic connection. Before he died, his brother-in-law corresponded with climate scientists in Moscow through a Russian professor. Maybe that would work. "Do you know his name?"

"Mmm, Vitaly Something. Uh, Simonov. Vitaly Simonov.

Megan knows him. I'll ask her."

"You ever meet him?"

"At the faculty fall barbecue two years ago. Seemed like a nice man. Quiet, but intelligent."

"The most important thing is if he can keep quiet."

"Well, I'll ask."

"Okay, if he looks good, set it up." He shifted the phone from his right ear to his left. "So, how's the baby?"

"Ten minutes ago she walked all the way across the kitchen. On her own. Pretty soon we can't call her a baby anymore. But I think she's coming down with a cold. No fever, so I don't think it's the virus. And she keeps asking for you. She says, 'Dada hold.' Meaning, Daddy hold me."

"Nice. Like I say, she's a budding genius." He smiled. "Tell her Dada will hold her when she's sleeping tonight, okay."

"Mmmm. Only if you hold me, too."

The thought brought a grin to his face. "You know, Eve, there's something very endearing about you."

"Oh, and don't I know it," she purred and blew a kiss through the phone.

TEN minutes after he'd sat down at a sidewalk table outside Caffe Trieste, Finch saw Agent Sandra Keely turn the corner from Columbus Avenue onto Vallejo Street. As she approached the coffee shop he slipped his mask under his chin to ensure she'd recognize him.

"Agent Keely," he said. "Care for a coffee?"

"After the swill at the office? Yeah. Give me five."

She returned to the table with an espresso cup in her hand

and sat opposite Finch, her face turned to warm in the sun.

"This must be your local café." She nodded toward Coit Tower.

"Yup. These days I don't go anywhere else." He rubbed a hand under the beard on his chin. "Thanks for seeing me on the fly. Last time we talked you said to call you if something comes up."

"Me, but not Agent Saxx. Why'd you cut him out?"

The question, delivered in her smooth, brassy voice, was calculated. He knew she'd come prepared to grill him. But he felt determined to deflect her probes until she understood what was at stake.

"How 'bout we pin that question and come back to it later." He pinched two fingers in the air as if he were pinning a note to a corkboard.

She rolled her shoulders with an indifferent smile. Maybe she didn't care for Saxx's company either. "All right. So what've you got, Finch?"

He glanced up and down the length of the street. "I know who the Orange Man is. And the woman called Musk."

She nudged her espresso cup to one side and gazed into his eyes with a warm expression. "Lovely. And now you're going to tell me who you think they are."

Her voice calm, deliberate. As if she already knew the answers. Despite her cover-model good looks, she could unnerve him with her self-control and inscrutable face.

"Hmmm." His eyes narrowed. "So you already know, don't you?"

"No." Her eyes brightened. "Absolutely not. But when you

called me, I guessed that *you do*. Why else are we sitting here?"

He smiled. "You guessed right."

"And how did you find this information?"

"That I can't tell you. Not right now. But when this breaks open, you'll know."

She took another sip of espresso and leaned forward. "Okay, so let's begin. I'm not recording this. And I'm not wired." She lifted both hands, palms up, and rested them back on the tabletop. "Just tell in your own way. If it clicks, don't worry, we'll get on it."

In all his years working in military intelligence, he'd never come across anyone so capable of controlling an interrogation. Without Saxx prodding her along with his bad cop persona, her style was all sweetness and light. Soon he'd be begging to confess everything Sheila had confided to him. He had to fight the urge.

"All right." He drained the last of his coffee and placed his mug next to her cup. "The Orange Man is Dr. Joseph Tull. He's a Stanford Computer Science PhD and a Fellow at the California Academy of Sciences in Golden Gate Park. His wife, Zena Smirnov, is also a Stanford doctorate."

"Married?" Her eyebrows ticked up. "Quite the pair."

"Tull is the Orange Man. And I'm sure Zena is the woman who interviewed me in the Drake Hotel."

"Which makes them prime suspects in the murder of Troy Hammond."

"Right. But it goes much deeper than that."

"Go on."

"They're both SVR agents who've been living here for twenty years."

"Okay." She paused. "So now you've got my attention."

"There's more. White Sphere has a bio-weapon. A synthetic virus built from Marburg Virus Disease. They can target specific DNA genes with it."

A look of disbelief crossed her face. She closed her eyes for a moment and Finch sensed her dread. She leaned forward and spoke in a whisper. "We've been warned this might come at us someday."

He was sure now that she understood the gravity of the situation. A disaster that could spread from San Francisco and infect anyone with the targeted DNA. They sat for a moment, absorbing the implications, each in their own way. When she turned back to him, he decided to reveal the one remaining card in his hand.

"And last, but not least … Tull is a contractor for the FBI in DC."

"What?"

He tipped his chin to one side. "Going on two years."

She teetered back in her chair as if someone had nudged her. "All right, Finch. Now you need to show me some evidence. Something I can touch."

"Tomorrow I can give you translated email transcripts between Tull and his handler in Moscow. And a thumb drive with all the original files."

"Tomorrow?" She glanced away as if she had to fit this piece of information into a 3-D jigsaw puzzle. "Okay, but I can't do anything until I see the transcripts. And have someone on our team verify them," she added.

"I know. I'm going through the same process."

"What does *that* mean?" She blinked. "Fuckin' hell. You haven't even read the transcripts. You don't have shit, do you?"

"Look. I've got their names." He leaned in. "And you can do something right now that I can't. One, profile these two mad-hatters. And two, put a tail on them."

"Okay, now *you* look." She opened her mouth, twisted her jaw to one side as if she might bite him. In a sudden shift, her attack dog lunged at him. She'd done well to hold a tight leash for this long. "Give me that name of yours. You tell me where you got all this or nothing happens."

"Sorry." He shook his head. "You don't get to pin the tail on the donkey until you verify the transcripts and arrest Joseph Tull and Zena Smirnov. Be patient. Tomorrow you'll have everything."

WALLY Gimbel sat in the wingback chair next to the bay window overlooking the city. From his lofty perch on Russian Hill, he had a magnificent view of San Francisco Bay, the Financial District, and the Golden Gate Bridge. All the icons of the city that he'd reported on during his forty years as San Francisco's preeminent journalist.

His hand trembled on the top of Ella's head. After his wife passed, Wally focussed all his love and attention on their chocolate Lab. Now Ella sat at Wally's side, the two of them studying the world below as if they might sniff out the next breaking news story. When Finch entered the living room, the dog turned her snout toward him. Finch could swear the dog had smiled.

"So that was Eve on the phone? Everything okay with her?" Wally notched his head toward Finch. The effort strained his face and Finch tried to hide his concern. What would become of Ella if she outlived Wally?

"Don't try to hide it," Wally muttered. "Anyone can see the Parkinson's got the better part of me today. Some days I win. Some I lose."

Finch sat in the chair opposite the round coffee table next to Wally. Ella padded toward him, lowered her head, and nudged Finch's hand onto her ears. He gave them a good scratch.

"Sorry, Wally. I just hate to think——" Unable to complete his sentence, he shrugged and gave the dog a final pat. Ella offered him a mournful glance and moved back to Wally's side.

"Yeah. I know." He shifted in his chair. An awkward shuffle that didn't change his posture at all. "Forget that. What did Eve say? She got the Russian translator lined up?"

"Yeah. Ready to go."

After he met with Agent Keely, Finch decided to wait out his seven p.m. rendezvous with Sheila Griffin at Wally's condo. He'd revealed everything he knew about Myfanwy Thomas, Saxx and Keely, the Drake, and now the Orange Man, Brothers of Vidar, and White Sphere. It was just like the old days back in Wally's office at *The Post*. Back when it was a real newspaper that published over 100,000 print copies every evening. Wally had listened carefully, his head shaking in little spasms that Finch interpreted as acknowledgments and gestures of support.

"Well," Wally said, "while you were on the phone with Eve

just now, I thought of something new."

Finch couldn't help but admire the old newshound. Still trying to determine the depth of the story. "I bet you did. Tell me."

"You know that platitude that came out of the Watergate investigations?"

"You mean, 'follow the money'?"

"Right. Woodward and Bernstein. For the last forty years"—he paused to re-calculate the passage of time—"make that forty-nine years, every reporter in the game had to follow the money. But this time it's not about the money."

Finch studied Wally's eyes as he spoke. Still clear and bright. Almost glowing.

"No. What do you think it's about?"

"Two things." He held up a finger, his hand now perfectly steady. "Geo-politics, which is on the verge of war." Another finger rose to stand beside the first. "And two, the insane revenge of Joseph Tull."

Finch drew a hand over his chin. "So what would you do?"

"All you can do about geopolitical threats is report them. That's our job. Hopefully, you can get to that before all is said and done."

Wally still held one finger aloft.

"But first, someone has to take Tull out." His hand curled into a loose fist.

Finch inhaled a long breath. Maybe Wally was right. Tull had to die. Maybe his wife, too. "Wally, you know what you're saying?"

"I know what I'm saying!" His voice rose with conviction.

"Look, there's only one thing you can do with a rabid dog. *Put it down.*"

Finch felt Sheila's Samsung phone buzz in his pocket. As he pulled the cell into his hand he checked the time. He felt a ripple of anxiety. Was she going to call off their meeting?

"They're here," she whispered, her voice restrained, but on edge.

"What? Who's there, Sheila?" Finch stood up and walked toward the kitchen with the phone pressed to his ear.

"Tull and his wife. I saw them drive up in a car. They're knocking on the door."

Finch tried to think. He pictured the layout of her house. Where could she hide? "Okay. Don't answer. Is there a safe place you can go inside the house?"

"I'm in the bathroom. But it just has a crappy slide lock."

In the background, Finch heard the knocking at the door.

"Sheila, can you make it to the back door? If you can, do it now."

"Fuck. I don't know." She gulped down some air. "I'm scared."

"Okay, listen. Either stay where you are or run out the back door. But no matter what, *don't hang up.* Leave the phone on. Keep the call open. Even if you don't hear me talking, just leave it on. And keep it with you, okay?"

"Okay. Okay, I'm gonna run."

"Sheila, do you have the thumb drive?"

Finch heard nothing more than a harsh brushing sound, a long, abrasive *shhhhhusssh* as if someone had rubbed the cell phone mic against a patch of rough fabric.

# Chapter Twelve

SAN FRANCISCO — 4 MARCH, 2021

Sheila opened the bathroom lock and sprinted toward the kitchen. She ran through the back door onto the deck when she realized she was barefoot.

"Shit," she whispered and scanned the porch landing. There. A pair of Myfanwy's slides that she'd tossed next to the garbage pail. She kicked her feet into the toe webbing and saw she'd got it all backward. Right foot in the left shoe, left in the right. Damnit. Just to run to the fence, climb into the Dawson's yard, then switch them.

She clambered down the porch steps. But when she hit the concrete walk her right ankle twisted over her heel.

*"Fuucck!"*

She braced a hand on the rail post and managed to stand. She inched forward then stopped when a bolt of pain arced through her leg. She let out a broken whimper and flopped onto the bottom stair. *"Fffuuuucccck."* A strand of hair fell over her eyes as she tried to stand. She grasped the post again, hobbled forward then stopped in her tracks when she heard the gate latch click open. A moment later Joseph and Zena appeared, their faces alive—almost burning, she thought—with manic energy. But when they saw her nursing a foot, their frenzied expression shifted to an air of victory.

"Sheila, are you all right?"

The edge in Joseph's voice only heightened her fear. She stood there wounded, completely at their mercy. They all knew it. Her brief flight now ended in defeat.

"Ohh, looks like you fell," Zena added and stepped past Joseph. "Let me have a look." She crouched at Sheila's feet and tugged up the leg of her jeans. "Ouch. That could swell up unless we get some ice on it. Do you have ice in the house, Sheila?"

How many times has Zena ever spoken to you, she wondered. Three, maybe four brisk acknowledgments of her humble existence. Now her voice dripped with sympathy.

"Here, let's get you inside."

Without another word, Joseph braced her under his left arm and helped her stagger up the steps to the kitchen. He sat her in a chair at the breakfast table while Zena rummaged through the freezer, found an ice cube tray, smashed the bottom against the edge of the sink. Five or six cubes clattered into the basin. She gathered them in a dishrag, soaked the bundle under the tap, then sat beside Sheila.

"Gentle now." Zena gestured with her free hand. "Give me your leg."

Sheila gasped and raised her foot above the floor. Her leg

hurt like hell because of them—but here was Joseph and his wife helping her. Maybe she had everything wrong. Completely upside-down and backward.

Zena clutched the cuff of Sheila's right pant leg and eased her calf onto her knee and began to massage Sheila's skin below the tibia and fibula.

"That hurt?"

Sheila felt daggers shoot up her leg. She covered her mouth to block a cry of pain.

"Mmmm?" Zena worked her hand toward the knee and back toward the ankle. "Hmm? Any pain in your leg?"

"A little. Mostly my foot."

"Yeah?" She began to ice her ankle and the bottom of the Achilles tendon. "Okay, I can't feel anything broken in there."

"No?" Strangely she felt relieved. Maybe everything would be okay now.

Zena touched the tarsal bones in the heel and watched the pain ripple across Sheila's face. "But that hurts, huh?"

"Yes—*shit.*" She clenched her teeth. "Yeah. I'm sorry," she whimpered.

"No need to be sorry," Joseph sat in the chair beside her. They had her sandwiched between them. She could smell them. The aroma of sweat, adrenaline, suppressed lust.

"We'll just ice this for a while," Zena continued to slide the ice over the foot. "If it swells up, then we better get you to the hospital. Sound okay?"

She nodded. "So, why're you here? Like, just out of the blue," she added.

Joseph hesitated then tipped his chin toward his wife.

"Should I tell her?"

"Why not. In the end it won't matter."

He leaned back in the chair as if it provided a more distant perspective to assess Sheila's situation.

"The truth is, we've discovered that you've been one very busy little bitch."

Sheila felt her guts flushing. She clutched her arms around her belly and let out a gasp.

"Now, now," he cautioned her, "Don't start shitting yourself. You asked me, and so I will answer you. All right?"

She tried to concentrate on Zena's ice massage. Up and down, side to side. "Okay," she muttered over the pain.

"Did you think for one minute that I wouldn't discover that you'd hacked into my computer?" He paused to let his words sink in. "Did you know the computer camera recorded your face as you gleefully sat in front of the screen? That I captured every keystroke you typed into my machine. Hmm, did you know that?"

She shuddered. "No."

"Well you did one smart thing, which I still don't understand." He frowned, with a mystified look. "And before we speak another word, I want to know something. How did you find my password and login ID?"

"From the wall mirror." She pointed to the space above his shoulder. "Anyone could see you typing it in the mirror."

A look of surprise crossed his face. "The mirror." He let out a pish of air as if he'd fallen into a pawn's gambit and only now perceived how the trap had sprung.

"A simple solution from a simple girl." His frown shifted to

245

a mock smile. "Well, sadly, your treason has landed you in some hot water. Boiling hot. Once I realized what you'd done, I hacked your computer, too. Tit for tat. Did you know that it's possible to spy on someone using the camera on their own laptop?"

She stared at him in disbelief. So that's what he'd done.

"But I think it's even more invasive to hack somebody's cell phone and turn the mic into a recording device. Don't you agree?" He smiled at Zena, then turned back to Sheila. "That's how we overheard your gossip with your roommate, Myfanwy. Everything about me. And about Zena. About the SVR. And yes, about the Marburg virus."

He paused as if he had to assess how to continue.

"But once we heard about Myfanwy's plan to confess to Will Finch, then—*poof.*" He curled two fingers and his thumb into the shape of a pistol then clipped them together in a crisp *snap*. "Fortunately, Zena got to her first."

He studied her face to ensure she was absorbing everything so far.

"So we decided to let your worm squirm on the hook, so to speak. Up until today when we listened in on your meeting Will Finch. The second Joel Griffin. Brass Shoes." A weak chuckle escaped his lips. "Your *father* of all people!" Another laugh. "But when we heard your plan to give Finch a thumb drive. Well then"—he shook his head as if he'd allowed her to take one too many liberties—"then we knew we couldn't let you do that."

He stood up and drew a roll of duct tape and a Swiss Army knife from his jacket pocket. Sheila watched in horror as he unspooled a six-inch swatch and cut it. Before she could protest, he taped it across her mouth. Then he taped her wrists together and yanked her to her feet. When she stood, Zena noticed a bulge in her pants.

"Wait a sec." She stood up and pressed her hand against the zipper in Sheila's pants. "What's this?"

Zena unzipped the jeans, shoved her hand into Sheila's underpants, and tugged out a cell phone. "This must be the burner."

"Is it on?" Joseph asked.

Zena nodded, threw the phone to the floor, and crushed it under her boot heel.

"Where's her personal phone?"

"On the counter." She tipped her head toward the sink. "Leave it there. Otherwise, they'll track it."

When Sheila heard the cell snap into pieces, she tried to scream. As she squirmed to wriggle out of Joseph's grip, he drew back his fist and cuffed her across the face. It took two, three—then a heavy fourth blow to silence her. A final punch knocked her unconscious.

FINCH walked back into the living room and stood next to Wally.

"Something's come up. That was Sheila." He gazed out the window to the city below. He had to find a way to help her. He dug his own phone out of his back pocket. Within seconds he had Agent Keely's ear. As soon as she heard his voice she blurted out the news.

"You're right. About all of it. Joseph Tull is a contractor to the FBI. And his parents died on flight 655. Looks like—"

"Forget that for now," Finch interrupted. "They've got her on the run."

"Who?"

"Tull and Smirnov. Just listen. I've got an open line to Sheila Griffin's cell phone. From her house on Lyon Street. But she started to run. Have you got a way to track her?"

Finch could hear Keely talking to someone in the background. Saxx probably. After a moment she came back on the line.

"We can try to track it. But we need your phone to do it. Where are you?"

Finch gave her Wally's address on Russian Hill.

"Okay, Finch. Ten minutes. And don't hang up the phone."

Finch waited at the curb outside Wally's building. When an unmarked, 2018, smoke-gray, Dodge Charger pulled up to him he climbed into the back seat. Saxx was at the wheel. The car's siren was mute but a pair of interior dashboard lights flashed red and blue.

Keely turned to him. "Give me the phone."

"Be careful with the power button," he said. "The small one on the side."

"All right." She checked the number on the call display screen and noted it on a clipboard. "Got it. I'll call this number in. If we're lucky it will link to her phone."

She set the Samsung phone on the dashboard then dialed the regional FBI line. While Keely waited to talk to the FBI technician, the three of them sat in silence, the lights blinking blue and red, the car engine idling with the distinctive Charger growl. Saxx glanced at Finch through the rearview mirror. An air of discontent bubbled between them. When Keely finally spoke to the phone tech, she conveyed the cell number. It took another two minutes for him to identify Sheila's last location.

"122 Lyon Street," she said, the phone still pressed to her ear. "In The Haight."

"That's her house," Finch said. "She never made it out of there."

"Boot it, Saxx." She waved a hand toward the hill. "Her line just went dead."

Saxx cursed, then gunned the engine, pulled a U-turn, and steered the car toward Van Ness.

As they approached the traffic lights, he activated the siren and forced the Charger through the intersection. He rolled left on Geary and left again onto Stanyan. When they pulled up to Sheila's house, Keely unbuckled her seatbelt and swung around to Finch.

"You stay here."

She read the skepticism in his face. "I mean it, Finch. You get that?"

"Yeah, yeah. Of course."

He slumped against the upholstery and watched Saxx and Keely jog up the sidewalk and try the front door only to discover that it was locked. Then they scrambled down the steps and around the west side of the house to the backyard gate. The same gate Finch had entered when he stole into her home. Moments before he was busted by Saxx and Keely's team.

AS Keely approached the back deck and peered through the

door, she saw a shattered phone on the kitchen floor. "I guess this explains the dead phone."

"I guess."

"They could still be inside," Keely murmured and pulled her weapon from her shoulder holster.

Saxx nodded, drew his weapon, and tried the door handle. It clicked. "Doubt it would be unlocked if she's inside."

"Still, we gotta check," she said and nudged the door open with her foot.

They entered the house and Saxx kneeled over the shattered cell and took a picture of it. Then he drew an evidence bag from a pocket, scraped the pieces into the bag, and sealed it.

"Forget the phone," she said. "I'll take the left side. Meet you at the front door."

She swept through the kitchen pantry, the sunroom, then opened the door to the hall bathroom. Saxx moved to the opening that led to the dining room and living room. When he reached the front door, he turned and pointed his gun at the top of the staircase landing.

"Clear down here," he called.

"Saxx, take a look at this."

"What've you got?"

"She's in trouble." Keely stood in the hallway bathroom, a tidy two-piece with a sink and toilet. She pointed at the mirror above the washbasin. Two words—one above the other—were scrawled on the glass in pink lipstick.

*HELP*

*TULL*

"Tull's got her." She shook her head then added, "Finch

was right."

"Goddamnit," he muttered.

"Why didn't they shoot her right here?" A puzzled expression crossed her face. "They shot Myfanwy on the street. Why wait to kill Sheila?"

"Maybe they're saving it for something worse."

Keely studied his face a moment, unsure if his spite was directed at Sheila's abductors—or the fact that Finch proved to be correct.

"We have to put out a BOLO to the SFPD," she said.

"For what? *If* they can source Tull's car. Or hers. Who knows if they even have a car." He shrugged his shoulders with a scowl of defeat. They both understood they'd just taken a giant leap backward.

She could see his determination unraveling. "Hey. *Procedure*. First we call it in, then assess options."

"Yeah, yeah, yeah." He slammed his open hand against the wall and led the way through the back door and around the house to the Charger.

FINCH could barely contain his impatience while Keely called the regional FBI unit and they put together a Be On the Look Out order. He knew BOLOs could be effective when a criminal was on the run. But listening to Keely's patient efforts to work the bureaucracy felt like Chinese water torture. Drip, drip, drip.

"You're wasting time," he pleaded. "From the moment Sheila called me, it took us twenty minutes to drive over here."

"Shut up, Finch," Saxx muttered as he scanned an iPad, searching the vehicle registry for a connection to Tull. "Let us

251

handle this."

"Give them another twenty minutes," Finch countered, "and they'll be gone."

"I said stuff it."

Finch could feel the pulse throbbing in his temple. He forced himself to recline against the upholstery as he watched the two agents work through their separate protocols in the front seat. As Keely finished her consultations on the phone, Saxx's search sputtered to a halt.

"They share a joint motorcycle registration. A Honda CBR650R. But no cars linked to either of them." He turned to his partner. "What'd you get?"

"They're writing a BOLO based on the images from their drivers' licenses. The BOLO includes Sheila's pic. It'll go state-wide within the hour."

Finch leaned forward and rested his forearm on the back of Keely's seat. "Obviously they didn't walk Sheila down the street hand-in-hand. With no car, that means they likely stole a vehicle. Why not check SFPD for any thefts over the past day?"

Keely glanced at Saxx. "Worth a try," she said and made another call.

As she called in a stolen vehicle request, Finch turned to Saxx. "What about Sheila's phone?"

He shook his head. "One's destroyed. We left the second phone for the forensics team."

Finch took a minute to brainstorm the options. He looked at Saxx. "Let's think it through. Where could they take her in broad daylight?"

"Finch, I'm warning you." Saxx's voice slithered into a menacing hiss.

He ignored the threat. "One, their house on Shrader. Two, the Science Academy in the park." He notched his thumb in the direction of Golden Gate Park. "Three, the Drake Hotel."

Keely finished her call. "Three car thefts this morning. One over on Delmar Street. A blue, 2018 Chrysler 300."

"Jesus. That's less than a mile from Sheila's house." Saxx squeezed his hands on the car's steering wheel. "Better add that to the BOLO."

"Already done." She turned to Finch. "I didn't catch what you were saying. About the Drake."

"Let's play it from their side." Finch turned his hand in the air. "Look, say they've locked her in the trunk of the stolen Chrysler. Then where to? Their house on Shrader? The Science Academy where Sheila and Tull work? Maybe the Drake where they know all the ins and outs. Those are my best guesses. Name two more."

"The coast highway," Saxx said. "Just before Mendocino. They step out of the car and it rolls over a cliff. Maybe they've got their Honda stashed there. They hop on, drive home, shower off. Then drink a fifth of vodka." He let out a bleak chuckle.

"My guess? She's already dead. They shot her, same as Myfanwy," Keely said. "Then they wait until dark and dump her in a park. Someplace big, like the Presidio."

Finch nodded. "Okay. Both those ways, it's already game over. There's nothing we can do. But if it's Shrader Street, the Academy, or the Drake, we can go there right now. If she's still alive, we can save her."

"Shrader Street? No way. They're too smart for that. And the Drake's too far," Keely said, pondering the options. "If they want to put her down fast, then the Academy."

"Yeah, maybe." Saxx tipped his head toward the park with an easy shrug. "the Academy's like ten blocks away. Couldn't hurt to look."

Keely nodded. "Okay. Go."

Saxx fired the ignition, clicked on the siren and flashers. Six minutes later the Charger turned off Nancy Pelosi Drive and pulled into the service bay at the back of the California Academy of Sciences in Golden Gate Park.

"All right. End of the road, Finch." Saxx stepped out of the car and opened the rear door. "The rest is up to Keely and me."

"What?"

Keely stood beside the open door. "Thanks for your help, Finch, but Saxx's right. At this point, you're just a liability." She cranked her hand toward the curb. "Out."

Finch swore in contempt and stood next to the car. He watched the two agents jog across the sidewalk and around the north side to the front entrance. After they ran out of his view a new thought struck him. The burner phone that Sheila gave him at Pier 23. Keely had stowed it below the dashboard. No matter what happened next, the phone might prove useful to track his side of their communications. He reached into the front seat of the squad car and slipped it into his jacket pocket.

He shut the passenger door and walked across the service bay ramp toward the benches in the outdoor café. At times like this, he knew his best choice was to sit and think. Consider the variables, make a plan. He ambled over to the café entrance hoping to buy a cup of coffee. When he discovered the obvious —that it was locked down—he sat at a bench, wondering if he'd get used to the closure of all the public facilities in the city. The whole country felt like it was teetering on collapse. He zipped his jacket collar up to his chin and realized he had no way to find Sheila on his own. Everything depended on Saxx and Keely now.

He set his elbows on the table, wove his fingers together, rested his chin on his steepled hands, and gazed at the Rhododendron Garden on the other side of Martin Luther King Drive. Even in the mid-winter dusk, the waxy leaves of the shrubs radiated a sense of enduring life. On the right stood the Japanese Tea Garden. Years ago he'd explored the site with his five-year-old son Buddy. Buddy, dead for over seven years. Gone longer than the years the boy ever lived, Finch thought. He pressed his hands to his eyes as he recalled the adventures they enjoyed together. The kid had a knack for finding obscure hiding spots among the bamboo stands and exquisite dry rock beds. Those jaunts now felt like a lifetime ago. How could it all pass so quickly? Time had a way of churning life into a stream of fragmented memories. Eventually, the memories themselves slipped into an endless mist.

"Finch, they found the car."

His reverie broke as Keely and Saxx ran past him across the empty terrace toward their car.

"What?"

"SFPD just called in. The Chrysler 300," she added. "On Irving near Twenty-first."

Finch trailed behind them, then picked up his pace until he

matched them step for step.

Saxx jumped into the driver's seat. When he noticed Finch at the back door, he swung around. "Hey! I already told you. You're done, Finch."

He raised his arms and shook his head in disbelief. "Come on, Saxx. I'm the one who got you here."

Keely closed her door and glanced at him with a sympathetic shrug. "Uh-uh," she muttered as the car backed away, then turned toward the south side exit from the park.

# Chapter Thirteen

## THE ACADEMY OF SCIENCES — 4 MARCH, 2021

It took almost an hour for Sheila to regain consciousness from the blows to her head. Joseph and Zena had carried her from the stolen car into the storage chamber next to the exhibits preparation workshop in the deserted basement of the Academy. The "vault," as the staff called it, was a wide, windowless room containing scores of steel racks loaded with veterinarian supplies and supplements—provisions required to maintain the diet and health of thousands of creatures living in the building. Everything from the leafcutter ants to the monkeys and sharks had unique medical needs. All of them accounted for in the Academy database which Sheila, as the Academy's tech specialist, routinely monitored and updated.

As her eyes focused on the solitary light above the vault door, she gasped for air, then tried to steady her breathing. *Where are my shoes?* Her eyes swept across the floor looking for her shoes. The pain coursed through her foot and it all came back to her. She'd been beaten and abducted, then bound with tape to a steel chair in the far end of the vault. As she rolled her lower jaw she realized her mouth was sealed with duct tape. At least her legs were free. She kicked her right foot forward and nudged the post of the nearest storage rack. An excruciating arc of pain coursed from her ankle through her leg. She snorted a long draft of air through her nostrils. *Fuuuck.*

She straightened her spine. All right, *think,* she implored herself. You know where you are. The clock. Above the door, the digital clock ticked through another minute. 6:40. Which means the prep workshop is closed and the few maintenance staff still on site are already gone for the night. Any moment Joseph and Zena could return. Or not. Maybe they've abandoned you. In which case you can sit here until morning when someone opens the door. But more likely Joseph and Zena will return. They'd killed Myfanwy. Why would they spare you? Face facts. Today or tomorrow they will kill you, too. *You have to save yourself.*

She struggled to free her hands. Taped separately to the steel frame at the back of the chair, her wrists twisted against the duct tape. The tape gave a little, but not enough for her to pull free. Then she sensed a tiny metal burr on the metal frame. She turned her right arm and felt the sharp point press against her flesh. *Maybe.* As she rubbed her wrist against the abrasion her eyes focused on the veterinarian supplies on the shelf next to her knee. She knew the entire inventory. Medications, analgesics, syringes, sutures. *The scalpels.* There they were. Number 10, 11, 12 blades. And next to them an array of scalpel blade handles. She felt the pain shoot up her leg again. She let out a yelp and ground her teeth together. Use it. Use the pain to fight. She rubbed her wrist against the burr in a taut see-saw motion. Her skin began to burn from the heat. Then she felt the abrasion nick the band of tape. She worked her wrist harder. Faster. Then it cut through.

She lifted her hand and tore the swatch of tape halfway across her mouth—just far enough to draw a breath.

"Oh my God," she wheezed. "Please, please help me."

Now what? She knew when Joseph and Zena returned, the storage room door would swing open and she'd be at their mercy. She'd have to fight. With her left hand still bound to the chair, she stood on her good foot, leaned forward, and braced herself on the stock shelf. A drizzle of blood seeped along her forearm where the burr had grazed her skin. She adjusted her weight and with her free hand grabbed a number 12 blade and a scalpel handle.

She sat on the chair again, unwrapped the blade and handle, then assembled them with her teeth and fingers. She shoved the wrappers into her jeans pocket and carefully slipped the scalpel under her right thigh. With the weapon tucked away she felt prepared. Just in case, she told herself. In case they come through the vault door before she freed her left hand from the chair.

A wave of ambivalence washed through her. Why wait? In ten seconds she could cut the duct tape from her left hand and hide in the labyrinth of ceiling-high racks. She could make her way to the vault door, swing it open into the workshop, and run through the exit that opened onto the service bay. Then she felt her right ankle throb with a dull, heavy ache. Not broken, she assured herself, just badly sprained. She stood and tested her weight on the injured foot. A flash of pain forced her to sit down. Could she hobble across the parking lot? Then cross the road to the Japanese Tea Garden? Before the pandemic struck, she'd watched children scramble through the pathways and trails. Playing hide and seek in the warren of shelters and hideaways. Maybe she could make it that far. She knew a way through the fencing that surrounded the garden. The south gate.

She checked the wall clock. 7:10. *Damn it, girl,* make a decision. She nodded to herself and took the scalpel in her hand and leaned across her belly to cut the duct tape on her left hand. Then she heard the taut *click-clack*—the sound of the vault deadbolt turning in the lock cylinder. Before the door swung open, she pressed the duct tape over her mouth again. Next, she adjusted the blade under her buttock so it sat next to her right hand—as if it were still bound to the chair. Her breath came in short bursts as the panic compressed her lungs.

Zena walked through the door followed by Joseph. She paused while her eyes adjusted to the dim light. "It's okay. She's still on the chair."

"You sure?" He held the door ajar with one hand.

"See for yourself," she said and then asked, "You ditch the car?"

"Like we planned. On Irving Street." He tipped his head toward the far wall. "That was smart to park the Honda there first."

Sheila studied her captors as the light from the exhibit prep room cast their shadows across the floor toward her. They stood about fifty feet away. Could they see her face? Somehow read her plan to escape?

Joseph paused to assess the situation. "Okay. I doubt anyone's still in the building, but just in case, I'll take the service stairs up to my office. Then grab my laptop and some files we need to take to Moscow. Shouldn't take more than fifteen minutes."

Zena glanced at the clock. "I'll get her ready."

Sheila's heart jumped. *Ready for what?*

"You know where I stored the vials?"

"Yes." Zena glared at him. "Just go."

"All right." He nodded to himself as if to confirm their plans. "In a week all our contacts in White Sphere will have the virus."

"I still can't believe you thought of it." Zena couldn't suppress a grin. "Using Marburg to infect everyone in White Sphere. That, Comrade—*that's* pure genius. Now you'll have Vitvinin's full support."

She wrapped an arm around his waist. "Then back to Moscow."

"Yeah. Finally."

When the vault door swung shut behind Joseph, Zena tested the handle to ensure it was locked.

Zena held a coffee cup in one hand, took a sip as she stood next to the rack of shelves. As she approached Sheila her pace slowed as if she had to gauge some unknown danger ahead.

"Ahh. I see you're awake." Zena frowned. Perhaps she felt a wisp of empathy for her victim. The shimmer of guilt the executioner feels for the condemned woman as she mounts the scaffold. "At least your eyes are open." She sipped at her coffee, lost in her thoughts.

"Did you enjoy the drive over here in the trunk of the car?"

Sheila kept her head locked in place. Her entire body broke out in a sweat. She clutched the scalpel in her fingers, worried that it might slip from her hand to the floor.

"No need to answer that." Zena let out a light chuckle and gestured to the duct tape sealing her mouth. "I wouldn't be able to make out a word, would I?"

Her relaxed posture, the coffee—all of it suggested a casual chat in a trendy café. "You know, I had no idea the Academy coffee machines were working during the pandemic. They even make a decent latté. Who knew?" she said with a chuckle.

She stood two paces away from Sheila and gazed at her. She saw the sweating mass of flesh with a swollen welt on the face where Joseph had punched her. Her hair, a nest of knotted curls.

"When I look at you, I wonder what it's like to go through life with those scars on your face." She braced one hand on her hips. "I feel for you. I do. What man could want you? Believe me, I've had challenges of my own. Things you Americans could never believe. But men? I've had all I want and more. Dozens and dozens. I can't remember half their names."

She set her cup on a shelf and rolled up her left sleeve. "I'm marked too. But I *chose* my own markings."

Sheila glanced at the tattoo. *My Life, My Fate.*

"I have chosen everything in my life. My name. My fate." Her lips curled into a look of triumph. "Even how I will die. I know *how*—and I will pick the time. But you simply wait for the end, don't you? What do you think this is?" She waved a hand above her head. "You think your life is a TV sitcom? A Disney movie? Fuck! You're like everyone else. Terrified by their own shadows. Like your father. Someone told him to get a vaccine. And like a good boy, he does just as he's told. Next thing you know, he chokes to death."

Zena shook her head with an expression of pity. Of disbelief that anyone could let life pass by without seizing it in both hands. "Well, as it turns out, your death will be much different than your father's. You will be remembered."

Zena took another sip of coffee, turned away, and began to search the shelf housing the vials of injectable drugs. She reached behind a row of glass cylinders and extracted a glass vessel sealed with an opaque plastic top. An unlabelled medication that Sheila didn't recognize. Joseph had stored the vial where it could sit for weeks unnoticed. If it were discovered by chance, no one would question it. No one could link it to the revered Dr. Tull.

Next Zena selected a three-milliliter syringe and needle. She discarded the plastic needle cover and fixed the needle hub to the syringe.

"We both know what this is, don't we." She shook the vial between a thumb and forefinger. "No need to explain this to you. You have the good fortune to be the first person—patient zero—to begin our human trial of the modified Marburg Virus Disease. After you hacked his computer, Joseph wanted to bless you with this special honor." She smiled, amused somehow. "I'm sure the media will come up with a memorable name for you. The new Typhoid Mary."

She set the syringe and needle aside and paused to enjoy a

last sip of coffee, then parked the cup on a shelf. Now her expression took on a more serious look.

"It's important that you understand how you fit into our plans. You are about to become an asymptomatic carrier of a DNA-targeted variant of Marburg Virus disease. What does that mean? It means you won't suffer from Marburg, but you will pass it along to people with a DNA profile that causes heterochromia. Do you know what that is?"

She studied the glazed look on Sheila's face.

"No? It's when people's eyes have two different colored irises. About one percent of the population. Unfortunately, those people will be stricken with Marburg. And because of the variance we generated, it spreads by breath—aspirants—not touch. The good news is that those with heterochromia will not suffer for more than a few days. A week at most. The bad news? They *will* suffer. But wait. There is more good news. And that's where you come in, Sheila."

She examined Sheila with a hopeful expression as if she might be able to guess the pending good news. When Zena saw no sign that Sheila had followed her monologue, she continued.

"You will have a choice to make. You can go straight to your tormentors in the FBI and tell them you're a Marburg carrier. They will interview you, investigate you, test you. And much more, I'm sure. But by then, you will already have infected them. And they too will become asymptomatic Marburg carriers. And all their friends and family. Their colleagues. Unless they have heterochromia. In which case, sadly, they will perish."

She pouted to acknowledge what a shame that would be.

"On the other hand, you could run. Infecting everyone as you go. But within a few months, the CDC will understand the nature of the new pandemic. They will trace the illness to you and hunt you down. In which case, you will be reviled.

"So. It's decision time. Do you want to be remembered as a heroine? Or as the most hated figure since Adolf Hitler? It all depends on your choices."

Now Zena inserted the needle into the vial and studied the suction of the syringe as she drew the plunger through the barrel. Satisfied that the shot was duly prepared, she leaned against the steel shelving post opposite Sheila's free hand.

"This part will be almost painless. A short prick, then it's over." A sadistic smile crossed her lips.

All the muscles in Sheila's body grew rigid. Her breath now came in staggered puffs through her nostrils. Then she noticed the look of surprise on Zena's face.

"Say, what's that now?" Zena leaned forward to examine the track of blood on Sheila's forearm. A look of mock sympathy crossed her face. "Oooh. Did you cut yourself?"

She lowered her head to inspect the cut. Her eyes squinted as she drew next to Sheila's shoulder.

Sheila didn't wait. She drove the scalpel into Zena's left cheek and ripped the blade down toward her mouth and out through her lips. The shock sent them both into a frenzy. Zena dropped the syringe and clasped a hand to her face. She let out a cry of surprise, then a scream. She fell to the floor and slumped against the shelving racks. She screamed again as she examined the blood dripping through her fingers. She swung one hand out to snatch Sheila's leg. When Zena grappled for the injured ankle, Sheila sprung into action. She cut the duct tape from her left hand and leaped up from the chair. The sudden motion set her off balance and she tumbled onto Zena. It took two, three, four twists until Sheila tugged herself free from Zena's grasp and pulled herself upright along a stanchion. She gasped through her nose and ripped the tape from her mouth.

"You fucking bitch," she cried and stepped out of Zena's reach. As she prepared to cut another slice through Zena's face, she hesitated. *No. Just run.*

She braced a hand on a shelf and hobbled toward the vault door. Step-hop-step-hop. Her gait began to stabilize as she reached the door. She knew she needed to prepare for the worst. If Joseph entered the storage room now, her escape would end in disaster. She held the scalpel in her right hand, a dagger ready to plunge into his throat. She cracked open the door an inch and peered into the empty exhibit preparation room. No one. She hobbled forward and tried to find her bearings.

She leaned against a workbench and scanned the room. *There.* Near the south wall, on a table where an intern had constructed the giraffe exhibit. Like everything else, the pandemic had terminated the project. But on top of the counter lay a plastic front leg ready to attach to one of the baby giraffes. Sheila staggered across the room and fixed the fat end of the giraffe leg under her right armpit. Awkward, but better than nothing, she told herself. The makeshift crutch relieved the pressure on her foot as she made her way toward the EXIT sign above the service door.

Behind her, the corridor door swung open. She turned to see Joseph crossing the floor toward the vault. "What the fuck?" he yelled, his face swelling with confusion.

"Where's Zena?"

*"Fucking dying!"* she screamed.

He stood ten feet from the vault. Another fifty feet from Sheila. He had a choice to make. On an impulse he ran through the vault door to Zena.

Sheila gasped as the pain lit up her ankle. She turned at the waist and banged her hips against the crash bar that unlocked the steel case door. It didn't budge. She slammed into it again and the gate sprung open. One more step and she stood outside on the service bay pavement.

AS the service door burst open Finch turned toward the café garden. Twenty feet beyond the nearest table Sheila braced herself, one hand clinging to the door frame. She stood upright, teetering as she struggled to find her balance. Then her hand released the steel frame. The pneumatic piston exhaled a tight puff as the door automatically closed behind her. She took a tentative step forward.

"Sheila?"

As she limped along, Finch tried to make out what was pitching her forward. She held a long, curved brace clamped between her armpit and one foot. Where were her shoes?

"Finch." She waved her free hand and then doubled her pace along the asphalt toward him.

As she approached he saw the heavy bruise on her face. A black eye swollen above the acne scars on her cheek. The trickle of blood oozing from her wrist. Worst of all was the pain that wracked her body with every step she took.

He jogged toward her and slipped an arm behind her shoulders and snugged her against his chest. "My God. They did this to you?"

She wrapped her arm around his neck and began to sob. When the fear caught in her throat, she pushed herself away. "They're going to kill me."

Finch glanced at the service door.

"We've got to run," she said. "They're coming after me." She waved a hand toward the Tea Garden.

"Wait a sec." He tightened his grip across her shoulders as he tried to think.

"No! They're going to kill me. I know everything. *Everything!*"

When Finch saw the terror in her eyes he believed her. He thought of Myfanwy. She'd had no time to anticipate her fate. But Sheila knew everything. Joseph Tull, Zena Smirnov, White Sphere, The Orange Man. She held the key to it all. Above all else, he had to protect her.

"All right." He held up a hand to try to ease her panic. He tugged his phone from his courier bag. "Let me call Saxx and Keely."

"No! Look, *I cut her face.* She's going to fuckin' kill me!" Her eyes raged with anger and she wheeled away from him.

"Where're you going?"

"The Tea Garden."

With the crutch braced under her arm, she hobbled over the parched lawn toward the road. As he watched her scramble barefoot from the grass onto the sidewalk he rang Keely. Three, four rings, then his call bounced into her voicemail.

"Keely, I've got Sheila with me. We're on the run. Heading to the Japanese Tea Garden. Tull and Smirnov are on us." He paused, unsure what to say next. "Just fucking get here."


JOSEPH grabbed a box of gauze from a shelf and squatted next to Zena on the concrete floor. He wound a long strip around his palm, bunched it in his fingers, and pressed it against the open wound in her face.

*"Blyad'. Eto bol'no,"* she yelped.

"Just breathe," he whispered above her ear. "Breathe into the pain."

*"Ya sobirayus' ubit' yeye!"*

"Yes. Don't worry." He caressed her hair. "We'll kill her together. You and me together. But first I need to look at this. Okay? I'm just going to lift my hand and take a look."

She let out a gasp as he lifted the wad of gauze from her face. He took a moment to study the cut and had to glance away. When she saw the dread in his eyes she swore again.

"Just breathe into the pain, Zena. You know how to do it. Find the pain in your mind and breathe through it."

When she settled, he examined the gash, gently probing the tear with his forefinger.

"Not as bad as it looks. At the top of your cheek the cut is superficial." He tried to deflect the lie with a soothing smile. The wound was serious and they both knew it. "The open cut is just an inch into your lip." He applied the gauze to her cheek again. "I can tape this up. Here, hold the compress in place. If we can stop the bleeding, you probably won't need any stitches."

She pressed the gauze to her face and stared at the ceiling as he shuffled through the veterinarian supplies. She squeezed her tongue against the inside of her cheek and felt the warm blood ooze from her face into her throat. To distract herself she spun an image through her mind. *Cutting Sheila's face to ribbons.* Letting *her* weep with the pain. Then, to demonstrate her mercy, she'd shoot her in the forehead. One shot. Done like all the others.

After a moment he sat beside her again and lifted the back of her neck onto his lap. As he gazed into her face, their eyes locked together.

"You're going to be fine." He tore open a box of steri-strips and selected four, one-inch strips. Then he tugged on a pair of latex gloves, broke the seal on a bottle of disinfectant and pressed a cotton swab to the bottle opening, tipped it upside down until the swab was saturated.

"My face is going to be scarred."

"Doctors can fix that. They do it every day." He brushed the swab along the length of the cut.

She gasped as the disinfectant leached into her skin.

"Shhh. Stop. That's the worst of it. Over now." He tore open the paper wrapper on a steri-strip and peeled off the adhesive backing. "Lift your hand away. I'm going to start at the top of your cheek and work down to the corner of your lip."

He applied the first strip, then another. He daubed away the blood as he applied four strips in even rows along the gash. When he finished, he examined his handy work and let out an uneven sigh. "It's a clean cut. No infection." Then he washed a new disinfectant swab up and down her cheek and waited until he could see the blood begin to clot.

"You're good," he whispered and kissed the top of her forehead. "Can you sit up?"

"I think so." She pressed her weight onto her elbows and leaned against his chest.

"Stand?"

"Yeah. Help me."

He held onto a shelving stanchion to lever himself upright. He extended his arm to her. "Grab hold."

She took his hand, stood for a moment, leaning her hips against a shelf until she felt stable. She traced a finger up the ladder of bandages on her cheek. "Joseph, I have to see what this looks like."

He pointed to the EXIT sign. "There's a small mirror on the wall beside the door."

She grabbed her bag and he wrapped an arm around her waist and steered her along the aisle. When they reached the mirror she pulled away from him and stood gazing at her image.

He could see her dread transforming into an obsession. "Are you all right?"

"Nyet."

"Don't start fixating."

"I'm *not* fixating." She held up a hand as if she had to block herself from screaming.

"Okay. Stay here while I grab everything from the shelves."

He walked back to the chair and picked up the serum and

syringe. He collected the remaining nine vials of the Marburg virus—along with the precious antiviral vaccine. Then slowly, carefully, he sealed them in an impervious inner pocket in his shoulder bag.

When he returned to Zena he asked, "Did you get a chance to inject her?"

Her face blanched. With the gash on her face and the taut frown, she revealed her defeat.

"Doesn't matter. After we're done today, we'll send the virus to our friends. Like we planned. Nothing changes."

*Our friends.* White Sphere, she thought. Soon they would all be carriers. She took a few seconds to assess their situation. Joseph was right. She had to pull herself together, find Sheila, and be done with her. She shuffled through her bag, placed her Ruger LC-9 on the top of her wallet and cell phone then pulled the zipper tight.

"All right. You know where she went?"

"The one place she knows like her own face. The tea garden. Before the lockdown, she went to the garden for lunch at least once a week."

Her teeth locked together. He could see her face harden with the determination he'd witnessed so many times before. She was ready. More than.

"Do you have your gun?" she asked.

He ran a hand over the breast pocket of his jacket. "Yes."

"Good. Now we kill her."


AGENTS Saxx and Keely could only observe as two uniformed cops from the San Francisco Police Department began to search the abandoned Chrysler 300. Car theft fell within the SFPD's jurisdiction. Kidnapping, on the other hand, would promptly dump the case into the hands of the FBI. The legal niceties inspired a brief confrontation.

"The vehicle was used in a kidnapping," Saxx argued.

"Not until you prove someone was actually kidnapped," the SFPD officer replied. "Until then, this is a matter of theft. Probably a joy-rider. One of ten we get every day."

"Okay, okay. Pop the trunk," Keely implored them and led the way to the back of the car.

When the trunk lid sprung open all four leaned in to inspect the liner.

The light from the senior SFPD officer's flashlight swept the interior. He stood up and shook his head at Keely. "Sorry, but this stays on SFPD turf."

"All right," Keely conceded, "I'll update Regional," She pulled her cell phone from her belt. Then she noticed the message icon blipping on the top of her screen. She tapped it, pressed the phone to her ear, and heard Finch's message. She stepped over to Saxx and pulled him aside.

"Finch called."

"Again?" At the mention of Finch's name, Saxx's hands curled into fists.

"Says he's found Sheila. That Tull and Smirnov are on them."

"What?"

She played the voice message on the speaker.

*"Keely, I've got Sheila with me. We're on the run. Heading to the Japanese Tea Garden. Tull and Smirnov are on us ... Just*

*fucking get here."*

"Come on." Keely jogged back to the Dodge Charger. "They're in the tea garden."

"Goddamnit!" Saxx took a moment to regain his composure, then sat at the driver's wheel. "This is my last showdown with that a-hole. You get that?"

"Yeah, yeah. I get it." She buckled her seat belt and made a U-turn motion with her hand. "Flashers on. Let's go. I'll call for backup."

# CHAPTER FOURTEEN

JAPANESE TEA GARDEN — 4 MARCH, 2021

The skeleton crew that managed the security of the Japanese Tea Garden ran a final check of the five-acre site at 4:45 p.m. The two entrance gates were inspected at 5:00 and the manager posted his daily report at 5:15. After he left the garden he double-checked the front gate lock, walked over to the bus loop, and hopped on the line 28 bus for the ride back to his apartment in Chinatown.

When Finch caught up with Sheila, he saw that access to the garden was blocked by a ten-foot-high barrier that surrounded the property. "Locked up tight," he said as he looked for a breach in the wall.

Sheila gasped as she clung to his waist. She discarded the plastic giraffe leg, braced herself under his arm, and clasped the back of Finch's belt with her hand. "At the South Gate there's a turnstile exit. Just past the cherry trees. You can't see it from here."

"It's not locked?"

"Yeah, but there's a keypad lock. I know the combination."

"You do?" He turned his head to study her face. On her cheek the purple bruise had expanded into the bulb of her nose.

"Yeah." She adjusted her weight against his chest. "At least I used to."

He heard a doubtful tone in her voice. If she was wrong, it wouldn't take long for Tull and Smirnov to catch up with them.

Finch snugged his arm around her waist and steered her to the left. He guessed they'd spent five minutes crossing the road from the Academy. It might take another five to get to the turnstile and enter the garden. They turned right past the line of cherry trees and hobbled another fifty feet to the turnstile. The three wings of the wicket were mounted on a steel spindle. Each wing comprised ten parallel bars. The top bar rose a foot above Finch's head. Sheila nudged him to the right of the turnstile. She let go of his belt and leaned against a post obscured by a bamboo screen, and rested her hand on top of a punch-button keypad.

The keypad was well hidden. Finch watched as she tapped her fingers aimlessly against the buttons.

"Just let me think a minute," she whispered.

Finch gazed back toward the corner. No sign of Tull and Smirnov.

She punched in a sequence of six keys and waited for the sound of the gate mechanism to unlock. Nothing.

"No. No, no, that's not it," she admonished herself. "It's six, seven, *two*, nine, nine, two."

She punched the buttons with deliberate forefinger jabs.

When they heard the heavy thunk of the lock release she let out a yelp. "That's it!" She smiled, her face a dazed mix of bruises and joy.

"All right. Let's go." Finch steered her into the first yoke in the turnstile and followed her in the second. When they stepped onto the path inside the garden he pulled her against his side again. "How do we lock it?"

"It's automatic. Sixty seconds." She smiled again.

"Let's wait. Just to be sure."

As they stood together in silence, Finch felt her fingers weave around his hand. "Thank you," she murmured, then leaned closer and kissed the flap of his leather collar. He drew a breath, unsure how to respond. When the lock clicked shut he slipped his hand away and tested the turnstile wing. It didn't move.

"I haven't been in the garden for at least ten years." His voice caught in his throat as he recalled the memories with his son. "I used to play hide-n-seek here."

"Yeah? There's a good place to hide with boulders and shrubs. At the far end." She pointed past the top of the Temple Gate which rose above the pine trees on the left of their path.

"You mean the dry landscape garden."

"That's it."

"Okay, hold onto my belt. Let's go."

The labyrinth of garden paths was designed to inspire a walking meditation. No matter which turns you took, a new moment of peace awaited the attentive mind. Most of the sculpted trails led to a water feature. A murmuring brook, a lily pond crossed by a series of wood bridges or stepping stones, a pool full of spooling koi fish, a reedy cove with nesting birds. All of it evoked a dream of perfected nature. Wilderness tamed by the human hand—the human hand itself a perfectly evolved tool of nature.

But all that felt like a mere fantasy now as Finch guided Sheila along the trail to the Temple Gate which stood high atop wooden pillars where it faced the magnificent five-story Pagoda. Both were marvels of Zen craftsmanship: ornate, balanced, almost whimsical in their reverence for tradition. Against the trees and ponds, their colors radiated through the landscape. Salmon red, cloud white, and a teal blue—with gold highlights adorning the ornamental features.

Sheila leaned against one of the pillars supporting the gate while she caught her breath. As he waited Finch glanced at the wafers of clouds thinning overhead. The evening dusk had slipped away to darkness. To the east, a half-moon climbed above the city. Above and to their right, Venus floated in the heavens, a solitary speck of light. Soon the night air would skin the grass and foliage with frost.

He glanced at her feet. They looked raw and cold. "You all right?"

She ignored the question. "We go left," she said when she regained her composure. "Past the big lantern."

As they passed the narrow trail that led off to the lantern sculpture, he realized that her balance had improved. She still leaned against his chest but she no longer clutched his belt.

"There's a way to climb behind the back. We won't have to cross the gravel." She took his hand again and led him toward the boundary fence.

Smart not to tread along the dry gravel bed, he thought. And not just because of her bare feet. A single footprint would betray their hiding place on the combed pebbles that flowed from the two boulders toward a stand of maple trees on their right. Perhaps they would be safe here. At least they could rest.

After they squeezed behind the rocks, they sat under the high branches of a leafy shrub and stretched their legs toward the fence. Finch was sure this was the same place that Buddy loved to hide when they played together. He tried to think. Six, maybe seven weeks after his last visit here his son died in the car wreck. When Bethany had smashed his car into the concrete abutment in her drunken stupor.

He shook off his stupor. *Focus,* he murmured to himself. He pulled his phone from his jacket and dialed Keely again.

This time she answered on the first ring. "Finch?"

Before he could reply, they heard a sharp bang ring out from the far side of the garden.

"What was that?" Sheila held a hand to her mouth to muffle a cry.

Finch shook his head, uncertain. Two more shots split the air.

"It's them." Sheila's chest started to quake with fear. "Fuck. *It's them, isn't it?"*

"Finch, Where are you?" Keely's voice was insistent.

"The back of the Tea Garden. Behind the boulder in the Dry Landscape Garden. They've started shooting," he warned her. "You're going to need backup."

BY the time Joseph Tull and Zena Smirnov reached the main

gate of the Japanese Tea Garden, Zena's wound began to seep. A trickle of blood oozed down her jaw and dotted her jacket collar as she punched arbitrary codes into the gate keypad.

"Let me see that." Joseph held her jaw in his fingers and tipped her chin toward the street lamp. A fleck of blood fell onto his wrist. "The steri-strips aren't perfect. When we're done we'll ride the Honda over to Bolshov's place."

"You think I need a doctor?"

"Maybe." Another lie to dismiss her concern. "Just to take a look at you."

*"Blyad,"* she swore and slapped her palm against the gate. "Do you know the code?"

He studied the push-button lock, then entered a four-digit code. "No."

She watched his fingers as he continued to stab aimlessly at the buttons. "Then how the hell do we get inside?"

He held up an arm as if he could block her rants. "Zena, let me think."

He walked back to the curb to examine the long wall that barricaded the garden. While he pondered the possibilities, Zena pulled her pistol from her purse and fired a bullet into the latch.

"Zena! Don't be insane!"

She rammed her shoulder against the door. When it failed to open, she fired two more rounds into the bolt. A whiff of smoke leached from two smoldering holes in the shattered lock. She pushed it open and wiped a streak of blood from her chin. "Let's go," she said over her shoulder and stepped into the garden.

He caught up to her and spun her around by her shoulder. "This is madness. It's like you just launched a police flare into the sky. You don't think the cops won't—"

She yanked his hand from her shoulder. "We are going to kill her!" Her eyes were on fire. "Like those two Chicanos downtown. One shot and it's over. *Done.*"

He could see the madness twisting her face. Impossible to tame.

"Come with me now. Or not. *If not, then we are done.* Either way, she dies!" She jabbed her hand forward, her pistol pointing to the path on the left. She paused, then set off alone.

AFTER the sounds of the three pistol shots traveled across the gardens, it didn't take long for the background hum of the city to dampen the shockwaves in the air. But the unwavering urban static did nothing to soothe Sheila's rising anxiety. Moments later, uncontrollable shivering began to quake through her legs and up through her chest.

"I c-can't s-s-stop shaking," she stuttered and cinched both arms across her chest.

Finch wrapped an arm around her shoulders. "We're okay, Sheila." He knew they were well hidden, but as they sat against the base of the boulder, he realized that Sheila's nerve could break.

"Just breathe," he whispered. "Saxx and Keely know exactly where we are. They'll get here before Tull and Smirnov."

She nodded. Then her teeth started to chatter.

"Sheila, listen to me." He cupped her chin with his fingers. "If you don't stop, they'll hear you. Do you understand?"

She nodded again, but her body continued to tremble.

"Take a breath. I want you to feel your breath rising from your belly, through your heart, through your throat, and out your nose. Now do it with me." He pressed his hand to her belly, then let it hover over her chest and throat. "Now breathe out through your nose." He released an audible sigh. "Can you feel that?"

"Yes."

"Okay, let's do it again. Together." He pressed his hand to her belly, then repeated the sequence. They paused and exhaled in unison. "Okay, now that's all we're going to do until the FBI get here. Just breathe. Nothing else. Okay?"

She nodded.

"Say it."

"Ok-kay."

They continued the pattern of harmonic breathing for four or five minutes. Until they heard Zena's voice shatter the silence.

"*Sheila Griffin.* I'm coming for you!"

Sheila's eyes flew open and she let out a horrible scream. "*Whhhaaa!*" She clamped a hand over her lips and slapped her belly with the other. Her neck twisted from side to side as if she couldn't believe her stupidity.

Finch stared at her, unsure what to say. He'd witnessed the same reaction in Iraq. A replacement, nineteen or twenty years old, just flown in from the States, screaming in panic when the enemy AK-47s began to erupt. A boy so unnerved that he jumped up and ran blindly into the line of fire, shooting his weapon sporadically into the air.

"Sheila." He touched her forearm. Her eyes were disengaged, completely unfocused. He realized that he had a choice. He could stay with her until her cries brought the Russians to them, or he could try to distract them. Since they didn't know he was in the garden, with luck he could take them by surprise.

"Sheila, I want you to stay here." He waved a hand in front of her eyes. Her constant shaking made it impossible to acknowledge him. "Stay here and keep breathing. I'm going to draw their attention away."

No response.

"Do you understand?"

Her shoulders rolled and fell in mute reply. The best she could do.

He squeezed her forearm again. "Don't worry, I'll come back."

He slipped between the fence and the boulders and stood a moment to scan the ground. Two feet ahead lay two smooth stones the size of his fist. He stuffed the rocks into his jacket pockets and inched toward the path. He paused again to listen to the various sounds of the night. The splash of traffic washing over the garden from the Presidio Bypass, the steady 60-cycle buzz of electricity. He pushed all that into the background and tuned his ears for the slip of footfalls treading along the pathways. Nothing.

Where next? Somewhere nearby. Close enough to draw the Russians away if they approached the boulders. Somewhere that provided a line of sight to all three paths leading to Sheila. In the gray light he saw a tall ornamental lantern to his left. He took a step forward, listening to his Nikes squeeze along the path.

*"Sheila! You are going to die!"*

Finch turned his head to the right. They weren't too close. Not yet, he told himself. Maybe they were down near the massive Buddha statue. Feeling reassured, he stepped past the lantern statue, over a low bamboo barrier and stood in the middle of a tight cluster of three maple trees. He pressed his chest behind the thickest tree trunk and looked along the path —the trail called Maple Lane—then turned his head back toward the Dry Landscape Garden. A perfect line of sight coming and going. Yes, this would do.

*"Sheila!"*

He felt certain Zena was approaching them from the Buddha. Trying to draw her victim out. And now she did.

*"Aaaahhh!"* Sheila's cry broke through the trees.

Certain as he was of Zena's hunting tactics, he was equally sure that Sheila had lost all composure. Once it begins to pump through your blood, the combination of fear and adrenaline can fuse in a deadly brew. He pulled the stones from his pocket and waited. Maybe it was better that Sheila lured the Russian toward him. Yes, if she approached from behind the cluster of maple trees, he'd wait for her to pass, then lunge at her. Three steps to the barrier, one step over, one more to his target. With luck, he could strike her head before she turned on him.

JOSEPH stood at the open gate to the Japanese Tea Garden knowing he had a choice to make. One, follow Zena into the garden to ensure Sheila was killed—and risk arrest by the FBI. Or two, abandon Zena now and immediately distribute the virus through White Sphere's network where it would infect everyone who touched the vials. If Sheila survived, her collusion with the FBI might disrupt White Sphere before he could deliver the fatal blow. But if killing her provided just one more day for him to attack—and succeed—the Kremlin would vindicate him.

But now he saw another option. A middle path. If he could quickly eliminate Sheila then flee the garden with the vials in his shoulder bag, then a delay of ten minutes might be acceptable. He listened to the wail of police sirens. Were they coming for him? In the heart of the city, they sounded an ever-changing alarm. Especially during the pandemic with its fitful cries for help.

All right. Go now, or not at all, he told himself. Every second of delay multiplies the risk. He drew his pistol from the shoulder holster and stepped onto the path leading past the ticket booth. Which way? *Guess.* He walked below the Drum Bridge and crossed the stepping stones over the main pond. When he reached the Long Bridge he paused to consider his next move. He mounted the bridge and stood midway along the open span, placed his hand on the rail, and stared into the gray evening air. He could see the moon and above it, Venus. After a moment he heard Zena calling out.

*"Sheila! I'm coming for you!"*

A feeling of despair washed through his belly. Zena's madness in full flight. Where would it land them? He flexed his fingers on the pistol grip and crossed the bridge.

*"Sheila!"*

The call of her voice led him past the Pagoda. Then he

heard Sheila's long, unbroken cry.

*"Aaahhhhhh!"*

He knew the desperation in her voice would trigger Zena's thirst for revenge. He could picture her salivating at the scent of the woman's fear.

Now he needed to run.

SAXX drove the Dodge Charger over the curb and parked in front of the main gate to the Tea Garden. As he stepped onto the asphalt he noticed that the gate stood ajar.

"It's open."

When they reached the barrier Keely brushed her hand over the damaged lock. "Looks like it took three shots."

"Jesus." He shook his head, his mouth tight with anxiety. "This's getting real."

"Real as it gets."

They both drew their service pistols. Now Saxx hesitated. "Should we wait for backup?"

"Are you serious?" She pointed to the broken lock with her gun. "Protocol, Saxx. We go in now. They follow."

"Yeah. I just wish Finch wasn't such a mutt."

Keely shrugged off the complaint and stepped through the gate. She led the way forward and paused to study the garden map near the ticket box office.

"You know where they are?"

"At the far end." Her hand traced a route to the Dry Landscape Garden. "We go left up to the pagoda."

She set the pace in a steady jog past the Drum Bridge and over the stepping stones to the Temple Gate. When they reached the Pagoda, they saw a sign pointing to two trails. Both led to the Dry Landscape Garden.

"Left or right?" Saxx asked.

Before she could reply, Zena's voice cut through the air.

*"Sheila. I'll make it better for you if you come out now."*

They traded a look, then heard Sheila's mournful reply.

"No, no. *Please don't hurt me. I'm coming out!"*

Keely pointed her gun muzzle to the path on the right. "Take the left," she whispered, "Maybe we can create a pincher."

Saxx nodded and watched Keely jog toward the sound of the shouting. He paused long enough to see her disappear into the shadows. Long enough to let his doubts swim through his mind. Finch, Finch, Finch. Somewhere ahead, Finch waited for him. The man had become a monster. But if Finch died, every-thing he'd discovered about Saxx's crimes would be revealed. Finch had ensnared him in a leg-hold trap. He couldn't win. Not tonight. Above all—more important than rescuing Sheila Griffin—he had to ensure that Finch survived. He moved through the shadows along the left trail. After a few steps, he broke into a heavy jog.

STANDING in the center of the tight triangle formed by the three maple trees, Finch could see the boulders where Sheila hid under the shrubs. To his left he spotted Zena coming to-ward him, her pistol clutched in both hands, elbows bent, her posture upright as her feet swept forward. Finch had to admire her training. Confident, prepared, covert. She could match any of the Seal team fighters he'd seen in Iraq.

As she closed in for the kill, Zena continued to call into the cool breathless air. *"Sheila! I'm coming for you!"*

Finch pressed his torso against the trunk of the heavy maple. When Zena crossed his line of vision he saw the slash in her cheek. The wound was patched together with four steri-strips—one of them torn loose, hanging by a thread. A drizzle of blood splattered onto the collar of her denim jacket. As she paused to press her sleeve to her cheek, her pistol tilted in the air. A break in her concentration. Now she moved past Finch's screen in the trees and anchored her feet on the path. She stood about ten paces past Finch and leveled her weapon at the boulders at the far end of the trail—another fifty feet ahead.

*"Sheila. I'll make it better for you if you come out now."*

Finch noticed a shadow appear on the track that came in from the Pagoda. Who? He narrowed his eyes. In the dim light he spotted the patch of flaming hair. Joseph Tull. For the first time since he'd heard of the criminal mastermind, he recognized the Orange Man. Tull took another step forward and signaled Zena. She tipped her gun toward the twin boulders. He nodded and held up a hand, a gesture to hold fast.

Then Finch saw the shrubs behind the rocks shake as Sheila called out again.

*"Please don't hurt me. I'm coming out!"*

"Then come out where I can see you." The urgency in Zena's voice tapered off. The little fish was hooked and swimming into the net. Zena adjusted her stance. All she needed now was patience and a gentle touch.

Sheila hobbled onto the trail. Her hands swept up in front of her chest to ward off the pending blow. Finch was too far away to see the tears streaming down her face. Did she see Zena's pistol aimed at her head? Or Joseph Tull, one foot on the trail, one hand gripping a pistol, the other waving Zena to back off.

"Wait, Zena," he called. "Not here. Not now. We go back to the plan."

*"Blya net!"* she cried. "Both here *and* now!"

Sheila fell to her knees, pleading hysterically. "Please, please, please!"

"I said, *no.*" Tull took a step into the middle of the path, blocking Zena's line of fire. "No noise!"

"All right. Then we do it this way. Maybe is better."

Finch watched as Zena's left hand pulled a barber's razor from her jacket pocket. She pressed her thumb against the tang and a three-inch blade locked into place. Razor in one hand, pistol in the other, she walked toward Sheila.

Now, Finch whispered to himself. *Now.* He stepped out of his cover, measuring the distance to Zena as he crept forward. She and Tull stood side by side, too far away for Finch to strike her directly. He set his feet and pitched the first stone at her head. The rock struck between her shoulder blades.

*"Blya!"* She staggered forward, then turned. When she saw Finch she swung her pistol around and fired two wild shots in his direction.

Finch dropped to the ground and scrambled back to the protection of the trees. He held the second rock in his left hand. He hid behind the tree trunk and drew a breath. He knew she would come for him as soon as she killed Sheila.

*"Blya!"* she called again and pivoted back toward Sheila.

Finch nosed his head around the tree trunk. The blow from the rock left Zena teetering from one foot to the other. Stunned, she dropped the barber's razor at her feet. The wound in her cheek was now broken open. A stream of blood coursed down her throat. Tull clamped his hand to Zena's shoulder to hold her steady.

"Drop your weapons!"

Keely's voice.

Finch rose to his knees and peered around the tree. Keely stepped onto the trail then jogged forward from the boulders and positioned herself beside Sheila. Keely leveled her weapon at Zena. At the same moment, Saxx appeared on the narrow trail on the left. His gun at the ready, he began to shout.

"Drop your guns. On your knees. Guns down! On your knees!"

Joseph and Zena held their ground. From the maple tree Finch could see them adjusting their posture. They stood poised, ready. Sheila, still on her knees, whimpered in soft, quiet jags. Beside her, Keely aimed her weapon at one of the Russians. Then Saxx stepped forward to stand no more than ten feet from Keely. Finch watched Joseph Tull and Zena shift again—one aimed at Keely, one at Saxx.

"Guns down!" Saxx repeated and pointed the barrel of his pistol to the trail.

"No. We're walking out of here," Tull countered. "We all walk—*all of us*—and everyone lives. Including the girl."

"I've got Zena," Keely said, her voice dead calm.

"I said *guns down*." Saxx's voice hardened.

"Fuck you. *Amerikans.*" Zena spat out the words. "You

think we are afraid to die?"

Saxx's hand began to tremble. "Look." His voice faltered. "Both of you down on the fuckin' g-ground."

The break in his nerve triggered Zena. She fired two rounds. One knocked Sheila backward, the second flew wide to the right.

Then an explosion of pistol shots erupted. Saxx fired three rounds into Joseph Tull's chest. He fell onto his back and his head smacked against the ground with a heavy thud.

Zena dropped to one knee, raised her pistol, and fired two shots at Saxx. Both penetrated his skull and knocked him into a shrub. Her face torn and bloody, Zena seemed poised for the inevitable. But when Keely hesitated, Zena tried to steady her hand and fired a round past Keely that flashed off the far boulder with a loud whine. Inflamed—*incensed*—Keely fired four, fast shots. *Crack-crack-crack-crack.*

Every bullet struck the Russian in her chest. Zena Smirnov slumped backward and fell dead across the garden path.

# CHAPTER FIFTEEN

EPILOGUE — 11 MARCH, 2021

When Sheila Griffin appeared at the front door of her house on Lyon Street, Finch felt surprised by her appearance. Despite the pair of crutches and the fading bruise on her eye, she radiated a sense of life. A faint smile expressed her gratitude for his help.

"Thanks for picking me up," she said and stepped onto the front porch. A blue medical mask dangled from one hand. "There's no way I could get over to the funeral on my own."

"No problem, Sheila." He returned her smile. "And don't worry about the mask. I'm okay without it if you are." He pointed to his gaiter gathered under his chin. "Besides, it's a graveside service, we won't need to wear them at the cemetery, either."

She nodded and took a tentative step forward.

"So how's the shoulder?" he asked.

She locked the door and slipped her crutches under her

armpits. "The bullet never hit the bone. Just nicked the top of my left deltoid. Took two stitches to sew me up. It's fine now, but it stung like hell when she shot me."

Finch tipped his head to one side and pointed to the missing lobule of his ear. "I know what you mean. I lost the soft part of my ear five or six years ago. I still remember it like yesterday."

"Huh." She studied his ear as if it might be a museum artifact.

"So what's the verdict on your ankle?"

He backed up as she took a step toward the staircase. Just in case she lost her balance and he needed to brace her.

"A broken tarsal. It's called a Lisfranc's fracture."

"Lisfranc's fracture," he repeated. "So how long do you wear the cast?"

"Four weeks. Hopefully. But could be six."

He watched her struggle to the steps and grasp the railing. "How 'bout I carry those sticks down the steps for you."

She passed him one of the crutches and kept the other to steady herself. When she reached the sidewalk, she wedged both under her arms again and followed him to his RAV4. After she'd settled in, he sat at the steering wheel and paused before he turned the ignition.

"Listen, Sheila. After what we went through I need to be honest with you. The FBI didn't want me to talk to you. And I know they debriefed you after they spoke to me."

She shifted her torso so she could face him. "Yeah. They questioned me for two days while I was in the hospital. Told me the same thing."

"I'm sure they did. But look … we spent that night in the

293

garden." He waved a hand as if he were sweeping away a cobweb. How to ask her what he needed to know? He believed they now shared an unbreakable bond. Maybe she did, too. Their reward for surviving together. "I've got some questions. And you're the only person who can answer them."

"Maybe." She glanced away. "Maybe not."

He had to accept her reticence. The last thing he needed now was to trigger a bout of PTSD.

"Not about you. About Joseph and Zena. About what they *had.*" He studied her face. Now that he was closer to her he noticed the bruise under her eye was still ripe. Nonetheless, he couldn't let his sense of compassion stop him from questioning her. "I mean about what they were planning with White Sphere."

"That's exactly what the feds *don't* want me to talk about. They don't want anyone to know."

He let his hands drop from the steering wheel into his lap. She needed to realize that they weren't going anywhere until she answered him. Just wait for her, he told himself. Don't say another word until she speaks on her own good time.

She hissed and shook her head. "What?"

He gazed into her eyes. Wondered how long it would take.

"I'm not a fool. You're a reporter and we both know what that means." Her lips pressed together as if she had to button them up. "Okay. So if I tell you *anything* I want you to promise to keep it off the record until the feds make it public."

This was all he needed. He could prepare the story before the FBI press conference. At some point, they'd make their investigation public. Could be months, maybe years. Eventually, the day would come and he'd be first to break the news.

"Yes. You have my word. I promise."

She gazed through the windshield, studied the house next to her own home. "Did you know that Janis Joplin once lived next door to my place?"

"Janis Joplin?"

Gabe Finkleman had disclosed that weeks ago. But Finch knew that if he feigned ignorance, she'd be more likely to tell the story in her way.

"Yeah. When she first moved into The Haight in the sixties. 122 Lyon Street. The Summer of Love." She shook her head and let out a dreary breath of air. Perhaps she felt she'd been born into the wrong era. Too late to dance under the stars with the hippies next door, blissful smiles on their lips, hands waving merrily to the universe.

"Before my time," he said. "But yeah, back in her day, Joplin was the queen of the scene." He smiled at the spontaneous rhyme.

"And now she's gone." She turned back to Finch. "But everyone remembers her, right? Because she *went* for it. She just got on stage and screamed out loud."

Finch blinked. Where was Sheila going with this?

"Look. *People have to remember this, too.*"

Now he understood. "You're right. They need the truth. That's why I have to get the facts straight."

"But I have your word? You won't print anything until the FBI makes it public."

"Sheila, you're my protected source. You have my word, and the legal protection that goes with it." He looked into her eyes, held a hand to his heart. "But no matter what, I need to record this."

Another hesitation. "Yeah, I guess you do." Then a nod. "Okay."

Finch took out his phone, clicked the record icon, and set the phone on the dashboard. "So first things first. Did Joseph and Zena distribute the Marburg virus to their network in White Sphere?"

"I think they ran out of time." Sheila took a moment to gather her thoughts. "Zena was going to inject me with it in the vault. She had it right there." She held up one hand to suggest the needle about to jab into her arm, then shook her head as if she still couldn't believe her battle with Zena. "But like … it didn't happen."

Finch nodded. Now that she'd started to talk, he didn't want to interrupt.

"Just before that, she said the synthetic virus targeted a specific DNA molecule. It zeroes in on people with genetic heterochromia. She said they'd tested it on animals. Most likely, dogs, since there're enough dogs in the Bay Area with heterochromia to mount a statistically reliable test."

She paused to consider Finch's reaction. He tipped his head to one side—a gesture of encouragement—and waited for her to continue.

"Since I got out of the hospital, I've been on the internet researching the increase in local dog abductions. Compared to other urban areas in California, the 67% jump in regional dognapping here can't be explained by the overall spike in pet ownership credited to the pandemic lockdown. You know, loners like me"—she let out a terse laugh—"in need of a new best friend."

Good. Finally, she was thinking straight, he thought. And she possessed the self-discipline to work for hours on some pretty esoteric research. Obviously, she'd made a substantial recovery since the Russians attacked her.

"All right," he said. "Second question. Who did the lab work, Sheila? Was Zena capable of this on her own?"

"Agent Keely let it slip. The FBI is tracking them down. Them and the members of White Sphere."

"You think they have that? Their names?"

She nodded. "Hundreds of them. It's all in the files. It had everything. And I mean *everything.*" She turned to him with an ironic grin on her face. "On the thumb drive I was supposed to give you."

Finch recalled their aborted rendezvous. She'd promised to meet him at Pier 23 at seven p.m. Perhaps if they'd met on schedule, her foot wouldn't be in a cast. Her deltoid, unharmed. Perhaps Agent Jeremey Saxx would still be alive, his funeral postponed for two or three decades.

"So what happened to the thumb drive?"

"The FBI took it. Keely and maybe a dozen other agents. They took the thumb drive, my computer, and phone. Even my Kindle reader."

He offered a sympathetic look. "Once they download everything, they should return it."

"You think so?"

He wasn't so sure, but why belabor the point.

"Let's get back to the lab work. Did Zena do the microbiology alone?"

"Maybe it was her idea. But the lab tech was another Stanford PhD. Everyone called him Psycho Rats. His real name is Spiro Ratzman."

"Spiro Ratzman." Finch rolled his lips between his teeth. He now had enough information to break the story the minute the feds started their press conference. He also knew the press conference would only occur after they collared Ratzman *and* seized all of the re-engineered Marburg virus supply. The FBI would close the game with a double play—when they could make a two-for-one announcement. Their triumph would be tainted, however, by the sacrifice of Agent Saxx.

As he digested the dimensions of the conspiracy, Finch envisioned the headlines rolling out day after day. The stories he'd write in sequence.

*America Saved from 'Unthinkable' Attack*
*Domestic Terrorists Arrested*
*Store of Bioweapons Secured*
*Terrorist Org—White Sphere—Under Investigation*
*White Sphere Led by Married Russian Spies*

After a moment, he turned back to her.

"When it comes out, Sheila, you'll need to be ready. For the courts, the press. Everything," he said.

"I know. I've thought about that. Maybe you can help me figure it out."

He saw this new anxiety etch a narrow crease under her mouth.

"Don't worry. I'll be there for you."

She fluttered a hand in the air, then let it settle in her lap. What could she do? Nothing but wait for the storm to pass.

"All right. You ready to meet Agent Saxx's widow?"

She shrugged. "I have to. He saved my life, Will. Without him, I'd be dead."

You and me, both, he thought. But he wouldn't admit it. Not yet. Maybe never.

He turned the key and when the engine started, he eased his car onto the road and drove toward the Presidio.

FINCH steered his car along Lincoln Boulevard and turned left onto Sheridan Avenue. When he reached the Fisher Loop, he found a parking spot about fifty yards from the Presidio Chapel.

He turned to Sheila. Her face was solemn, almost inanimate. No telling what she was thinking now. "Can you walk from here?"

"Yeah. Of course." She forced a laugh. "After walking barefoot from the Academy all the way through the Japanese gardens? Ha! Ha! This is a piece of cake."

Even if her laughter was forced, he was pleased to hear it.

"Which reminds me. How did you know the combination to the tea garden gate?"

"From a friend who worked there."

"Myfanwy?"

"No. Someone from the before times."

Finch sensed her remorse. Like everyone, she now divided her life into two parts. Before and after the pandemic. He wondered if the friend was a man or woman. None of your business, he told himself and decided not to ask.

"Let me get the door." He stepped onto the asphalt and walked to the passenger side of his car. The air was clear and fresh. Two isolated clouds floated high above the Golden Gate Bridge. A light breeze, fragrant with a hint of impending spring, rippled over the lawn of the San Francisco National Cemetery. Perfect weather for an outdoor memorial.

"Let me grab your crutches." He tugged them from the footwell in the back seat. "Here."

As he watched her fit the crutches under her arms, he could see her struggle. She let out a curse and limped along beside him toward the chapel.

To their right thousands of white, marble gravestones rose across the manicured grounds in perfect ranks and files. The cemetery, reserved exclusively for military veterans, command-ed pride of place in one corner of the Presidio Park. In 1776 the Presidio had been fortified by the Spanish to guard the passage into San Francisco Bay. Now a 1480-acre national park, it had been transformed from a wilderness outpost to a public play-ground.

An honor guard comprised of five men in formal military dress stood at attention outside the chapel door. Between them and a polished oak coffin sitting on a casket roller, stood Ellen Saxx and her son, Frank—their arms wrapped around their waists, shoring one another up. Beside them, a chaplain and the chapel manager swayed from foot to foot, offering whispers of comfort to the bereaved—all of them waiting with an air of restlessness. Arrayed on the nearby lawn, a phalanx of at least two hundred police and FBI agents gathered opposite the coffin and the mourning party. Most wore dress uniforms, crisply pressed for the ceremony. The solemnity of the occasion was further muted by the black masks covering their faces.

"Quite a farewell," Finch whispered to Sheila. About twenty feet away he spotted Agent Sandra Keely. He nudged Sheila's arm and led the way. "Let's head over there."

As the service began, Finch and Sheila stood together five or six paces behind the assembly. The ceremony followed a prescribed order of events. An introduction by the chaplain, his sober reading of the Twenty Third Psalm, a wreath laid upon the coffin by the FBI Director, roses set in place by Mrs. Saxx and her son, as they leaned together arm-in-arm. A formal farewell was recited by Captain Willard Mazza from the U.S. Army Corps of Engineers. Then a moving eulogy was spoken by the head of the regional FBI office, Special Agent in Charge, Desmond Simms.

According to Simms, Saxx had entered the FBI following five years' military service in Germany. While his name would soon be added to the Wall of Honor in FBI Headquarters in Washington, "he wanted to be buried next to his brothers in arms, here in his home town."

When he concluded his speech, Captain Mazza signaled the honor guard, a message relayed to a line of seven soldiers arrayed on the hill. They raised their rifles and each man fired three rounds in quick succession. Saxx's final hurrah—a twenty-one gun salute. No matter how many times he heard the final shots echoing in the air, the shock always caught Finch by surprise. A book slammed shut in mid-sentence.

It took several minutes for the funeral party to break ranks and dissolve into the less formal round of condolences. Groups of two and three approached Saxx's wife and son to shake their hands and whisper words of sympathy. Sheila stirred at Finch's side then took a step toward the coffin. "Coming with me?"

"Yeah. Of course." He glanced at Sandra Keely and waved a hand at Sheila. "No, wait a sec. You go ahead. I'll meet you there in a few minutes."

A puzzled look crossed Sheila's face. She shrugged and limped toward the coffin.

When Keely saw Finch approach she took a step toward him and drew her mask under her chin. He wondered how she'd dealt with the shootout in the tea garden. Killing Joseph Tull and Zena Smirnov. Losing Saxx. Whatever her reactions, none was apparent in her face.

"I'm almost surprised to see you here."

"Sheila called me and asked for a ride." He tipped his head toward her as she shuffled across the lawn. "She wanted to express her thanks for Saxx saving her life."

"You think she'll be okay?"

"Hard to tell. She's one of the walking wounded." A frown turned on his lips. "But yeah, she's going to be okay."

Keely's eyes narrowed. "And did you two ... talk?"

He glanced over her shoulder. The soldiers who'd fired the twenty-one gun salute were marching toward the chapel in line, rifles braced on their shoulders.

"Don't worry, we know the rules." Not the answer she wanted, but the only one he was willing to give her. "Look, have you got five minutes?"

She coughed up a skeptical chuckle. "If it's got anything to do with Tull or Smirnov or White Sphere—then, no—I don't. You're off the case, Finch. We'll let you know what we know at the press conference. Not before."

As she turned to leave, Finch took a step past her.

"It's about Saxx," he said. "About the fraud he used to manipulate me." He scanned her face to see if this triggered any apprehension.

"Fraud? What are you talking about?"

"The brass. And the note. Remember the note he sent me?"

A look of confusion crossed her face. Her expression made him wonder, was she in on it, too?

"It said, 'Play the game, or you'll end the same.' "

"Of course I remember that. But what are you talking about?"

"He sent it. Saxx. It was his play to entrap me. That, and your threat to arrest me on charges related to South Dakota. That's what you used to lure me into the meeting at the Drake."

"Saxx?" Her confusion now turned into anger. "You're sick, Finch. On a day like this"—her hand swung around to point at Saxx's coffin being wheeled into the back of a hearse —"you want to raise some BS about fraud? Really? You need help. Seriously."

She turned away again. Finch pulled a flash drive from his pocket and stepped in front of her once more.

"It's all here." He held the drive between his thumb and forefinger. "Take it. Saxx's DNA and his fingerprints. All certified by a notarized forensic expert. Don't worry, I've covered enough forensic documentation in court to know it'll withstand any defense arguments from the FBI."

She stood motionless, her eyes fixed on the thumb drive. "Am I implicated in this?"

"Well … you were his partner." He shrugged his shoulders. "My guess is you'll be investigated. Maybe tarnished."

Her head notched backward as if he'd spat at her. She recovered her composure and pulled the cuffs of her jacket sleeves to her wrists. "What exactly do you want, Finch?"

"Considering the burden of evidence, not very much."

"What exactly?"

"A truce."

"A truce?" Her cheeks fluttered as she expelled a light hiss. "What kind of truce?"

"I won't reveal what's on this drive. In exchange, you'll ensure the FBI never brings charges against me for what happened in South Dakota."

He could see her mulling the offer over, the tip of her tongue shifting from side to side between her lips. "How do I know it's worth it?"

"Take the thumb drive, Keely. In five minutes you'll realize this is more damaging than your worst nightmare."

He held up the drive again and she took it in her hand, examined it briefly, and slipped it into her jacket pocket. Then she turned away and began to walk toward the chapel.

"Call me when you decide," he said as she continued across the lawn.

When she didn't reply, Finch watched the attendant close the back of the hearse, open the driver's door and take the wheel. The engine coughed a puff of exhaust from the tailpipe.

Then Saxx was driven up the hill to take his place among the thousands of fallen soldiers.

"HELLO."

"Finch?"

One word and he recognized her voice. The call he'd been waiting for. "Agent Keely. Good to hear from you."

"I thought you might have the phone."

The accusation made him smile. He knew the missing burner phone would force her to call him. "Right. I guess I do."

"It's evidence, Finch. You know that."

"Good thing I hung onto it."

"No more games, Finch." She let out a wheeze of exasperation. "I want it today."

"Okay, but I'm not coming down to your office again. Brings back bad memories."

She hesitated then said, "All right."

He imagined her considering two or three options.

"How about that café you like in North Beach. Caffe Trieste. Say, three o'clock."

"Sure. I can do that."

"Don't be late, Finch."

He didn't appreciate the tone in her voice and decided to turn it back on her.

"Don't *you* be late."

FINCH sat at one of the tables outside the Caffe Trieste nursing a double espresso. Just as he checked his watch for the third time, he saw her round the corner on Columbus Avenue. A purse hung from her right shoulder and she carried an N95 mask in her hand. When she sat in the chair next to him he put on a smile.

"If we sit outside, we won't need these," she said and tucked her mask in a pocket. She glanced across the empty road. "Sorry, I'm late."

"Well, my guess is it's not because of traffic. More likely the White Sphere investigation is running hot twenty-four-seven."

She blinked as if she had to shuffle off another sleepless night. Finally, she turned to look directly at him. "Not gonna say you're wrong."

"As I said before, anything I can do to help, you let me know."

She shook her head. "You can start by giving me the burner phone. You bring it?"

"I did."

She reached inside her purse for an evidence bag and Finch slipped the phone into the clear plastic container. She closed the zip seal with a look of gratitude.

"I'm not breaking any protocols in telling you that securing this phone is the best thing I've done all week."

Her gaunt expression revealed that she now felt the full impact of killing Zena Smirnov. He knew there was no way to predict how long the effects might linger. Days, months, a lifetime? Sometimes it depended on the emotions attached to a shooting. Guilt and remorse could lead to an agent's resigna-tion—even a change of career. A sense of triumph could gener-ate the opposite effect. Rededication to the job. Promotions.

Rank. In Keely's case, Finch couldn't hazard a guess.

"That bad a week is it?"

"You have no idea."

He glanced up the length of the Vallejo Street hill. Where it all began. Where Myfanwy drew her last breath.

"You want a coffee?"

She held her fingertips to her forehead as if she had to block a migraine. "One too many already."

"All right." He waited a moment, knowing he had to get down to business. "So when're the feds going public with this?"

"After the CIA clears it." She pulled her upper lip between her teeth as she considered what lay ahead. "Then Homeland Security and the NSA. Then the Secretary of State. Maybe the day before the president reams out the Russians live on CNN."

Finch scratched at his beard. He'd been growing it out since the pandemic started but cropped it to a taut, half-inch trim. At moments like this, it provided a good distraction.

"You have a chance to look at the thumb drive?"

She turned and studied his face, gazed at him for an uncomfortable length of time. Despite the pressure on her, maybe because of it, she could still dig deep and grasp her unwavering determination. Maybe she'd rise above killing Zena, after all.

When he couldn't tolerate the silence he pressed her. "Well, did you?"

"Yeah, I did. It looks pretty damaging for Saxx." She ticked a finger against the tabletop. "I'm still not sure how it affects me."

"You know there'd be an investigation. That's a given. As

his partner, you'd be questioned. What did you know? When did you know it? And rest assured, they'd question me very closely."

"Yes. They would," she whispered.

"But only if it gets out."

Her eyes narrowed. "So what *exactly* do you want from me?"

"The more important question, Sandra—even though Saxx is dead and gone—is this. Can he still drag you under with him?"

"He knew about this. That you had the thumb drive?"

"He knew. We met outside City Hall. I showed him what I had."

"And?"

"He was hooped and he knew it. We made a deal. If he blocked any charges against me related to South Dakota, the thumb drive would never see the light of day."

"And you want the same thing from me."

He nodded.

She mulled this over, knowing any loose threads could easily entangle her. "What else? There had to be more to it."

"We kept it simple." He paused. "Except that—"

"Except *what?*"

"That if I die—or my wife or my daughter dies—from unnatural causes, my lawyer releases the files. Everything comes out. It's still like that."

"You're joking." She hesitated, unable to fathom her partner's motivation. *"What the—what was he thinking?"*

"Probably about climbing the FBI ladder. If he busted

White Sphere early in the game it'd give him leverage."

"I guess. Maybe." But she sounded doubtful. She now realized that Saxx lived a double life of some kind. That she never really knew the man, her partner for the past four years.

"All right. All right, Finch." Another pause. "Look. How do I know I can trust you?"

He'd anticipated this question. "You can't. But I'm risking something, too. If I break the story about Saxx, then somebody in the Bureau could come after me about South Dakota. Maybe you," he added.

"You can bet on it." Her voice hardened. "That same day." Like Saxx, she could be unforgiving.

He waited for her to continue.

"Look, if you want a deal with me, first you have to revoke the death clause. No way I let this thing go public when you die."

A reasonable request, he thought. An easy concession to secure her agreement. "Consider it done. I'll call my lawyer this afternoon."

"Look, don't insult me, Finch," she said. "You think I trust you based on your word alone? I want to see the retraction clause in writing. Signed by you and the lawyer."

"I'll personally deliver a notarized copy to you tomorrow."

A knot of silence tugged at the dead air between them. He could see her trying to bottle up the anger in her face, especially in her mouth. No matter how hard a man fell for her good looks, she'd be an angry lover. He waited another moment for the heat to cool then decided to cut through the tension.

"Let's get back to basics. I'm not here to insult you. Quite the opposite. I'll protect you if you protect me. All we do is keep our mouths shut. Both of us."

He could see her calculating the options. Considering the points and counterpoints. He knew she understood that his plan provided a way to safeguard herself from Saxx's bent schemes. She expelled another heavy sigh. He'd been counting them. Five times since she sat down beside him.

"All right, damn it." Her voice was now soft. "No one talks. But first, you give me the retraction letter from the lawyer."

"Like I said. You'll have it tomorrow."

"Okay then. So, deal?"

"If you're sure that's what you want."

Her lower jaw clicked to one side as if she had to release a muscle cramp. "What? So now you won't take *yes* for an answer? Damnit, Finch, you're impossible."

She continued to glare at him as her jaw now shifted to the other side. *"Yes, that's what I want."*

He needed to hear her say it like that. Begging him. He knew he'd never get an apology from the feds—no commendation for his role in bringing down White Sphere. No remorse for endangering him and his family. And thank God, no mention of his thousand-dollar consulting fee. That was blood money. Filth. Given all the options, hearing Keely begging him was the next best thing. The only reward he'd get.

"All right, Agent Keely." He suppressed a smile. No need to gloat. "Yes. We have a deal."

**FIRE EYES**


Read D.F. Bailey's first stand-alone thriller, **FIRE EYES**
a W.H. Smith First Novel Award finalist.


Born by chance.
Fueled by madness.
Ignited by love

CHAPTER ONE

The bomb went off a little after one in the morning. It was a beautiful thing. There was blues and greens and thick yellows that blended in with the smoke to make it all look like mustard gas in some World War I movie. And the sound of it was much louder than I thought. I guess it could have been the noise alone that brought the cops. But the look of it—the colors—they were much more than I hoped for. Damn it, they were *beautiful*.

But what happened to Renee, that's something else. It was the last thing I expected. She tried to make everything so casual, carrying the bomb the way she did under her arm. First she spins around and smiles like there's no care to the world and moves up the sidewalk in her dream of ballet. She points her toe to the ground once, twice—then, as she turns on one foot, the bomb explodes and breaks the night into a thousand smoking greens and yellows and reds, with a huge blast like a rocket burst echoing off the walls of the mountains. And then it's all over before you can really see it and in the end she's worse than dead because the bomb blew everything apart. There's a crater gutted into the sidewalk and suddenly all the lights in the First City Electric building black out. A minute later there's a flicker of light in the windows and then the power surges back to life. Only the front door has any sign of damage, two windows shattered from their steel frames. And along the sidewalk, halfway up from the road, her handkerchief rests where it fell. Except for that, there's nothing left at all. Not even the baby.

Yes, *she's* the one that didn't come back. I remember her saying it would be like a war, and in a war there's always some that don't come home. I always thought she was talking about me. Specially when I put the bomb together in the lab.

"No, no," I tell her, "I'll be careful. I always tamp real careful when I'm making these things."

Making the bomb is when the Power comes into my mind. That's when the danger is worst. So I tamp the guts of it down into the shell with cotton balls. Cotton's best because it keeps the moisture of my fingers away from everything so none of the electrics can short out. And it's soft enough so I can build the most dangerous parts in a gentle way.

"Just be sure," she says and backs to the corner of the room near the mattress. She thinks she can dive under it if anything triggers accidental. She doesn't know that if something triggers she'd be dead before she could even *see* it.

"I am," I tell her, "just don't even breathe." I can hear her footsteps backing to the mattress. It's the kind of noise that gives me the Power. Everyone else backing off and there I am doing the impossible. Nobody else can touch it but me.

"Steady out your fingers," she says.

"Just quit your talking." Any interruption's like poison. Finally I tamp the last of the explosives into the canister and seal the shell off with a waterproof cap. That way I can leave it outside in a pinch and if rain comes there's no problem. Just wait her out till I'm ready. And I can either set it automatic or by remote. Hell, the remote's a dream these days. Some even do it with one of those garage closers. I heard of one guy who's triggering them with remote-control TV channel changers. That's a tough one to believe. But can't you see it? Parking a block down the road and just waiting till the cops come, then click it to channel 13 and *WHAM!*—they're goners.

But there wasn't a remote on Renee's. I should've put one in but it was her fault, because she wanted it timed for thirty-three-and-a-third minutes. Just like a record, she says. That's rule one. Never allow no one else in the lab. But she was a forceful one. She'd come in anytime she pleased and stick around and seldom do as I told her. You've got to admire that in a way, because most of these modern women's bitches are just hot air and no bras. Not Renee, though, she'd stick it out to the end whether there was shit in the hole or not.

That's why she took the shell instead of me. That and the fact she could pass the security check. It's the one thing they gave her for working there three years: a little plastic badge with her picture on one corner that pins to her shirt so they don't stick a knife in her guts just for walking in the front door after hours.

We drove there together and had the banger rolled in flannel blankets in the back seat. We even borrowed one of those baby harnesses that lock into the seat belts. If the cops stopped us then it'd look like some baby sleeping on the way home. Even cops wouldn't disturb no baby.

"Roll it up nice and easy," I tell her when we're setting out.

"It's so cute," she says, "what'll we call him?"

"Nothing. And you shouldn't fix yourself on the idea of having a kid." But to keep her happy I add on a new touch. "Or we could call it Billy Junior, if you really want to."

She starts laughing like this is the joke-of-the-week. "When you name it after yourself it shows you're egotistical."

"Nothing wrong with a little pride," I tell her as she pulls the blanket right over the baby's head so he can sleep like a newborn kitten.

We drive to the electricity offices in the Camaro. It takes about an hour and a half altogether, when you add in the time for the stop at the 7-Eleven and then the half-hour stop we made when she started crying. At least that's how it began. After that I think she went a little crazy on me. She was looking up at the stars and her whole face was wet from the tears and then she tried to explain everything between us. It's the kind of thing you don't want to dwell on. People will stop trusting you if you talk about the truth. Especially when you lay everything out person to person.

Anyway, we just about forget the bomb, it looks so much like a baby and the music blasting out of the radio is such a lure away from what we're really doing. When we get to the building she grabs it up very softly, just like a kid, under the ass and around the belly. I sit back and watch her go up the sidewalk. She starts to dance a little, like she's got one of those Fifties songs in her head, and pretends to be dancing at the prom. Christ, how ridiculous. Then a handkerchief slips from her pocket and drifts to the ground. She turns around without noticing it and pulls the baby to her chest and shows me how she's breast-feeding the newborn like a good mother should do. For a second I even think about being that little baby and sucking on the mother-nipple and how good it's got to taste.

She strides up the walk and does a little ballet turn. But it's no place to play ballerina, so I get out of the car and whisper up to her as loud as I dare.

"Stop that assin' around, Renee. Just drop the baby off and stop that jerk-off stuff."

She smiles that devilish smile she uses when she knows she's gone one step farther than I ever would. It's like a contest between us. Sometimes we'll try to out-chicken the other. When someone finally backs off, it shows where all the nerves really are. The winner gets to leer it into the loser and it's a big deal until the next time comes. Then it's really up to the loser. He's gotta *shine*.

But with this baby there shouldn't be no goof-assing. I've seen guys lose anything from their fingers to their life in one sudden flash. It'd be so quick you'd blink to shut it away, then open your eyes and the whole world has changed. A guy dead here. One guy with a hand off there. Maybe another guy with his stomach ripped open and his kidney flopped onto the ground. And it happens from no cause at all. Maybe God says, "Okay, now you blow up those combat engineers in F-squad. Them soldiers don't matter no more." Then the bomb just flashes and it's over.

"Gentle that baby," I whisper, "until you get inside."

Then she smiles more heavenly than I've ever seen. The Devil part turns into something sweet and she does another ballerina turn along the sidewalk.

And that's where it blows. The gas colors pour out like mustard steam and for some reason my eyes don't blink at all. They just suck it in like a mind volcano so I get to see everything flying apart.

First her smile washes out. Those angel lips fall off like the great hotels dropped by the real demolition experts. They're there one second and the next they're just gone. The whole wall of her face, smooth and clear as it is, turns into rubble and falls onto itself until there's nothing left but a pile of broken bricks and bones. There's no look of sadness, no idea that the end has come.

I run up the sidewalk after the first shock passes and look into the smoldering crater. I'm balanced there on the sidewalk, on my toes with one knee bent forward, like a wild deer in the forests ready to disappear into the night bush. But something pulls me in closer, down to where her body should be. The Devil is flying out of her and I squat over and take a good sniff of the blasting powders steaming up from the pit, then I look around and see everything perfectly. The brown brick building with two shattered front windows, the parked car, the grass and sidewalk, those prickle bushes next to the link fence. I know *exactly* how to run and break away like that deer in the woods, straight down the sidewalk jumping the lawns and shrubs, I hop the last bush and duck into the car and close the door tight and just listen. If there's squad cars coming you sit tight and tell 'em sweet dick when they ask. But if there's no cops then turn the key soft and pull out as sweet as you please.

And it works just like that. There's no sign of a soul, so I pull out unnoticeable. I dump the baby harness off at the welfare office and no one knows the difference. It's somebody's free donation. Far as they're concerned, some big-heart left it without a trace. They might even give up a prayer in the morn-

317

ing. Who knows how they think it through?

Then I drive round like a bug that just found some dead squirrel. Don't know where to go. Just take all the green lights and whenever there's a red one turn right and keep going. After a while I sort of come to, come right out of this automatic driving and realize how useless it is. Following the lights is crazy cause no one ever took the time to organize it so the lights'll take you somewhere. They don't lead nowhere. Just around.

Then I figure, okay, let's drive back to the building and see what's going on. It's an hour later and I'll just be a guy driving by on his own time. A guy who couldn't sleep specially well and is out for a simple drive. Even at two in the morning that's not so suspicious.

But it's like pulling the plug in a washtub that's full to the top with dirty water. At first, nobody knows the drain's free. Then a minute later the water starts sucking down and the surface rolls back and forth until the whirlpool starts. That's when you know it'll never stop and you can see the tiniest speck caught on the edge, right on the lip of the whirlpool at the one point just after any possible escape. There you are. On the lip. Right on the lip. Then one, two quick swirls and down into the guts of some black animal with no eyes. That's how it is driving back there—a dizzy hell.

When I'm a block away I can see the place has gone crazy with cops. There's at least six squad cars with their lights flashing all blue-red, like the Devil's still with Renee.

I slip the car into neutral and pull up at a coast. They've got a roadblock set up, and two cars ahead of me a cop has his nose poked through the window, yapping at the driver. I take a good clean breath.

After a minute the cop motions for me to unroll my window.

"Evenin'," he says.

"What's the trouble, officer?" I crane my neck and make sure I look surprised to see a roadblock set up so late at night.

"Routine." Then he turns more serious. "What brings you by here tonight?"

"Just out for a drive. Changed my shift today and I couldn't sleep so good."

"Let's see your license and registration," he says.

I lean over to the glovebox to get the papers and he sticks his head in all the way and starts sniffing the air. You hear him do it twice. Sniff-sniff, just like Porky Pig.

He holds the papers and license in one hand and checks my face against the picture, asks my name and address and checks my answers against the card. Then he goes to a squad car and makes some notes and radios into headquarters and lingers around his car a while.

If they had the brains for it they might've read my thoughts while I was waiting in the car lineup. But that's not too likely. Usually cops aren't good enough to read your thoughts. Not like the shrinks and special doctors. With a little training some of them could maybe handle it, but on the whole the cops are useless buggers. They're much better at reading how you sweat or how your eyes twitch if there's any little pressure inside you. And that's what I'm doing my best to control. My face is smooth as ice. It's just now that the sweat's starting to come into my palms.

"Okay, on your way."

"Thanks."

He passes the papers to me. I roll the window back up and take a deep breath. With the window up it's like sealing him off and turning him into something stupid and ignorant. Like a cartoon.

Then I drive off slow, obeying all the traffic rules as though I just took my driver's test. When I get close to it I look up the sidewalk to see Renee. But the funny thing is that there's hardly any sign of the bomb. They put a few barriers around the crater, but apart from that there's nothing. Even the building lights are lit up like nothing ever happened. You almost wonder why the cops bothered to show up.

But it's probably another trick of theirs to lure me out of what's really happened. It's the kind of trick that might work on anybody else. It might work on me, too, except that my memory's near perfect and I remember *every* little detail. Up to a point, anyhow.

Made in United States
North Haven, CT
12 March 2022

17055091R00195